Anonymous

A Tale of the Times

Vol. II

Anonymous

A Tale of the Times
Vol. II

ISBN/EAN: 9783337137403

Printed in Europe, USA, Canada, Australia, Japan

Cover: Foto ©Andreas Hilbeck / pixelio.de

More available books at **www.hansebooks.com**

A

TALE

OF THE

TIMES.

BY THE AUTHOR OF A GOSSIP'S STORY.

DEDICATED, BY PERMISSION, TO MRS. CARTER.

IN TWO VOLUMES.

VOL. II.

Nor shall the pile of hope God's mercy rear'd,
  By vain philosophy be e'er destroy'd :
Eternity, by all or wish'd or fear'd,
  Shall be by all or suffer'd or enjoy'd.
    MASON's *Elegy on the Death of Lady Coventry.*

Dublin :

PRINTED BY WILLIAM PORTER, GRAFTON-STREET,

1799.

A

TALE

OF THE

TIMES.

CHAP. I.

Then gay ideas crowd the vacant brain,
While peers and dukes, and all their fweeping train,
And garters, ftars, and coronets appear,
And in foft founds " Your Grace" falutes the ear.

POPE.

FITZOSBORNE's thoughts were now fo engroffed by his intended attack on the principles and honour of lady Monteith, that he felt as little interefted about the event of his engagements with lady Arabella as if the marriage ceremony had really taken place. He was roufed from this infenfibility by the noble vifcount his brother, who, having procured a copy of the redoubtable fettlement, which I have before mentioned, fwore upon his honour (his lordfhip, though very fond of this oath, was never known to be forfworn) that the terms were too hard for any man above a fhoe-black to abide by. " I would have you " by all means, Ned," faid he, " make a better " bargain for yourfelf. The girl is immenfely " fond of you, that is evident; and a fellow with

" a

" a tenth part of your addrefs would make the
" pretty driveller accede to any thing. Can't
" you give her a little fentiment upon the occa-
" fion, and tell her, that by referving all her for-
" tune in her own power, it will be abfolutely
" impoffible for her ever to enjoy the fublime
" gratification of receiving obligations from the
" perfon fhe loves? Can't you flourifh too upon
" the provifion in cafe of feparation and divorce,
" and declare that the frigorific idea petrifies
" your whole frame? Be malter of her fortune,
" however, at all events; for let me tell you,
" my dear lad, a wife's affections in this age are
" but a transferable commodity of little perma-
" nent value, I affure you."

Edward felt too well convinced of his influence to doubt the poffibility of his acquiring the
glittering prize upon his own terms; and he
fketched in his mind the only conditions upon
which he would confent to give the lady the honour of his name. Thefe conditions were re-
markable for nothing but their being a direct
contradiction to lady Madelina's plan. But on
his firft converfation with lady Arabella upon the
fubject he difcovered, that he had greatly miftaken her character when he attributed to it any
degree of pliability in pecuniary matters. She,
indeed, loved to fquander with thoughtlefs pro-
fufion; but that very love of fquandering fuggefted the propriety of retaining the power of
doing fo; and the lovers parted with great mutual diffatisfaction: Edward convinced that his
merits would confer honour upon any lady on
whom he beftowed his hand, and lady Arabella
perfuaded that a younger brother has no right to
expect a higher office than to be his wife's fteward, if he be fo lucky as to engage the good opinion of a woman of fortune. Both feemed inclined

clined to bring their matrimonial pretensions to a
fresh market. He thought that his person might
attract some fair one equally rich and less mercenary; and she knew, that when people calculate upon good matches, there is always as great
a difference between present possession and rever-
sionary expectation, as there is between the comparative splendor of a baronial and a ducal coro-
net. The gentleman pondered upon the propriety of discontinuing his addresses; but the
lady hastened his deliberations by informing him,
that if his visits at Portland-place were upon her
account, she begged she might not in future
interrupt his important avocations; and thus
Mr. Fitzosborne was suddenly reduced to the situation of a *rejected* swain, a condition which the
versatility of his talents knew how to improve.

Lady Arabella's frivolity, selfishness, and avowed expectation of making superior conquests, did
not discredit the tale which Fitzosborne told
of his dismission. The blunt integrity of lord
Monteith's character took fire at his sister's evident dereliction of the principles of honour, con-
stancy, and female delicacy; and the reluctance
with which the specious Edward appeared to discover her caprice irritated his ardent temper still
more. He charged her with base infidelity and
gross indecorum; and she evaded the charge by
urging, that she was a free independant being,
and accountable to no one for her actions, which
were the result of her opinions; and no one had
any right to scrutinize the opinions of others.
The earl raved against this heterodox doctrine,
because it militated against his wish of supremacy, without discovering that there was a degree of ingratitude in the application of these
principles against the interest of the master from
whom she had acquired them; and her ladyship
　　　　　　　　　　　　　　　　　　resolved.

refolved never to miflead her hufband by fur-
nifhing a previous inftance of her fubmiffion to her brother's authority. She removed on
the very evening of the difpute to the houfe of
lord vifcount Fitzofborne.

In order to explain the reafon of her choofing
that afylum, I muft unriddle a little Machiave-
lian policy. The fituation of the noble houfe of
Fitzofborne was become fo very precarious in
point of credit, that the reprefentative of its
honours, like Shakefpeare's Percy, had long "caft
" many a northern look to fee the Frazer bring
" up his powers." The illuftrious vifcount indeed could not give himfelf a legal title to that
fpacious inheritance which now centered in lady
Arabella; but his fraternal wifh of transferring
it to his own family was not quite difinterefted.
Edward had ever appeared too abftracted, too generous, and too fuperior to low mercenary views,
to deny a brother the loan of a few thoufands,
and his indifference to money was in the vifcount's opinion the caufe of his prefent difappointment; for had his whole heart been engroffed by the defire of advancing his fortune, the
pretty bird might have beat her gay plumage in
ufelefs vexation, at finding herfelf furrounded by
too many toils ever to hope for recovered liberty.

In oppofition to thofe faturnine cenfors who
affirm that a genteel pair never think or act in
concert, I have to relate a fcheme in which the
vifcount and his lady cordially co-operated, and
which, though it might not terminate in an in-
vocation of Venus's antique doves, promifed to
produce a modern pigeon. The farce commenced with a vifit from the vifcountefs to her dear
friend; during which fhe heard with mingled furprife and grief that Mr. Fitzofborne's expectations

tations were so very illiberal, and his temper so
very uncomplying, that the connection was dif-
solved. She commended the laudable spirit which
dictated lady Arabella's resolution of sooner break-
ing her heart than submitting to unjustifiable
demands; but when she added, that, by thus acting with proper regard to female dignity, she had
excited the resentment of her brother, the indignation of her sympathizing friend exceeded all
bounds. With bitter sarcasms on the indelicacy
of lord Monteith's interference, she intreated
her to remove directly to lord Fitzosborne's, and
assured her, that offended beauty would find a
protector in the viscount; who would either compel Edward to make proper concessions, or dis-
own him for a brother. There was something
truly *Roman* in this sentiment. It was expressed
with becoming dignity; and the viscountess, still
farther to enforce it, added, "You will get a
"little more into the world, my dear, from which,
"it is certain, you have lately been too much
"secluded. We have frequently little private
"parties, at which you cannot object to taking a
"card, for nobody will know any thing about it,
"so that there cannot be any indecorum. I pro-
"test, I think you grow more bewitching every
"hour. Your mourning becomes you so ex-
"quisitely, that in pity to the world I ought to
"propose keeping you shut up; that other belles
"may have a little chance; but I own I am ma-
"licious enough to wish to give a little fillip to
"Edward's fears. Nothing is so animating as a
"strong fit of jealousy, and I know that to make
"fresh conquests you need only appear." So
friendship urged; and its arguments were con-
clusive.

The parties might now be said to be fairly
drawn up in battle array; for, not to yield to the

Fitzofbornes in hofpitality, lord Monteith had infifted that Edward fhould become his gueft; and, though their taftes and difpofitions were by no means in unifon, he fancied himfelf highly gratified with the companion he had felected; and he was much too warm an advocate for what he efteemed an injured character to permit the countefs to continue neuter. Fitzofborne's affected dejection foon interefted her feeling heart; and, though fhe could fcarcely confider the lofs of an Arabella to be a misfortune, fhe felt that great allowance fhould be made for the force of difappointment upon a mind fo ftrongly fufceptible. Still incredulous as to the reality of his attachment, fhe was inclined to believe, that after he had acceded to the propofals of his friends, a fenfe of honour and the force of habit had produced in his refined difpofition a recurrence of the fame images, which might be almoft fuppofed equivalent to preference. The void which female caprice had left in his imagination muft be at prefent painful, and, though an enlightened underftanding would foon occupy the chafm with a more brilliant fet of ideas, delicate fenfibility might be allowed to ftart at the illiberal ridicule which a cenforious world is ever ready to beftow on a jilted fwain or a forfaken damfel. Befide, without being mercenary, might not a prudent man regret the lofs of a fplendid eftablifhment? To foften that regret fhe exerted all the brilliant powers of her mind, and all the fafcinating graces of her numerous accomplifhments. Charmed out of his pretended melancholy, Fitzofborne feemed to beftow a liftlefs attention, varying the contour of his expreffions as the ftyle of her attractions required: Sometimes terminating his filent adulation by exclaiming,

ing, " Happy Monteith !" At another expatiating in praife of friendfhip; or, if he aimed at, making the moft forcible impreffion, he only interrupted the vivacity of her tones by the frequency of his fighs. But in either inftance he was equally careful that lord Monteith fhould hear both the exclamations and the fighs.

Difappointed by perceiving that his dejection did not yield to time, and more than ever convinced that love could not have made fuch an incurable wound, the countefs began to fufpect that this diforder was conftitutional, and fhe propofed his applying to fociety and change of fcene, the ufual recipe for a melancholic humour. His conftant rejection of invitations induced her to pique his pride. " Do you know," faid fhe, " that lady Arabella flourifhes in the firft circles, " and is become fo very irrefiftible, that not only " wits and beaus write madrigals to her, but a " certain young duke of our acquaintance is " thought to be ferioufly entangled ?. They are " to be at the opera together to-night in his " grace's box. Now I intend to go, and take " you for my *cecifbeo*. What. fay you to my " fcheme ? It will be generous to fhew the " young adventurer how Armida metamorphofes " her knights before he is irrecoverably enchant.. " ed."

" I am very willing to exhibit my woe-begone " face, if the publication of it will afford you any " amufement," returned Fitzofborne. " The " duke and I fhall not exchange any angry " glances, and I honour lady Arabella's fincerity " too much to feel any refentment at her conduct. " She has only exercifed the indubitable right of " every human being. Her heart has changed " its poffeffor, and fhe has obeyed its dictates."

A 3

" Does

" Does not your candour grant rather too
" great a latitude here?" inquired the countefs.

" Confidering the prejudices of the times, I
" certainly do. But is there not a great degree
" of cruelty in requiring conftancy from thofe
" minds that have not fufficient fortitude to be
" really immutable? And after all, as we can
" only affume the appearance of it, is it not alfo
" unjuft, and wicked too, as we create a necef-
" fity for hypocrify? To difeafes in different
" conftitutions we prefcribe different remedies;
" but the diforders of the mind muft be all cured
" by one univerfal panacea. Surely it is only
" the tyranny of cuftom that prevents us from
" adapting our moral code to every character,
" inftead of ftretching diffimilar minds on the
" gigantic iron couch defigned for a Procruf-
" tes."

Lady Monteith felt ftartled. She recollected
that where much was given much would be required; yet this text related to diffimilar powers
of doing good, and could not poffibly be urged
in extenuation of any vicious action. But Fitzofborne interrupted her mufings by affuming a
gayer air than he had lately exhibited. " I fee,"
faid he, " I fhall have fome difficulty to recon-
" cile you to *all* my opinions; But, no matter;
" when I legiflate for the world, don't flatter
" yourfelf, that I fhall propofe a lax fyftem to
" you. I know how to eftimate your mental
" ability, and *your* code fhall be rigorous and
" coercive."

" Dare you repeat this fpeech to-night at the
" opera in the hearing of lady Arabella?" faid
the countefs.

" There requires no courage to repeat an un-
" difputed truth in the hearing of the whole
" world."

" world." Lady Monteith forgot her difapprobation of the novelty, fingularity, and laxity of Fitzofborne's opinions ; and as fhe drove to form her party for the evening, fhe only remembered his happy talent at a compliment.

CHAP. II.

It is Jéaloufy's peculiar nature
To fwell fmall things to great ; nay out of nothing
To conjure much...

YOUNG.

THE polite world were fo engroffed by engagements, that lady Monteith found it impoffible to form a party to her fatisfaction. Exclufive of the pale votaries, who facrifice peace, health, fortune, and honour at the fhrine of Pharo, feveral were engaged to the Quizzes, and more to the Cabinet of Monkies; which was juft opened. The fair countefs could fcarcely get any body into her party but thofe who were left out of all others: and they who refufed her fecretly laughed at the rufticity of fuppofing any body, who lived in the world, could defer till two o'clock the important bufinefs of fixing the evening occupation. She was forced to be contented with an antiquated belle of the laft age, and a would-be fine lady of the prefent, to whom fhe was lucky enough to add a beau, fir Hargrave Nappy, a gentleman, who though known by every body to be incurably deaf, had long laboured under the tantalifing defire of wifhing to be thought a connoiffeur in mufic. With this defign he conftantly attended the opera,

were

where his unvarying countenance and fixed pofture procured him the appellation of the pillar of melody.

Surrounded by the group I have deſcribed, and eſcorted by the gallant Edward Fitzofborne, lady Monteith entered a ſide-box oppoſite to that which was occupied by lady Arabella's party. Had Geraldine intended to have ſelected foils for her own perſon, the females in her train were moſt happily gifted by nature for that purpoſe ; and in point of celebrity they were juſt enough known to make it difficult for any lady to decline being their companion. Repeated mortifications had taught them the arcana of high life; and the protection of a counteſs was ſufficiently flattering to confine them to that humble part which they ſuppoſed her ladyſhip intended they ſhould ſuſtain. Claiming ſir Hargrave for their ſhare of the beaus, they invited him to ſeat himſelf between them, and they addreſſed all their obſervations to him, without once turning their heads to liſten to the converſation which paſſed behind them. But ſir Hargrave was ſo abſorbed in opera ecſtacies, that unleſs his eye happened to inform him that he was peculiarly addreſſed, all the *ſmart things* paſſed utterly unnoticed. Indeed the only honour that they ever received was a half bend, after which the amateur reſumed his former erect poſition, and with one hand in his boſom, and the other (on which was a fine antique) beating time on the front of the box, he repeated, like Shakeſpeare's Lorenzo, " Mark " the muſic."

It is a very great pity that theſe unfortunate *ſmart things* ſhould be wholly loſt. The preſcient muſe at leaſt muſt be ſuppoſed to have heard them; but I feel ſo anxious to return to

the

the rest of the party, that I must defer the re-
capitulation of them to some other opportunity,,
promising, if possible, either to interweave them
with the history of my travels, or, if I have no
other means of introduction, to give them to the
world in the form of " More last words of Mrs.
Prudentia."

The blooming Geraldine never appeared so
enchanting. She perceived, with a degree of
pleasure, in which she did not suspect any criminality, that the adventures of her box proved infinitely more interesting to lady Arabella, than
the devoirs of the noble duke whom she wished
to exhibit as her captive. Fitzosborne was in
excellent spirits. The countess enjoyed the circumstance. She thought he had been extremely
ill used, and she applauded the spirit which could
return insult with contempt. His attentions to,
herself, considered in this point of view, gave her
sincere satisfaction. She returned them. Her
natural vivacity, combining with accidental circumstances, hurried her into a degree of mirth,
which, to those who were unacquainted with its
motives, appeared to border upon coquetry, more
than the innocence of her heart and the rectitude
of her principles would have permitted.

. But while the lamb, basking in the blaze of
noon, bounds over the flowery hillock, the wolf
watches its haunts and meditates its destruction.
To exemplify my pastoral simile: Fitzosborne
saw with diabolical exultation, that Geraldine's
behaviour had attracted general attention. He
doubted not but calumny would be ready to frame
some malignant whisper, and he understood the
maxim which teaches that " virtue rarely survives
the loss of reputation." Though he conceived
that the powers of his own invention were fully
equal

equal to overthrow any defence which lady Monteith might make, he did not difdain adventitious aid. His watchful eye, though feemingly only fixed on the lovely form which was feated by him, had difcovered lord Monteith in the pit. He perceived too that he was attentive to his lady's behaviour, and he fancied he read difpleafure in his countenance. " Can this thoughtlefs ani-" mal," faid Fitzofborne to himfelf," " have " any thing like jealoufy in his compofition? He " feems lefs carelefs than ufual. If fo, it is in-" deed above my hopes."

While he ruminated on this idea, the door of the box opened, and a young man of fafhion ftepped in. He was an intimate friend of lord Monteith's ; and, feeing the countefs in what he thought a new point of view, he was defirous of fharing the pleafure which her converfation afforded. This did not increafe the gaiety of the party. The appearance of a ftranger cauf-ed a temporary interruption. Geraldine recollected her thoughts, and her natural delicacy feemed to fhrink from an intrufion which, though fanctioned by the freedom of our prefent fyftem of manners, feemed inconfiftent with ftrict politenefs. His ftyle of addrefs too was bold and familiar, very different from the infinuating fenfibility of Fitzofborne, who, though confcious of diftinction, never appeared to prefume upon favour. She determined to mark her approbation of his behaviour by her own conduct, and, inftead of the confidence and vivacity which marked her deportment previous to the entrance of her new gueft, fhe became as cold and circumfcribed in her anfwers as the rules of civility could poffibly admit.

Lord

Lord Monteith now entered the box; and, as he never concealed any fentiment, the difpleafure he felt was ftrongly marked in his countenance. He had heard his lady pointed out as uncommonly beautiful by a ftranger who fat next him; and though he was very well pleafed with that plaudit, the fubfequent obfervations were not fatisfactory. To the words " Charming creature !" were added " and fo gay, fo lively too in her " manners ! what a happy man that gentleman " muft be !" The ftranger was juft arrived from the country, and unwittingly fuppofed that a married pair would not forfeit their claims to celebrity by appearing at the fame entertainment in the fame party. Every exclamation which he uttered in compliment of the affectionate attention of this peerlefs couple increafed the earl's reftleffnefs; and, no longer able to conceal his own right to the charmer who thus fafcinated all eyes, he fuddenly rofe and joined her. He had feen nothing in her manner which cuftom did not juftify, and Fitzofborne was of all others the friend in whom he could moft confide. Yet, without knowing what to blame, he thought the laws of cuftom required revifal.

Geraldine had not that fpecies of fortitude which fees difpleafure on a hufband's brow without any fentiment but exultation. She was ignorant of thofe principles which teach the diffipated wife who has long renounced the power of pleafing to exult in the capacity of giving pain. The light heart which had prompted the gay repartee became loaded with fudden depreffion, and the frolic fmile vanifhed with the unaffected vivacity which had given it birth.

The world had much to fay on the adventures of this evening. Poor Arabella ! every body was

was very forry for her. Lady Monteith had certainly fpirited away her lover. Her exultation upon the occafion was rather, too marked for a woman of prodigious decorum; and really, if fhe did continue to flirt it fo notorioufly in public, fhe muft renounce her pretenfions to fuch *very* ftrict propriety, and confent to be thought no better than other people.

At coming out of the opera Fitzofborne tapped lord Monteith upon the fhoulder, and afked him, how he difpofed of himfelf for the evening. " At home, if you have nothing-better to propofe:" was the anfwer. " There is a " fpirited fet juft gone to Brookes's," continued Fitzofborne; " fuppofe we follow them to ob-" ferve manners and characters." His lordfhip had no objection.

Early in lord Monteith's life his name was unfortunately familiar to the frequenters of the gaming-table and the heroes of the turf. His attachment to the lovely Geraldine leffened that dangerous propenfity; and, though fhe had failed in her endeavours to infpire a love of elegant pleafures, indifference for his former purfuits had gradually increafed to difguft: the lefs pernicious fports of the field, and a boyifh turn of amufement, fucceeding in occupying a mind too volatile to feek pleafure out of its own refources. But fince his lordfhip's difguft and forbearance arofe more from the abfence of temptation than from any fixed principle, the fight of the card-table and the rattle of the dice-box excited paffions which increafed the unfubdued emotion that he had felt at the opera.

He propofed to Fitzofborne to form a party. Edward pleaded a total want of fkill; protefted, that he had a fixed abhorrence of the gaming-table;

table; and declared, that he never vifited thofe
fcenes, except to ftudy the human character, and
to moralize on the fatal effects of the impetuous
paffion of avarice. His reflections were foon
finifhed that evening, for in a little time he profeffed himfelf wearied with the fcene, and he
propofed to lord Monteith that they fhould retire
to a private room. There too he felt the moments drag heavily, and it was mutually agreed
to enliven them by a friendly game at picquet.

The ftake firft propofed was trifling. Monteith was unfuccefsful. He transferred his latent refentment to the cards, which he ftamped
under his foot; called for a new pack, and infifted upon doubling the fum they played for.
The events of the evening put feveral hundreds
into Fitzofborne's pocket; and his fuccefs might
ftill have been greater, but neither his friendfhip
nor his honour would (he protefted) permit him
to urge his good fortune any further. "Your
"temper," faid he, "is too warm; and I hope
"the little vexations of this evening will con-
"vince you of the neceffity of felf-control, or
"at leaft prevent you from trying your chance
"with thofe who might take the ungenerous
"advantage of your agitation, which I fcorn to
"ufe."

"I value not money," faid Monteith an-
grily; "nor can the curfed cards agitate me. A
"truce with your morality, therefore, Edward;
"when I want a monitor, it is time enough for
"you to inveft yourfelf with that dignity."

"I am not in a refentful humour," returned
Fitzofborne fmiling. "I fhall therefore very
"gladly refign my dignity, as you term it. In-
"deed, I have been a little unlucky in the exer-
"cife of it this evening. Yet if my well-meant
"admonitions are but remembered by my
"friends,

" friends, the difintereftednefs of my attachment
" will enable me to fupport a little tranfient acri-
" mony."

" Where elfe did you play the lecturer ?" inquired Monteith, carelefsly.

" Where I faw a little-impropriety," replied
Fitzofborne, with fuppreffed fignificance.

" And did you fucceed no better than you
" have done with me ?" continued the earl, with
increafing anxiety.

" I don't know. The character I had to deal
" with was more *guarded* than you are."

" What caufed your reproof ?" faid his lordfhip, with affected eafe, and apparently occupied
in forting the cards into three divifions.

" I believe nothing but 'too great nicety of
" my own feelings; for on reviewing the affair
" I cannot fee any thing effentially wrong ; and
" I begin to think thofe rules which impofe
" fuperior caution on perfons who are objects
" of public admiration unneceffarily fevere."

" The fentiments of ladies," refumed Monteith, " are generally more delicate in thefe points
" than thofe of men. Suppofe you make Geral-
" dine your cafuift in this bufinefs : She will tell
" you if you went too far in your admonitions."

" By no means," faid Fitzofborne, fnatching
the cards. " Come, enough of one fubject.
" Shall we have another game ?"

" No ! I am tired ; and as I love to have every
" doubtful bufinefs cleared up, we will go home
" to fupper, and I will mention your uneafinefs
" to lady Monteith, that you may fleep with a
" difburdened confcience."

Fitzofborne ftarted. " How came *you* to dif-
" cover, that the hafty opinion which I injudi-
" cioufly uttered, really difpleafed her ? Let me
" conjure you, my lord, by all our friendfhip,
                                        " endea-

" endeavour to reftore me to her favour, and be
" convinced that I can only have forfeited it
" through inadvertence."

Lord Monteith fmiled with the confcious fuperiority which attends a fuccefsful feint, and affured the alarmed Fitzofborne, that, if he would
candidly acknowledge the nature of his offence,
he might depend upon his interpofition.

" It really," returned Edward, " was nothing
" of confequence. You have often charged me
" with poffeffing a ftoical fternnefs, and I con-
" fefs fome of my notions are auftere. The
" countefs was in very lively fpirits this even-
" ing."

" Was fhe?" faid Monteith, biting his lips.

" I faid fomething to her, I forget what, re-
" fpecting the eafe with which Britifh matrons
" publicly permit the advances of notorious li-
" bertines. I beg your pardon, Monteith, I know
" he is your friend; but I muft own, I repeated
" this with more energy when fir Richard Ver-
" non came into the box. You know his noti-
" ons are avowedly licentious."

" It was very friendly of you," exclaimed his
lordfhip, with a voice convulfed with paffion.
" Did he talk to lady Monteith in an improper
" ftyle?"

" By no means. Yet there was fomewhat
" freer in his addrefs than I fhould have approv-
" ed had the lady been my wife; and I felt for
" my abfent friend. The blaze of your Geral-
" dine's charms, my lord, is loft upon me.
" Beauty can never more affect my heart. But
" I too well recollect the emotions it has caufed
" not to wifh fir Richard to avoid lady Monteith,
" at leaft if he refpects his own tranquillity."

" And could Geraldine refent your friendly
" obfervation?" interrupted Monteith.

" She

" She only anfwered, that I was grown fple-
" netic, for public places fanctioned thefe intru-
" fions. I however obferved, that fhe did not
" fpeak to me any more during the whole even-
" ing."

" I deteft caprice. She fhall acknowledge
" the friendlinefs of your motives."

" Oh! for heaven's fake! do not interfere in
" that ftile. You will alarm her pride, and fink
" me for ever in her opinion. Befide, you will
" utterly prevent any future effort on my part
" gently to reftrain thofe very agreeable fpirits
" which may be liable to mifconftruction. To
" own the truth, I thought to-night fhe attracted
" particular attention."

" Her prudence," exclaimed the earl, who,
though he had imbibed the poifon of infinuation,
was yet offended by a direct attack, " is as ex-
" emplary as her character is fpotlefs."

" True," replied Fitzofborne, " but think of
" the malignity of the world."

" Who dares to impeach her conduct ?" continued her lord, with increafed violence.

" What does not envy and calumny dare ?"
cried the fentimental torturer. " But I fee my
friendfhip is troublefome. However, Monteith,
recollect, that you artfully wound the fecret out
" of me, and therefore have no right to be dif-
" pleafed at the difclofure."

" Your hand, Edward. Excufe my warmth.
" My wife is too dear to me, to allow me to hear
" the leaft cenfure caft upon her behaviour with
" indifference. I venerate the excellence of
" your heart, and I love your franknefs. I am
" frank myfelf, though I own I did ufe a little
" circumlocution to difcover what you certainly
" never intended me to know. I was too fubtle

" tle there. Was I not? But come, think no
" more of it. Perhaps lady Monteith might be
" a little wrong; but I know you both meant
" well, and she will readily forgive you."

" Then, as a pledge of your renewed esteem,
" let me entreat you never to mention this affair
" to her. I may have been too susceptible, and
" have mistaken her silence for resentment; for
" I am convinced I misconstrued her preceding
" behaviour."

Monteith pledged his honour for secrecy, and
endeavoured to dissipate his chagrin by humming
an air. But the idea that Fitzosborne had seen
something wrong in Geraldine, and his recollection of the stranger's conversation, sunk deep into
his mind, and clouded the gay vacuity of his
thoughts with spectres fearful as " the green-
eyed monster" which haunted the frank and noble Moor, who, like lord Monteith, " thought
" men honest who but seemed to be so."

C H A P. III.

No might nor greatness in mortality
Can Censure 'scape; back-wounding Calumny
The whitest virtue strikes.

SHAKESPEARE.

VICE always appears to be more alluring
when its machinations are crowned with success.
During the dangerous period of youth, while the
passions are warm, the imagination lively, and
the judgment weak, the spectator feels a bias in
favour of that adventurer whose course (marked
by

by ingenuity) leads to a fpeedy attainment of his
defires.   But could inexperience reflect, and impetuofity paufe, the couch of even the moft profperous villain would prefent no alluring fpectacle.
Fitzofborne's plans had hitherto anfwered his
wifhes.   His fpecious manners had acquired the
efteem of the countefs, and the unbounded confidence of her lord.   He had obtained a firm foot-
ing in the family; had fown the baleful germ of
fufpicion, fo fatal to domeftic peace; and the
difpleafure and gloom which occafionally pervaded
lord Monteith's countenance convinced him that
it had taken root.   Calumny was prepared to
doubt the ftability of Geraldine's honour; and
calumny, like a peftilential blaft, can taint the
innocence it affails.   To thefe engines of feduction might be added the fophiftical principles of
falfe philofophy, which, though cautioufly adminiftered and often rejected, ftill, like the delved
mine, poffefs a power capable of fubverting the
firmeft moral virtue, if not founded on the rock
of religion.

Yet Fitzofborne was wretched.   The atrocity
of his defigns haunted his pillow, not with a fenfe
of remorfe, but with the apprehenfion of danger.
The fituation of the lady was exalted; her character was exemplary; her connexions were refpectable; her hufband, as he had lately difcovered, was not only tenacious of her reputation,
and vain of her attractions, but alfo confcious of
her merits, and fincerely attached to her perfon.
Though the earl's apprehenfion was peculiarly
flow, his paffions were as remarkably vehement;
and his fkill at the various offenfive weapons was
fo great, that his opponent could have very little
chance of efcaping with life, if called to make the
amende honorable.   Fitzofborne's fortunes were

almoft

almoft defperate. Worldly prudence feemed, therefore, to point out the neceffity of applying his ingenuity in devifing fome plan of improving his circumftances, inftead of wafting his talents in a purfuit which only promifed danger, or, to fpeak according to his ideas, " barren honour."

Notwithftanding the appearance of open hoftility, he held a private correfpondence with the vifcount's family; and his intelligence from thence confirmed his own opinion, that the breach with lady Arabella was not totally irreparable.— Her vexation at his attention to lady Monteith was too lively to be concealed, and too fincere to yield to the hopes which the noble duke's increafing admiration infpired. In vain did fhe recollect detecting him incognito at the theatre, looking at her through his opera glafs. In vain did fhe remember her more fplendid triumph, when he prefented her with a ticket for lady Fillagree's fancied ball, infcribed " To the faireft." Fitzofborne faw his affiduities without emotion. The noble duke's fentiments were known to be inaufpicious to marriage; and no lady, who had not abfolutely determined to be a duchefs, could even affect to find fatisfaction in his converfation.

Fitzofborne poized the chance of lucrative advantage with precifion; and as he had no inclination for fleeping in the bed of honour, he beftowed fome forethought on the hazards he ran by purfuing his illicit defigns againft the lovely countefs. Since he deemed his fuccefs certain, it was unneceffary to examine the effect of a difappointment. Great prudence, great caution, and great morality, might prevent a *rencontre*. He might be unwilling to lift his arm againft the life of his friend; he might refpect the laws of his country;

or

or his health might impose the neceſſity of a tour for its reſtoration. The laſt ſtep would be the moſt convenient, in caſe lord Monteith applied for legal damages, ſince, however large the ſum given by the verdict, abſence and incapacity would be a receipt in full. The next ſtep of the injured huſband muſt be a divorce, and the deſerted lady could not object to taking refuge in a ſecond marriage, which was the only chance of reſtoring her again to the world, if not with untainted, at leaſt with a convaleſcent character. Geraldine was an heireſs, and it was to be ſuppoſed that her ſettlements were made with proper precaution. Even as a wife ſhe was infinitely more deſirable than Arabella; and, though the illiberality of huſbands might wiſh to ſecure their domeſtic poſſeſſions by an impaſſable incloſure, modern ſpirit had proved itſelf able to ſurmount every fence; and the lady might give away herſelf and her property ſeveral times over, without calling upon death to cancel a former bond. The world indeed would at firſt be angry; but the times were very liberal. People would allow for the force of *irreſiſtible* temptation. They would plead, that it was impoſſible to forbear adoring ſuch a charming creature. The blame would be happily transferred to my lord, who ought never to have admitted a friend into his family, or to have truſted her out of his ſight; and in a little time every body would viſit Mr. Fitzoſborne and his lady, and perhaps even find them out to be a very worthy and exemplary pair.

Confirmed in his deſigns not more by his own inſidious inclinations than by the falſe notions which prevail even amongſt the more principled part of that important circle called the great world, Fitzoſborne proſecuted his nefarious

plans;

pians ; and he determined, that if fear, or as he
called it prudence, did not check, compunction
should not dissuade. Chance, and the credulous
confidence of Lord Monteith, favoured his
wishes. Cards of invitation to lady Fillagree's
petit foupé had been sent to the Monteiths, and
the countess had not only chosen her character,
but she had also decorated an Italian tiffany with
festoons of violets, in which dress she intended to
personify the Perdita of Shakespeare. Her anxious entreaties had prevailed upon her lord to accompany her in the habit of the royal Florizel ;
and this mark of attachment on her part, and
condescension on his, promised the renewal of
domestic harmony. The expected evening approached, when a note from the minister requested lord Monteith's attendance in the house of
peers. Business of great importance was to be
agitated ; a violent opposition was expected ; and
the honour of his lordship's support would confer
a lasting obligation. The earl was not in the habit of courting ministerial favour ; he disliked
the task of attendance ; and the labour of listen-
ing to a long debate was always sufficiently ter-
rific to make him prejudge the question. Yet
though no one ever took less pains to acquire real
authority, he was very well pleased to be thought
a man of consequence ; and the minister's request
was too pressing to be declined. Geraldine
wished to give up her engagement ; but my lord
had fixed upon a plan that would settle every
thing, and to which his own dislike of masked
balls and fancy suppers gave a determinate stabi-
lity. It was, that Fitzofborne, instead of spend-
ing the evening alone in the library, should be
her escort. My lord's dress would fit him pretty
exactly, and Edward's excuses answered the end

for which they were defigned, which was to fix my lord moft pofitively in his determinations.

The entertainment was to be given at a villa a little diftance from town. Geraldine dreffed early; but her heavy heart feemed to anticipate fome difaftrous iffue. My lord came into her dreffing-room to fee if fhe looked her character; and while he contemplated the fimplicity and ex-quifite adaption of her ornaments, the apprehen-fions with which he had been lately tortured returned. " Do not," faid he, " dance with " Vernon, nor any of that fet, if they fhould afk " you. Plead that you are engaged to Fitzof-" borne, or elfe fay that you are tired."

" Will not that have a " fingular appear-" ance ?" inquired the countefs.

" You have a ftrange apprehenfivenefs of fin-" gularity, Geraldine. Don't you remember " your father's words, that there is no fhame in " being the only perfon who acts as fhe ought to " do ?"

" Suppofe then," faid her ladyfhip, " I do not " dance at all."

" What ! when all the world knows that you " are very fond of dancing ? Is that the way to " avoid fingularity ? " And why this averfion to " my friend ? Cannot you forgive him for offer-" ing you fome advice which you was too care-" lefs to attend to ?"

" My dear lord, there has been fome little " mifunderftanding, certainly. I am far from " having any averfion to Fitzofborne, and as far " from being offended at his giving me any ad-" vice. I do not even recollect the circumftance."

" O ! you give it that turn, do you ? But " you underftand my prefent prohibition, I fup-" pofe, and you will remember it."

" Undoubtedly.

" Undoubtedly. And do you recollect, that
" depending upon your accompanying me, I
" have not formed any party. If poffible come
" away from the houfe, and join me at Rich-
" mond."

" You are grown a coward, Geraldine.—
" However I will come, if I can; but Fitzof-
" borne is furely a fufficient guard. Tell Ara-
" bella to do that worthy fellow juftice, or I
" fhall difown her for my fifter."

The vivacity of lady Monteith had received
fo fevere a check that fhe could not recover her
fpirits during her ride to lady Fillagree's. Fitzofborne difcovered her dejection. " I know,"
faid he, " fuch folitude is often very trouble-
" fome ; yet the fervency of my friendfhip will
" not permit me to fee you difpirited without en-
" quiring into the caufe of your depreffion."

" It is fo wholly feminine," returned fhe,
" that it is abfolutely undefinable, and muft be
" fet down in the catalogue of my unaccounta-
" bles, unlefs I fhould give as a reafon, what I
" am very unwilling to admit; I mean, an idea
" of my lord's, that fome time or another I did
" not treat your good advice with fufficient de-
" ference. Pray, Fitzofborne, when did you
" play the moralift ; and when was I fuch a re-
" fractory pupil ?"

" Ah Monteith ! this is one of thy mifconcep-
" tions. I will explain the whole affair, ma-
" dam, though it is too ridiculous to merit repe-
" tition. You recollect the night we were to-
" gether at the opera."

" Perfectly."

" And that in return to fome obfervations
" which I made on the behaviour of lady Ara-

" bella,

" belly, you said, disappointment had made me
" splenetic ?"

" I do."

" Lord Monteith heard your answer as he en-
" tered the box; and he will persist in his opi-
" nion, that my expressions were pointed at you,
" as a reproof for something in your manner to
" Vernon. I must excuse him by saying, that
" he was a little flustered. I followed him to
" Brookes's, where we soon adjusted——"

" To Brookes's! Does my lord frequent
" Brookes's ?"

" O you tempter! No; I have too much ho-
" nour to reveal secrets. The affair was soon
" explained, I was going to say ;—for Monteith
" really has a very good heart, which excuses a
" little accidental puzzle-patedness."

Geraldine coloured ; but her Proteus companion gave her no time to resent. Looking out of
the chariot window, he relapsed into sentiment.
" See, dear lady Monteith," said he, " how the
" giddy throng hasten to this festival of ostenta-
" tious vanity. A reflecting mind, on contem-
" plating this crowd of carriages, must feel other
" sensations than those of pleasure. Not to men-
" tion the sufferings of those noble animals who
" draw the vehicles of tyrant man, the situation
" of master and servant, as exhibited upon the
" present occasion, is enough to cure the most
" obdurate heart of its partiality for those distinc-
" tions of rank which corrupt society now exhi-
" bits. How repugnant to the feelings of uni-
" versal love is that pale emaciated footman, who,
" exposed to the inclemency of the seasons, sus-
" pends the flambeau over the carriage of his vo-
" luptuous master! How remote must that man
" still be from the ultimate perfection of his na-
" ture,

" ture, who can enjoy the pleasures of a crowded
" assembly, while his coachman quakes in the
" warping wind, or shrinks beneath the pelting
" storm ! It is the cruelty of a Mezentius : The
" living body is united to putridity."

" There is some justice in your observations,"
said the countess ; " and it behoves us as *indi-*
" *viduals* to lessen the evils of that inequality
" which public good requires." The carriages
now stopped ; and as Fitzosborne led her to the
gay assemblage of beauty, fancy and elegance,
her reflections on his character concluded with
an observation, that " his very failings leaned to
" the side of virtue."

The ball went on very much like other balls.
Sir Richard Vernon and several gentlemen of his
cast of character were present, and Geraldine
complied punctually with her lord's injunction,
either to sit down, or to dance with Fitzosborne.
She had forgot to account for his appearing in a
dress so correspondent to her own ; and when
some ladies, by pointing it out, alarmed her sense
of propriety, her explanation was embarrassed,
and consequently suspicious. As at the opera,
Fitzosborne's attentions were confined to her ;
and his elegant address and polite vivacity added
the sneer of envy to the whisper of detraction.
Lady Arabella had indeed the honour to move
down one dance with the duke ; but his grace was
so fatigued by the exertion, that he was obliged
to renounce dancing, and to have recourse to
Cassino for the rest of the evening. Her succeed-
ing partners ranked no higher than commoners,
without possessing any of the innate distinctions
which gave celebrity to the partner of Fitzosborne. He had only bowed to her in the most
distant manner possible. Her smile of invitation
was

was unanſwered.; and ſhe began to think a fainting fit was the only chance of rouſing the monſter's attention. She performed it in the greateſt perfection ; but on opening her eyes ſhe felt a little mortification to find, that neither he nor the counteſs appeared in the circle which had gathered round her. Another glance convinced her, that they were not in the room.

" The heat of this apartment," ſaid the lovely ſufferer, " is inſupportable. Do, my deareſt " Harriet, lend me your arm, and let me breath " a little pure air in the veſtibule." The viſcounteſs complied, and the miſtreſs of the ceremony with ſeveral other ladies accompanied the fair invalid.

Lady Arabella caſt a ſcrutinizing glance upon the ſuite of chambers through which ſhe was led ; but ſhe deſcended into the veſtibule without making any diſcovery. It had been converted into an orangery for the occaſion, and decorated with a variety of lamps taſtefully ſuſpended. The many-coloured light trembling on the fragrant exotics, the freſhneſs of the air, the ſtillneſs of the ſcene, and the extenſive view which it admitted of the " ſtars in all their ſplendor" and " the moon " walking in brightneſs," afforded a ſtriking contraſt to the glittering but artificial ſcene which they had juſt left. Lady Arabella and her friends were not the only admirers of its enchanting effect, for at the upper end ſtood the counteſs and Fitzoſborne.

" Pray let us go back," ſhrieked lady Arabella, who however did not much doubt their identity. " I am quite frightened. Somebody is " here." The lady of the houſe declared, that it could be nobody whom ſhe could object to, while

while the charitable vifcountefs whifpered, " that
" it would be rude to interrupt a private party."

" O! not for the univerfe," exclaimed Arabella. I would die a thoufand deaths rather than
" be rude."

The countefs advanced with an air of eafy dignity, which the inquifitive looks of the other
ladies foon difcompofed. " Blefs me," fifter,"
faid the candid Arabella, " I really did not think
" it was you."—" And Edward too," continued
the fignificant lady Fitzofborne; " how do you
" do? There is no fuch thing as catching your
" attention for one moment this evening. How
" came your aufterity to condefcend to vifit thefe
" tinfel amufements?"

" Pardon me, madam," faid Edward, bowing
refpectfully to lady Arabella, " thofe amufements
" cannot be tinfel which have the power of at-
" tracting fterling merit." Her ladyfhip did not
deign to take the leaft notice of his fubmiffion,
but continued whifpering the countefs: " So you
" have one conftant *cecifbeo* I fee, and Monteith
" ftays at home. Very fingular, I vow. But
" was you not afraid of taking cold during this
" long converfation?"

" No," replied Geraldine with recovered
compofure; our converfation was too interefting
" for me to think of cold. What if I fhould tell
" you, Arabella, that fome part of it related to
" yourfelf. " But you really treat your faithful
" fwain's advances in too contemptuous a ftile
" for me to begin my requefted interceffion, or
" even to deliver to you a meffage from your
" brother on the fame fubject."

The party had now re-entered the houfe, when
the countefs, turning, faid to Fitzofborne, " You
" forget Mifs Parker."—" Where is Mifs Parker?"

" ker?" was the general inquiry. " In the
" orangery," faid lady Monteith. " No, ma-
" dam, I am here," echoed a fhrill voice, which
iffued from one of the ladies who accompanied
lady Arabella.

" Mifs Parker could not have been left in the
" orangery," obferved the vifcountefs. " Your
" ladyfhip was certainly miftaken. She came
" down ftairs with us."

" And fhe was the firft who fupported me
" when I fainted," faid lady Arabella, who, in
her eagernefs to detect a fuppofed criminal, forgot, that fainting people do not always know
what paffes.

" She accordingly accompanied me into the
" orangery," repeated lady Monteith.

Mifs Parker, who was no other than the " an-
" tiquated belle" at the opera, now came forward, and with a refpectful curtefy begged leave
to explain : " I certainly accompanied your lady-
" fhip and Mr. Fitzofborne down ftairs, when
" you did me the honour to afk me ; but while
" your ladyfhip was engaged with him in look-
" ing at the ftars, I found it was very cold, and I
" was afraid of my old attack in my fhoulder ;
" fo I thought I would ftep and fetch my pellice ;
" and I believe your ladyfhip and the gentleman
" were too much occupied to perceive that I was
" gone."

A farcaftic fmile, which lady Fillagree's politenefs could fcarcely reftrain her from joining, followed this narrative, when Edward, like Jofeph
Surface, promifed to give a full and fatisfactory
account of the matter. He faid, that on his mentioning that he had obferved a beautiful Jacobea
lily in full blow as they entered, lady Monteith
and Mifs Parker had expreffed a wifh to pay it
more

more attention; that he had the honour to efcort them; and that, after admiring the flower, her ladyfhip was fuddenly ftruck by the fplendor ot fome particular conftellations, when lady Arabella entered.

Another general fmile enfued, and Geraldine, no longer able to rally her fpirits, ordered her chariot; and, telling Mifs Parker fhe would fet her down at her own door, fhe relieved the ladies from the pain of fupprefled merriment, by taking leave.

C H A P. IV.

Confcience, what art thou? Thou tremendous power!
Who doft inhabit us without our leave ;—
How doft thou light a torch to diftant deeds !
Make the paft, prefent, and the future, fhown !
How, ever and anon, awake the foul,
As with a peal of thunder !

YOUNG.

THE fuppofed fecret, mentioned in my laft Chapter, was of too much importance to be confined to the difcoverers. By means of the happy art of innuendoes, the initiated foon diffeminated it through the whole circle, in the politeft manner imaginable. One lady obferved, that the adventures of the third Eloifa would foon be publifhed : another affirmed, that it would be called Werter the Second, with a different cataftrophe : a third wifhed to read the Chapter on Botany : a fourth thought that that on aftronomy would contain the moft aftonifhing difcovery : a fifth

B 3

allowed,

allowed, that aftronomy and botany were both very fuitable ftudies for fhepherds and fhepherdefles; and every body hoped that the adventures of the poor little lady, who had loft her pellice, and got the rheumatifm, would be inferted. The farcafms of the vifcountefs were peculiarly piquant; for hers was the moft fufpected character in company; and it is an invariable rule with ladies of her caft, that the odium with which you befpatter a neighbour's reputation has a retroactive effect in furbifhing your own. Her indignation was chiefly pointed at lord Monteith, who, fhe faid, was certainly anxious to obtain the honour of being a cornuto; and her idea was thought to be the more judicious, as it was known to correfpond with the fentiments of the noble vifcount her hufband. Envy, idlenefs, the love of faying good things, and a dearth of converfation, affifted her to propagate the ftory. For two days the town talked of nothing elfe, and every relater could add circumftances of frefh atrocity. In two days more, the truth of thefe adventitious circumftances became doubtful, and, being proved unfounded, the whole fabric fell with them to the ground. At the end of the week every body was heartily forry for the dear mifreprefented countefs; and every body, forgetting the part they had themfelves taken, heartily wifhed that fome law might be invented to prevent defamation.—But to return to the object of thefe inquifitorial proceedings.

The lovely Geraldine plainly perceived the malicious explanation that had been given to an incident which Fitzofborne had faithfully explained. The love of diftinction was, as I have before obferved, one of her ruling foibles; but fhe fought to gratify it by the nobleft means. Her

fpotlefs

spotleſs fame added luſtre to the ſplendor of her
talents and the attractions of her beauty. She
had ever been named as one of thoſe few, who,
in a degenerate age, afforded a happy inſtance of
the poſſible union of propriety and faſhion. To
have the goodly edifice which ſhe had reared with
ſuch aſſiduous care at once deſtroyed; to have
her unſullied name become the jeſt of witlings
and the aſſociate of wilful depravity, was inſupportable. Even ſuppoſing that the candid hearer
would reject the calumnious aſſertion, ſhe could
not endure the very idea of having her character
expoſed to ſuſpicious diſcuſſion. She ſat ſilent in
the chariot, the tear of anguiſh ſtealing down her
cheek, incapable of attending to Miſs Parker's
narrative, whoſe regret about the peliſſe furniſh-
ed her with a ſubject of lamentation till they arrived in town.

Fitzoſborne read lady Monteith's ſentiments.
He rightly judged that this keen ſenſibility would
prove injurious to his audacious deſigns; and he
determined to exert his inſidious arts to ſubdue it.
The earl was not returned from the Houſe. The
counteſs wiſhed him good night, and paſſed on to
her dreſſing-room. Fitzoſborne followed her to
the door. "Excuſe my anxiety," ſaid he;
"your look does not indicate a wiſh for repoſe.
"Will you allow me to ſit with you till Monteith
"returns?" She replied, that ſhe was not in
ſpirits for company; and after a pauſe, "It is in
"vain," ſaid ſhe, "to diſguiſe my feelings, Fitz-
"oſborne; and you know the cauſe of my diſ-
"treſs."

"I know nothing that can juſtify, or at leaſt
"deſerve, thoſe tears. Deareſt lady Monteith,
"for Heaven's ſake, conquer that emotion, which
"increaſes the miſanthropy I long have felt at
"the

" the narrow prejudice and illiberality cf the
" world."

" You are always tilting againſt thoſe wind-
" mill giants," returned Geraldine with a languid
ſmile. " It is of the ſpirit of detraction and in-
" conſiderateneſs that I complain; of that cruel
" levity, which ſports with what is dearer than
" life."

" Nay, now you urge your ſenſibility too far.
" It is weakneſs, not delicacy, to put our hap-
" pineſs ſo much in the power of others. Have
" you forgotten that beautiful ſentiment, ' The
" conſcious mind is its own awful world ?'

" I grant its propriety only with reſpect to the
" tortures of guilt; for can innocence be inſen-
" ſible of the value of reputation ?"

" It may diſprove ſlander by deſpiſing it, and
" by acting with marked contempt of its petty
" machinations. The tale you ſeem to appre-
" hend is too poor, too contemptible for belief.
" I have but one fear reſpecting its public ex-
" poſure."

" What fear ?"

" If lord Monteith ſhould hear it."

" If he ſhould, what have I to dread ?"

" The warmth of his character; his irritable
" impetuoſity; his ſuſpicious——"

" Suſpicious, did you ſay ? How muſt I be
" degraded, Mr. Fitzoſborne, in his opinion !
" To ſuſpect me after four years experienced
" confidence ! And what muſt the world think
" of me, if even my firſt, my deareſt friend
" doubts my rectitude ?"

" I know that angels are not purer; and when
" Monteith recollects himſelf, his judgment will
" tell him the ſame. He is now a little warped;
" an unhappy ill-grounded apprehenſion—a ſmo-
" thered ſpark nearly extinguiſhed by reaſon,
" which

" which this ridiculous ftory may revive;—and
" fufpicion in a character like his muft be terri-
" ble."

Geraldine leaned almoft fainting againft the
wainfcot. A deadly palenefs was diffufed over
her intelligent face, and her heart panted with
apprehenfive terror. None, except a Domitian
or a Fitzofborne, who delight in torture, but
muft have pitied her agonies.

The traitor did indeed affect to pity. He
dropped upon his knew, and uttered every rhapfodical expreffion which the moft guileful art
could dictate. " Deareft lady Monteith, for
" Heaven's fake be compofed—my tortured heart
" bleeds to fee your anguifh—moft injured—
" moft lovely fufferer—Oh richly worthy of a
" better fate—Impart your anguifh to the faith-
" ful friend who would die to relieve it."

The laft words recalled her recollection.
" Rife, fir," faid fhe with becoming dignity.
" My fituation does not call for the active offices
" of friendfhip. You fay I am injured. In
" what? From what motive do you torture me
" with fufpenfe? You feem to poffefs fome fatal
" fecret refpecting me. If I ought to know the
" evil you allude to, tell me at once, that I may
" arm my foul with fortitude to fuftain my tri-
" als, or detect the calumny which fports with
" my peace."

Edward was difconcerted. He had hoped that
fo much friendfhip might have furprifed her into
a little acknowledgment. And he perceived with
regret that many a fummer's fun muft ftill rife
to mature his villany. He had never yet encountered the refiftance of a firm fuperior mind,
or fo ftrongly feen the " lovelinefs of virtue in
" her own form," or " felt how awful goodnefs
is."

is." Yet, more remorfelefs than the Prince of.
Darknefs, " he pined not at his own lofs."

The fophifts, who in thefe evil days are falfely.
called enlightened, affect not to palliate their own
vices by pleas of neceffity and frailty, whatever.
difguife they may affume to expedite their fuccefs with others. Afpiring to a pre-eminence
in impiety, which former times feared to arro-
gate, they fin upon principle, promulgate fyftems
to juftify iniquity, and profcribe repentance by a .
morality which overturns every reftraint, and a-
religion that prohibits nothing but devotion.
Combining Pagan fuperftitions with the explod-···
ed reveries of irrational theorifts, they place at
the head of their world of chance a fupine ma-
terial God, whom they recognife by the name.
of Nature, and pretends that its worfhip fuperfedes all other laws human and divine. By the.-
fide of this circumfcribed Deity they erect the
idol fhrine of its vicegerent, Intereft; by the
monftrous doctrines, that " whatever is profit-
" able is right," that " the end fanctifies the,
" means," and that " human actions ought to.
" be free," they diffolve the bonds of fociety ;.
and, after conducting their bewildered followers
through the mazes of folly and guilt, in fearch.
of an unattainable perfection, their views termi-.
nate at laft in that fallacious opiate which infi-··
delity prefents, " the eternal fleep of death."   .

When pofterity fhall know that thefe principles characterife the clofe of the eighteenth cen-
tury, it will ceafe to wonder at the calamities.
which hiftory will then have recorded. Such
engines are fufficiently powerful to overturn go-
vernments, and to fhake the deep-founded bafe
of the firmeft empires. Should it therefore be
told to future ages, that the capricious diffolubi-

lity (if not the abfolute nullity) of the nuptial
tie and the annihilation of parental authority are
among the blafphemies uttered by the *moral* inftructors of thefe times : fhould they hear, that,
law was branded as a vain and even unjuft attempt to bring individual actions under the re-
ftrictions of general rule ; that chaftity was de-
fined to mean only individuality of affection ;
that religion was degraded into a fentimental effufion ; and that thefe doctrines do not proceed
from the pen of *avowed* profligates, but from
perfons *apparently* actuated by the defire of improving the happinefs of the world : fhould, I fay,
generations yet unborn hear this, they will not
afcribe the annihilation of thrones and altars to
the fuccefsful arms of France, but to thofe principles which, by diffolving domeftic confidence
and undermining private worth, paved the way
for univerfal confufion.

Stimulated by that zeal for making profelytes,
which marks the miffionaries of thefe doctrines,
Fitzofborne had hoped to goad his victim into the
fnares of infidelity by the corroding pangs of
previous guilt. Her unaffected agony at the idea
of her hufband's doubting the propriety of her
conduct and the rectitude of her heart, could
only be infpired by connubial tendernefs and real
delicacy. The blufh of generous indignation
which kindled upon her cheek at the fuppofition
that Edward's infinuations might proceed from
finifter views, and the calm contempt with which
fhe treated the little arts of feduction to which
female vanity has fometimes yielded, convinced
him that all his attempts to overturn her high-
feated honour would be ineffectual, unlefs he
could weaken the bonds of conjugal attachment,
or remove the ftrong bulwark of confcious immortality,

mortality, which gave energy to her principles
and ftability to her virtue. Her native fagacity
affured him, that all thefe attempts muft be made
with caution ; but his poifonous noftrums, once
introduced, would work with filent vigour. If
the conflict of the paffions fhould not be fufficiently ftormy in her temperate mind to erafe the
belief of future retribution, her thirft after know-
lege might entangle her in metaphyfical fubtilties. The love of diftinction and the allurements
of example might induce her to add one more to
thofe courageous females who conceive that the
character of a woman is not entirely divefted of
weaknefs till fhe defies Omnipotence ; while
unrequited tendernefs and unrewarded defert muft
eftrange an exquifitely fufceptible heart from its
unworthy mafter, and direct its affections to the
fpecious blandifhments of an unprincipled im-
pofture.

Fitzofborne's anfwer to Geraldine's fpirited
appeal was dictated by the moft confummate art.
He protefted that he had no fecret to divulge but
what fhe already knew ; namely, that lord Monteith had unwarily imbibed fome fufpicious apprehenfions from the marked admiration which
fir Richard Vernon had paid to her at the opera,
and to which the incidental circumftance of her
being in remarkably good fpirits that evening
might contribute. He fcarcely wondered at his
friend's alarm, when he confidered the free notions of the age, the baronet's libertine principles,
the impetuofity of lord Monteith's temper, and
his extreme fufceptibility in a point of honour,
which in his opinion probaby proceeded from
the warmth of his conjugal attachment. He
begged pardon for too deeply fympathifing in her
uneafinefs, but owned that his feelings were ne-

ver proof againſt the magic influence of female tears. The term "injured," which he perceived had alarmed her, was heedlefsly uttered, without any reference, at leaſt any deſigned one, unleſs it alluded to thoſe illiberal ſlanderers who attempted to aſperſe a character which he verily believed was the only exception to that general careleſſneſs of reputation too ſtrongly characteriſtic of the manners of the preſent race of married ladies.

"Calumny, my dear lady Monteith," continued he, "is now conſidered as the teſt of "faſhion; and, inſtead of ſhrinking from its peſ- "tilential attack, even women of virtue conceive "a ſlanderous paragraph in a morning paper to "be a kind of paſſport to celebrity; and, pleaſ- "ed with becoming an object of general atten- "tion, they wait very patiently for time to con- "fute what was untrue in the report. Your "extreme delicacy (for now that you are a little "recovered I cannot help remarking that it is too "exquiſitely ſuſceptible) and the peculiarity of "your lord's diſpoſition make me ſee the conſe- "quences of this affair in a more ſerious light "than I ſhould otherwiſe do: but as I am afraid "that neither of you will ever practiſe the philo- "ſophy which I ſhould aſſume on this ridiculous "occaſion, I can only ſay, that I ſhall be ready "to purſue any plan you ſhall ſuggeſt for my "conduct. Come, clear that penſive brow; "and be convinced, that Monteith may ſee other "men admire you without ſuppoſing that you "encourage their addreſſes."

This ſpeech had the deſired effect. It convinced the counteſs that ſhe ought to conceal from her lord every circumſtance in her own behaviour which excited the animadverſions of

others;

others : and while her agitated spirits were somewhat confoled by the hope that his difpleafure
was now wholly confined to Vernon, fhe faw the
neceffity of extreme caution, left it fhould ultimately point at her. Her apprehenfions of fome
criminal intention in Fitzofborne's paffionate
addrefs were tranfient. The extreme audacity
and guilt annexed to the bare idea of his having
formed an illicit attachment, and the abfolute
impoffibility of his even *hoping* for fuccefs, perfuaded her, that his paffionate language was only,
as he affirmed it to be, the unpremeditated fympathy of fincere friendfhip; and fhe now blufhed
at her own indelicacy in doubting, though but
for a moment, the rectitude of his heart.

Efteem and confidence are never fo powerful
as at the moment of removed fufpicion. She
wanted an advifer and confidant. Who could
feem fo proper to perform that office as the fagacious, fentimental Edward ? The firft fcheme
which lady Monteith propofed to ftop the cir-
culation of the flanderous tale was, that Fitzofborne fhould immediately leave the family.
The arch-tempter immediately fignified his perfect acquiefcence ; but with deference ftated,
that in his opinion fuch an apparent coincidence
with the prejudice of malevolence would tend
to confirm its cenfure ; and to his repeated advice to treat the whole ftory with indifference
and bravado, lady Monteith oppofed her own
poignant feelings, which would never permit her
to go into company while confcious that a whifper was circulated to her difadvantage. At length
a compromife was agreed to between the oppofite
opinions, and Geraldine determined to take leave
of the gay world with more than philofophic dif-
tafte of its levity and uncharitable afperity.

Forget-

Forgetting that retirement had sometimes sug-
gested the wish of introducing her brilliant talents to the notice of more accurate observers,
the envy, hatred, and detraction which impeded
her career, made her again wish to take shelter
in the quiet undisputed superiority which Powerscourt or Monteith presented. The presence of
caprice and affectation renewed her Lucy's remembrance, rendered the recollected sweetness
and ingenuousness of her character still more
pleasing, and stimulated her impatience to pour
her sorrows into the bosom of soothing friendship; or to heal her corroded heart by the gentle
balm of parental tenderness. The proposed alliance which had occasioned her journey to London being to all appearance entirely frustrated,
she wished to return to the pleasing occupations
of domestic life; and the claims of filial duty
determined her to take Powerscourt in her way to
Scotland. To prevent any suspicion, that her
retreat was in consequence of a breach between
the earl and Fitzosborne, it was proposed, that
the latter should continue at Portland place till
lord Monteith's parliamentary engagements terminated: and Geraldine entertained a private
hope, that her lord's interest with ministry might
procure some post which would tend to recon-
cile Edward to the severe blow which his fortunes had received by the rejection of lady Arabella; and at the same time convince the world,
that caprice was not the distinguishing charac-
teristic of all the Macdonald family.

Fitzosborne now recurred to the conversation
which had really been begun in lady Fillagree's
orangery; and he debated the probable event of
his renewing his addresses with so much seeming
anxiety, and acted the part of the mortified
swain

fwain with fo much adroitnefs, as entirely removed every fhadow of fufpicion from lady Monteith's mind, engaged her anew in the office of a
confoler, and even roufed a degree of felf-accufation at her having dared to fufpect that the morals of the virtuous Edward fell fhort of the perfection to which they pretended.　She lamented
with pathetic fweetnefs the depraved ftate of female tafte, which gave a coxcomb infinite advantage over a man of fenfe with the diffipated
belles of the day ; and Fitzofborne, refigning all
his hopes of conjugal felicity, with a profound
figh declared, that in future he muft tranquillife
his troubled foul with the endearing fympathy of
female friendfhip.　He proceeded with platonic
delicacy to draw the mental portrait of fuch a
friend as he wifhed to find : carefully including
in the enchanting compofition every grace which
Geraldine feemed confcious of poffeffing.　Superior refinement, and an apprehenfivenefs of
even juft praife, was mentioned with emphafis ;
and while the orator ftated the peculiar difficulty
in which this elevated faftidioufnefs would place
a fufceptible mind, impelled by warm efteem to
exprefs its admirrtion, yet reftrained from fpeak-
ing by the certainty of offending, the countefs
liftened with unfufpecting delight: fo true is the
maxim,

> And while he tells her he hates flattery,
> She fays fhe does fo, being then moft flatter'd.

　Lord Monteith interrupted the converfation
at a late hour.　He returned in very high fpirits,
not only elated by the triumph of his party, but
with his own particular fuccefs ; having made a
neat and appropriate fpeech, confifting of three
or four well-turned periods, which was honoured
with

with profound attention. His lordſhip was leſs quick in diſcovering improprieties than in reſenting them when pointed out by others. Fitzoſborne's ſitting alone with his lady, at five o'clock in the morning, alarmed him no more than Fitzoſborne's eſcorting her in a correſpondent dreſs to lady Fillagree's fancy-ball. He, recounted the events which had taken place in the debate with too much eagerneſs to liſten to the narrative of her adventures. He only heard with pleaſure, that Vernon paid no attention to her, and that ſhe was perfectly in charity with her *cecifbeo*. So many agreeable occurrences made him readily conſent to her propoſal of paying her annual viſit to Caernarvonſhire immediately; and he was too ſincere a friend not to enter with eagerneſs into her plan of rendering Edward ſome pecuniary ſervices. His late diſplay of oratorical ability ſeemed to enſure ſucceſs; "for," ſaid he, "though " I want nothing from Government, why ſhould " not my friends reap ſome advantage from the " fatigue which I endure in the ſervice of my " country? Do you think that they dare refuſe " me, Geraldine, when they know how much " I am courted by Oppoſition?" He concluded by obſerving, that Edward's talents would do honour to any adminiſtration. His appearing in a conſpicuous line would alſo mortify Arabella, and convince her that ſhe ought to have reſpected her brother's *deeper* knowledge of manners and characters, and not have diſmiſſed a lover who was infinitely too good for her.

CHAP.

CHAP. V.

Meanwhile, by Pleasure's sophistry allur'd,
　　From the bright sun and living breeze ye stray:
And, far in London's gloomy haunts immur'd,
　　Brood o'er your fortune's, freedom's, health's
　　　　decay ;
O blied of choice, and to yourselves untrue !
　　The young grove shoots, their bloom the fields
　　　　renew,
The mansion asks its lord, the swains their friend ;
　　While he does riot's orgies haply share,
　　Or tempt the gamester's dark destroying snare,
Or to some courtly shrine with lavish incense bend.
　　　　　　　　　　　　　　　　AKENSIDE.

WHILE the earl of Monteith, with all the blunt sincerity of his ardent character, pursued his friendly but unsuccessful design of serving Fitzosborne, the polite circles were very merry at his lordship's expence, every one wondering that he could not see what was so extremely visible to every body else. As lady Monteith had by retirement subdued the acrimony of competition, even the candour of her rivals returned, and the tide of popular opinion grew still stronger in her favour. Large allowances were made for a little vanity and a little indiscretion. Most people sincerely believed that, after all, her marked predilection for Fitzosborne was nothing more than a harmless flirtation, perhaps entered into out of frolic, or with a view to mortify Arabella.— These delicate extenuations were generally con-
　　　　　　　　　　　　　　　　　　　　cluded

cluded by a laugh at his lordſhip's ſtaying in
town to vindicate her character, and a fear, that
ſuch uncommon good-humour on his part might
encourage her to go greater lengths in her *mirth*
than ſhe at firſt intended.

The annihilation of domeſtic happineſs opening the faireſt views for Fitzoſborne's ſucceſs, he
determined to employ every engine for its de-
ſtruction. The guarded honour of Geraldine
had hitherto rejected his inſinuations to the diſad-
vantage of her lord with the warmth of confirmed
affection, and the indignation which a conſciouſ-
neſs of the inſeparable union between his reputation and her own muſt inſpire. But various inſtances had convinced him, that this " God of
" her Idolatry" was vulnerable in a thouſand
points ; eaſily deceived, eaſily ſeduced, ſoon irritated, and as quickly pacified. The preſence
of the counteſs, her ſuperior judgment, and the
reſpect for the decencies of life, which his ſtrong
attachment to her had inſpired, had hitherto preſerved him from any groſs acts of immorality,
and given a decorum to his conduct which juſti-
fied the confidence ſhe always placed in his behaviour. Fitzoſborne too plainly ſaw that there
was no innate principle to preſerve Monteith in
the hour of temptation, when his guardian angel
was abſent from her charge. Thoſe temptations
he reſolved to ſupply : he doubted not his own
ability to environ him with ſnares, from which
even a firmer virtue would find it difficult to eſcape ; and yet at the ſame time to conceal his inſidious interference, and to cover his machinations with the proſtituted names of friendſhip,
ſentiment and morality. Though lady Monteith's enlarged underſtanding had ſufficient diſ-
cernment to diſcover calumny, and to treat un-

founded

founded fufpicions with contempt, could fhe refift the evidence of truth? or could her feeling
heart fupport that cruel indifference which a diffipated hufband always affects to fhew to the amiable wife whom he injures by his vices? Her
ftrong fufceptibility at every circumftance which
threatened the diminution of their mutual regard
convinced him that fhe could not.   And furely
the refentment which a young and beautiful woman muft feel at fuch injurious negligence would
render her an eafy prey to the wiles of a feducer.
To fuppofe the contrary, was a paradox which
his knowledge of the human character would not
admit.

It is not my intention to pollute my page by
a defcription of thofe fuccefsful plans of iniquity
by which Fitzofborne fubverted the principles of
the man who really loved him, and felt anxious
to render him effential fervices.   Unhappily, the
world prefents too often the fpectacle of one immortal being alluring another to inebriety, or
plunging it in depravity, for me to excite furprife by adding, that fuch actions are not deemed
incompatible with the facred title of a friend.
Thefe feducers have not indeed always the deeper
motives which I afcribe to Fitzofborne; but let it
be remembered, that the principles he profeffed
gave a fanction to his more monftrous atrocity.
Private vices are public benefits.   It is not a general advantage, that property fhould be transferred from an indolent fenfualift to an active intelligent enterprifing citizen, who would turn it
to beneficial purpofes? Monteith would be juft
as happy with his dogs and horfes, the only fphere
of enjoyment which his limited underftanding
feemed capable of relifhing, though his beautiful
wife, and the fair poffeffions with which fhe was
endowed,

endowed, were refigned to fome clever fellow who had wit enough to acquire them. Suppofing the reftraint of confcience conveniently filenced by that fcepticifm which is now efteemed fo liberal, what other principle will you fubftitute to prevent fuch practices? Succefs foon reconciles the world to the profperous villain. A little declamation will fatisfy fentiment, and even the watchful dragon of honour may be charmed to fleep by honied words. Gratitude, which ufed to rank next to integrity in the fcale of virtues, is now, like its immediate predeceffor, degraded from its proud pre-eminence. Refinement has difcovered, that the giver beftows not from benevolent motives, nor from affection to the receiver, but merely to relieve himfelf from the pain of an uneafy emotion; and it has taught us to infer from thefe premifes, that it would be weaknefs to feel obligation for benefits which wholly proceed from the all-invigorating principle of felf-love.

Entangled in the mazes of an illicit amour, begun in a moment of inebriety, and purfued from want of courage to be fingular, and want of energy to be firm, the unhappy Monteith beheld his prefent fituation with horror, and contemplated his paft happinefs with vain regret. His little daughters, his Geraldine, his domeftic tranquillity, his rural amufements,—how forcible was the contraft between thofe guiltlefs pleafures, and the clamour of a Bacchanalian revel, the corroding inquietude of a gaming-table, and the venal allurements of a courtezan.

Thoufand after thoufand vanifhed at thefe midnight orgies. The image of his injured wife and fupplicating infants conftantly rofe to his view; but they only came to increafe his defperation, not to reftrain his madnefs. The words,

" one

" one more bottle, and another fong! What,
" Monteith a flincher? Come, my lord, luck
" muſt change; make one more ſpirited effort:"
and, " Can the deareſt of men, for whom I
" have refuſed ſuch liberal offers, deſert me?"
Such expreſſions formed the magic ſpells whoſe
powerful incantations enthralled a mind, reduced
to the deplorable ſtate of acting the part it ab-
horred, and adopting the vices it deſpiſed, left the
votaries of diſſipation ſhould ſuſpect that he wanted courage to be wicked.

Fitzoſborne did not expoſe his untainted reputation by *appearing* in theſe ſcenes of depravity.
He contented himſelf with pointing out parties
which he entreated his lordſhip to avoid, or with
mentioning inſtances of ſurpriſing turns of luck
at the gaming-table which it would be folly in
any one to expect. He exclaimed againſt Mrs.
Harley's infamy, but acknowledged that ſhe was
in the higheſt faſhion; that ſhe had rejected a
much larger ſettlement than what ſhe now folicited from Monteith, which he hoped his lordſhip would have reſolution to refuſe; and yet,
after all, as the ſtrong bias of the paſſions ſeemed
to point 'out that ſuch temporary engagements
were congenial to our natures, their criminality
muſt wholly depend upon the circumſcribed, and
perhaps erroneous, ſyſtems of political juriſpru-
dence. He always concluded theſe powerful diſ-
fuaſions by urging the peculiar ſeverity of lady
Monteith's principles, and the conſequent neceſſity of concealing his miſconduct from her. He
conjured him to haſten to Powerſcourt; and then
added, what he knew would negative the propoſal, " How will you ſupport the tears and the
" reproofs of that injured woman? For I fear,
" my friend, that in ſpite of every prudent pre-
                              " caution,

" caution, your pale dejected looks, embarraffed
" manner, and conftrained vivacity, cannot fail
" of attracting her apprehenfive obfervation."

While the cruel machinations of Fitzofborne
thus affailed the honour of Geraldine by vitiating
the mind of her hufband, the deftined victim of
his worfe than murderous defigns enjoyed the
foothing confolation of pouring her forrow into
the attentive ear of friendfhip. Ignorant of the
feverer trials which immediately awaited her, the
tranquillity of rural fcenes, the benevolent fimplicity of her revered father, the dignified refignation of Mr. Evans, and the interefting fweetnefs of the amiable Lucy, confpired to calm that
painful conflict which undeferved calumny and difappointed hope had excited in her foul. The early
carol of the lark, the dying fall of the nightingale,
the kindling glory of a fummer's morning, the
reviving frefhnefs of the evening zephyr, the various delights which the country affords, and the
attractive fimplicity of its uncontaminated inhabitants, infpired lady Monteith with ftrong indignation againft that faftidious tafte which,
while it degrades the majeftic operations of Nature with the epithets of ordinary and vulgar, or
paffes them with ftupid infenfibility, purfues the
celebrity required by the conftruction of a carriage or the adjuftment of a robe. Her cenfures
againft this petty ambition were, however, too
warm to be the dictates of cool judgment, and
evidently proved, that the fair declaimer had been
once included in the frivolous groupe who pay a
blind idolatry to popular efteem. Difappointment infpired other notions; and, guided by this
new impulfe, fhe appeared once in her converfations with Mifs Evans to lean to the dangerous
doctrines of Fitzofborne. " When I reflect,"

faid

faid fhe, " on the evanefcent nature of reputa-
" tion; that it is acquired without folicitude, and
" loft without guilt; that it is the fport of ca-
" lumny, and the battery from which envy mor-
" tally wounds the peace of innocence, I feel
" convinced that it is beneath the attention of a
" well-governed mind."

The converfation had been previoufly confined to the caprices of fafhion, and Mifs Evans
was furprifed that it fhould produce fuch a ferious
conclufion; for to this genuine child of nature
the eclat annexed to the invention of a becoming
turban, or even the honour of an innumerable
party, feemed unworthy of a moment's anxiety.
She therefore fixed her intelligent eyes upon her
friend, and afked her to what fhe alluded in this
reflection?

" My own fad ftory," faid Geraldine, " is
" ever predominant in my mind. Even while I
" am enjoying the delights of thefe beloved
" peaceful fcenes, I cannot for one moment for-
" get that I am now a mark for public ridicule;
" and I am endeavouring to derive fome confola-
" tion from thofe fentiments which a gentleman,
" a very fenfible man, and a friend of lord Mon-
" teith's, has frequently fuggefted."

" They can only apply," faid Lucy, " to the
" cafe of thofe who place their *ultimate* hopes in
" the applaufe of the world. They have nothing
" to do with the well-grounded mind, which,
" while it purfues the fteady path of duty, is
" pleafed with being encouraged on its journey
" by the modeft voice of well-earned praife.
" Far be it from me, my Geraldine, to feek to
" diminifh your confolations. Innocence allows
" you to poffefs a very fuperior one; and while
" your life difproves accufations, you have no
                                        " caufe

" cauſe to be depreſſed. Yet the watchful ſuſ-
" ceptibility of female honour cannot but feel
" every attack upon its character; and it moſt
" impatiently longs to refute the cenſures which
" its purity abhors. Lord Monteith's friend, I
" ſuppoſe, only made general obſervations. He
" could not allude to your particular ſtory."

 " They were the obſervations of Fitzoſborne,"
ſaid lady Monteith gravely.

 " Of Fitzoſborne? interrogated Lucy. " I
" have heard you deſcribe him as one of the moſt
" enlightened, uncorrupted, and amiable of men :
" the perſon, too, reſpecting whom your con-
" duct is cenſured."

 " It is exactly as you deſcribe. He is thus de-
" ſerving, and I am ſo accuſed."

 " Does a fixed contempt for the good-will of
" that maſs of his fellow-creatures which is called
" the world, imply this ſuperior merit? The
" world, I have heard my dear father often ſay
" judges right, but from wrong premiſes. It is
" haſty and raſh, not diſpaſſionate and reflecting.
" It kindles into indignation at a ſpecious tale : it
" loads a ſuſpected character with opprobrium;
" but however falſe its inference, however miſ-
" taken its judgment, its errors always lean to
" the ſide of juſtice and virtue. And I am the
" more inclined to pay a deference to my father's
" opinion, becauſe I find his idea of that aggre-
" gate body of which I am an individual con-
" firmed by my own feelings."

 " I ſhall only join the general deciſion of the
" world, which you ſo reverence," replied the
counteſs, " when I found the praiſes of Mr.
" Fitzoſborne. To the manners and the exte-
" rior of the moſt finiſhed gentleman, he adds
" the information of the ſcholar, and the profun-
" dity

" dity of the philofopher. Perhaps his ardent
" love of truth may urge him to too great a con-
" tempt for eftablifhed rules; and you know,
" Lucy, we muft not expect fuperior minds to
" pay a fcrupulous attention to the little puncti-
" lios which cuftom exacts from ordinary cha-
" racters. He is actuated by the moft exalted
" views, and his life is the nobleft comment up-
" on his opinions."

The limited obfervation of Mifs Evans had never difcovered fuch a being as lady Monteith defcribed ; and fhe regarded the delineation of its
diftinguifhed properties with fomewhat of the
fame kind of fcrupulous curiofity with which we
perufe the defcription of the unicorn and the kra-
ken ; not abfolutely denying that fuch things may
exift, but wifhing to have their reality more
clearly identified. Her wifh was foon gratified,
and this human phœnix was introduced at Powerfcourt by an event in which chance (the modern
term for Providence) had a fmaller fhare than
oftenfibly appeared.

The poft always arrived at fir William's in the
afternoon ; and though the good baronet had nothing of the bafhaw in his character, and was by
no means an adept in the fcience of politics, he
conftantly exercifed an unlimited authority over
the newfpaper, the contents of which he regularly recited, in an audible voice, to the party
affembled round his hofpitable board. The jour-
nal of paffing occurrences which found admiffion
at fir William's, was generally uncontaminated
by private flander, party abufe, or fulfome pane-
gyric, and fimply a plain narrative of the events
of the day. It *happened* however, that after lady
Monteith had fpent about four months at her father's,

ther's, the following paragraph found admittance :

" It is rumoured in the polite circles, that a
" certain ministerial nobleman, in the vicinity of
" P******d Place, finds sufficient attractions
" in the beautiful Mrs. Harley to console him
" for his recent disgrace; while a fair incon-
" stant is trying, whether the keen air of the
" C*********shire mountains may not be
" beneficial to a consumptive reputation. It is
" said, that lord M*******'s settlements on his
" new flame are uncommonly liberal."

Sir William was not versed in the language of
initials and asterisks ; and was not in possession of
the decyphering glossary which a knowledge of
polite scandal supplies. After two or three attempts to unravel the enigma, he delivered it to
his daughter, with a request that she would tell
him what it meant. A crimson blush and a dying paleness alternately took possession of her face
while she perused the paragraph. After coolly ob-
serving, that it was some very ill-natured nonsense,
she complained of faintness from the heat of the
room, a circumstance which her situation, being
near her fourth confinement, might render op-
pressive. Miss Evans's arm was ready to lead
her to her own apartment, at the door of which
she entreated her friend to leave her, and to su-
perintend the backgammon party in her room,
as she much feared she should not be able to re-
join them that evening.

No alarm was excited that night by this circumstance. Sir William's communications had
been too confused to convey any explanation to
his auditors, and any future appeal to the news-
paper for information was impossible, for it had
suddenly disappeared during the bustle occasioned
by

by lady Monteith's faintnefs. But fince the butler and the houfekeeper were both very great po-
liticians, and very anxious to infpect the conduct
of adminiftration, this circumftance too frequently happened to bear at this time any myfterious
air.

Geraldine's indifpofition wore next morning a
more ferious afpect. Her maid owned, that fhe
had been extremely reftlefs and agitated all night,
and her pulfe indicated confiderable fever. Sir
William's parental tendernefs took alarm. The
moft eminent medical affiftance which the country afforded was called in, and an exprefs was
difpatched to town to fummon her hufband.

The petrifying power of vice requires time
before it can render the heart completely callous.
Lord Monteith had not yet forgot his inimitable
Geraldine, the mother of his pretty little girls,
the founder of James-town, and the benign
enchantrefs whofe magic powers had converted
the wild unfrequented fhores of Loch Lomond
into the refidence of plenty, elegance, and happinefs. His recollection of the guiltlefs pleafures
once enjoyed in her fociety aggravated his fears
for her fafety; nor could a thoufand Mrs. Har-
leys detain him from her bedfide. Endeavouring
by the fpeed of his return to atone for the criminality of his abfence, relays of horfes were
ordered upon the road, and the exertions of the
poftboys were ftimulated by additional douceurs.
But lord Monteith is not the only furious driver
that has found it impoffible to travel from himfelf. New to the fuggeftions of remorfe, yet
unable to divert the pain of its fcorpion-fting by
the fallacious juftification of comparing his own
conduct with that of other men of fafhion, his
troubled imagination continually placed before
his

his eyes the frightful image of an amiable wife murdered by his vicious indifference; and his thoughts were alternately occupied by curfing his own folly, and frantickly addrefling Heaven to fpare a life which he now felt to be infinitely dearer than his own.

Such a fituation called for the ameliorating offices of friendfhip, and the fentimental, difpaffionate Fitzofborne had claimed that pious tafk. To abate the reader's indignation againft that gentleman's conduct, I muft affirm, that it was afterwards fatisfactorily proved, that the fatal paragraph which I have quoted was not communicated to the newfpaper editor in a hand-writing that bore the *leaft* refemblance to Edward's. I will alfo own, that his emotions during the journey to Powerfcourt were almoft as poignantly diftrefling as thofe of his fellow-traveller. Confcience, indeed, was lefs loud in her accufations, becaufe her fenfibility had by frequent repreffion been rendered more callous. But the probable difappointment of thofe plans of aggrandifement which he had purfued with fuch wicked diligence, haraffed his apprehenfion; and he regretted, that human fcience had not yet reached its fummit of perfection, by prefenting to him the immortalifing elixir that would enable him to difpute with death for the poffeffion of the victim whom he had marked for a more dreadful deftination.

CHAP. VI.

Dang'rous conceits are in their natures poisons,
Which, at the first, are scarce found to distaste ;
But, with a little act upon the blood,
Burn like the mines of sulphur.

SHAKESPEARE.

THE appearance of lord Monteith, when the carriage stopped at Powerscourt, was sufficiently deplorable to excite commiseration even in those bosoms which felt the strongest abhorrence of his former conduct. Pale, and trembling with apprehension, he asked if his lady were still alive. On receiving an answer in the affirmative, he flew to her apartment, not reflecting upon the effect which his sudden return might have. Fitzosborne, possessed of a greater command of his own feelings, stopped him at the door, and, dragging him into an adjoining room, whispered to him, that prudence and composure were highly necessary. "If you see lady Monteith in "your present perturbation of spirits," said he, "you will certainly become your own accuser, "and perhaps lay the foundation for much fu- "ture misery. Remember, possibly she knows "nothing of Mrs. Harley's affair. For shame ! "my friend, how you unman yourself by these "emotions."

"She lives," said Monteith, lifting up his eyes, which, to the extreme mortification of Fitzosborne, were suffused with tears. "If she "had died, murdered by my infidelity, I would "not have survived her."

Can

" Can you tell how her illnefs and your infi-
" delity can poffibly be connected ? If it pro-
" ceeds from her knowledge of your weaknefs,
" you have certainly caufe to dread feeing her.
" I muft entreat you, if you regard your repu-
" tation as a man of the world, or your autho-
" rity as the mafter of a family, do not let even
" your valet witnefs your diforder."

He was prevented from proceeding by the appearance of fir William Powerfcourt, whofe benevolent heart had been deeply penetrated by a
defcription of his fon-in-law's diftrefs, though his
paternal pride had previoufly ftimulated to refent
the abfence which even his unfufpicious temper
had confidered to be a neglect of his beloved
daughter.

" Be compofed, my lord," faid the good baronet, fhaking him affectionately by the hand ;
" my dear child will do well, don't make your-
" felf fo unhappy—fhe will be very glad to fee
" you, I affure you. She always names you
" with the greateft tendernefs."

" Dear injured excellence !" febbed Monteith.

" She never made one complaint of your ftay-
" ing fo long in London," continued fir William. " Sometimes, indeed, fhe faid, The
" houfe fits late thefe turbulent times. Then,
" after parliament broke up, you had fome bufi-
" nefs to get through to ferve a friend. The
" phyficians give us great hope of her to-day ;
" and when you are a little more compofed, I
" will let her know that you are come. Depend
" upon it, there will be no reproaches."

" Reproaches," reiterated Monteith, his eyes
fparkling with indignation ; " I cannot bear re-
" proaches. Thofe of my own heart are fuffi-
" ciently

" ciently excruciating. I won't see her. Order
" my horses."

Fitzosborne, who had watched every expres-
sion with serpent wiliness, here observed to sir
William, that travelling post with no rest, and
scarcely any refreshment, had greatly deranged
his friend's mind. "And I am fearful," said he,
" of some bad effects from the indiscretion of a
" servant, who hurried into lady Monteith's
" apartment to announce the earl's arrival."

No other hint was necessary to remove sir
William; while Monteith, with clenched fist,
traversed the room in an agony which increased
every moment.

" Am I expected to beg pardon?" exclaimed
he to Fitzosborne.

" If you go on accusing yourself, and yield-
" ing to these extravagancies, you invite imper-
" tinence, and must expect mortification. Lady
" Monteith must be destitute of the ruling pas-
" sion of her sex, if she does not make you feel
" that she knows her power over you. Remorse,
" my lord, like religion, is certainly a business
" between a man and his own heart; yet, possi-
" bly, as sir William lectures you upon one
" head, Mr. Evans may think it right to treat
" you with a little clerical freedom upon the
" other."

" It is all known then," said Monteith,
throwing himself upon a sofa; "and I am to be
" stared at by country boors as a reprobate and
" a libertine."

" Nothing is known, or can be known, if you
" act with common propriety. Sir William
" only talks of your staying in town, and at-
" tending parliamentary business, when you
" ought to have been nursing your wife in the
" country.

" country. Come, come, Monteith, go and
" afk her how fhe does, without entirely aban-
" doning all fenfe of dignity. But that I fcorn
" to probe a penetrated heart, I could remind
" you, that attention to my *former* counfels
" would have prevented your prefent pangs."

Lord Monteith fighed, and made another effort to vifit his countefs. The high tone of ecftafy to which his feelings had been elevated on
firft hearing of her fafety, was now confiderably
lowered; and he almoft wifhed that the fepa-
rating diftance which he had fo rapidly paffed
were ftill between them, to protect him from the
foul harrowing fight of an injured, yet ftill beloved object. " If," faid he to himfelf, " fhe
" utter one fevere expreffion; if fhe look at
" me with lefs tendernefs, nay, if fhe do but
" even betray a knowledge of my folly, I am
" loft."

His apprehenfions, however, were groundlefs.
Geraldine received him with that fmile of inef-
fable fweetnefs which generally irradiated her
countenance. It was, indeed, no longer play-
fully animated; but its penfive languor conveyed
even to his alarmed attention the idea of bodily
fuffering, rather than of mental anguifh. After
thanking him for the folicitude he had expreffed,
and which, fhe faid, her dear father had pathe-
tically defcribed, fhe congratulated him upon the
birth of a fon, who, though prematurely hurried
into the world by her indifpofition, (here fhe
ftifled a figh,) was yet, fhe was happy to find,
likely to live.

When Providence gratifies the clamorous
wifhes of us fhort-fighted mortals, it muft not
only give us the good that we afk, but it muft
alfo adapt the time of its bounty to the moment

of

of our defires. Eight months ago lord Monteith thought nothing but a fon wanting to gratify all his wifhes. He now ftarted with deep remorfe and difmay at the birth of a being, who feemed to rufh into exiftence to reproach him for having wafted the fair poffeffions to which his anceftors had left him heir, in the frenzy of the gaming-table and the haunts of diffipation. The too fufceptible countefs read in his embarraffed manner a refutation of all the hopes which a defcription of his lively emotions on his return had infpired. She could no longer flatter herfelf with the idea that envy and falfehood had fabricated the paragraph fo fatal to her peace, and nearly fo to her life. She covered her beautiful face, pale as the pillow on which it refted, and, fobbing out an apology for an hyfterical weaknefs which would not permit her to fupport the fight fhe had fo earneftly defired, fhe entreated to be left alone. To recruit her enfeebled fpirits was the plea that fhe urged; but her real defign was to lament unobferved the peculiar hardfhips of her prefent fate.

The obfervations fhe made upon her lord's character had hitherto difclofed much inconfiftency, weaknefs, and imperfection; but fhe had ever been confoled by the conviction, that his heart retained many traits of native goodnefs, and that his ftormy paffions, even in their wildeft uproar, confeffed the power of her gentle influence. Her delicacy fhrunk at the thought of dividing his affections with a venal wanton; and the rectitude of her principles infpired the livelieft concern, when fhe recollected the guilt which her ftill-beloved lord incurred by purfuing an illicit attachment. Weak in body; enfeebled in mind; reduced by fufferings, and dif-

appointed

appointed in her deareſt hopes ; her pride wounded in its moſt fuſceptible part, ſlighted by him
whom ſhe moſt wiſhed to pleaſe ; and traduced
by that world whoſe applauſe ſhe had ſo ſedu-
louſly courted, what was there to bind lady Monteith to life ?　Surely I might now call in Ar-
ria's dagger, Portia's firebrand, or ſome more
faſhionable quietus, with very good effect.　But
my heroine was a *mother*, and though man, poſſeſſed of firmer nerves and a colder heart, is often
unjuſt to female merit, and falſely ſuppoſes that
name to be ſynonimous with weak ſuſceptibility,
maternal feelings have frequently inſpired ſuch
long-ſuffering quiet fortitude as would add luſtre
to the annals of a martyr.

　Four innocent helpleſs creatures, who derived
their exiſtence from her, taught Geraldine that
ſhe had more to do than to lie down and die.　In
proportion to the hazard of their being deprived
of paternal tenderneſs and protection, they poſſeſſed ſtronger claims upon their mother's heart,
and urged her to exert every faculty to preſerve
their morals, their fortune, and their happineſs.
Hope revived with the determination of diſcharg-
ing theſe ſolemn duties, and whiſpered, that patience, gentleneſs, and undeviating rectitude of
conduct, ſometimes produces a further reward,
over and above the certain eulogy of approving
conſcience.　A reclaimed huſband *has* been re-
ſtored to virtue by the mild allurements of a
blameleſs wife ; and a joyful mother *has* had the
glory of leading back a repentant father to his
abandoned children.　" Be ſuch my lot !" ſaid
the counteſs.　" How poor is all other praiſe !
" How contemptible every other purſuit !"

　Theſe reſolutions, though formed in the ſecure privacy of a ſick chamber, might have re-
ſiſted

fifted common temptations ; and lord Monteith,
if left to his own natural character, would have
evinced his penitence for his paft faults by a more
attentive tendernefs ; but Fitzofborne knew too
well the advantages of difunion to permit the
wounds which he had inflicted on the conjugal
felicity of the Monteiths to be thoroughly healed.
His influence over his lordfhip's mind was as unbounded as vigour, duplicity, and craft can acquire over a weak, open, unreflecting character.
It had been interrupted by the ftrong alarm which
lady Monteith's danger excited ; but as the returning health of the charming countefs relieved
all anxiety for her fafety, her hufband grew weary
of the trouble of thinking for himfelf, and, vo-
luntarily furrendering the intellectual liberty of
which he was fo tenacious, permitted his falfe
friend again, " with devilifh art," to " reach
the organs of his fancy.

The moft accurate judges of human nature
have obferved, that we feldom forgive thofe
whom we have injured ; and though the word
forgivenefs may be here mifplaced, it is certain
that the pride of human nature, fond of juftifying
itfelf, always endeavours to find an excufe for its
own mifconduct in the behaviour of thofe who
are fufferers from its faults. Almoft perfuaded
that his infidelity and extravagance had efcaped
difcovery, lord Monteith wifhed to filence the
pain of felf-accufation by excufes better calculated to ftifle remorfe than the poor apology which
the more enormous guilt of others fupplies.—
While his imagination continued to unite the
ideas of Geraldine and perfection, the behaviour
of his grace the duke or the moft noble marquis
to their refpective ladies afforded no extenuation
of his own folly. But when his jaundiced eye
began

began to think her mirth levity, and her gravity fullennefs, the load of his own guilt was at once removed. Though the opinion of the world ftill prefcribes forbearance and decorum to the wife, it allows the hufband to recriminate, and a defect in temper on the part of the lady is a received excufe for the vices of the gentleman :—a cruel and unjuft conclufion, yet recommended by its univerfal prevalence to the moft ferious confideration of the inftructors of female youth.

Fitzofborne increafed all Monteith's extravagance by faint praife, affected filence, or ftifled obfervations. But his chief attention was now directed to the countefs. Her forced gaiety and frequent abfence of mind plainly told him, that the newfpaper paragraph had done its office, and he not unfuccefsfully endeavoured to communicate to her his knowledge of her fituation, and his commiferation for her fufferings. Every inftance of her lord's neglect or inattention was rendered more excruciating to Geraldine by Fitzofborne's watching her countenance, or marking Monteith's behaviour by fome flight fign of difpleafure. In his converfations with her, he frequently introduced fubjects which he knew muft harrow up her foul. Reverting again to his favourite maxim, that " the con- " fcious mind is its own awful world," he commented on the prefent perverted ftate of fociety, in which merit generally mourns in filence, from the injuftice or mifconception of others. The omnipotence of beauty, when united with its rare affociates fenfibility and intelligence, was another favourite theme. He ridiculed the illiberality of annexing an idea of guilt to the allowable admiration of what is " perfect, fair,

" and

" and good." And he continually affirmed, that minds of a fuperior ftamp ought to fhape their conduct by their own innate fenfe of decorum, and not by the rules intended for more grovelling capacities. He condemned the indelicacy and want of tafte of many men of fafhion with warmth bordering on feverity, for deferting the fociety of women of refinement and information, and forming grofs attachments, in which intellect could have no fhare. But the only remedy which he could devife for this evil was, he faid, to relax, inftead of bracing, the feverity of our fyftem of divorce : and he frequently concluded with expatiating upon the folly of legiflators, in not accommodating their inftitutions to the varying humours of the people whom they meant to control. To fome of thefe fuggeftions lady Monteith's mind gave an unqualified affent. She doubted the tendency of others ; but they were fo difguifed in the veil of fuperior zeal for the improvement and happinefs of the world, and fo fweetened by the adroit mixture of oblique flattery, that fhe feemed rather willing to blame the limited powers of her own underftanding than to queftion the infallibility of Fitzofborne's all-fapient mind. Sir William, who was fometimes prefent at thefe orations, was at firft extremely puzzled to know what the gentleman meant ; but when he found that fomething was wrong in that palladium of juftice which he had ever been accuftomed to venerate, the Britifh Conftitution, and heard the propofed improvement, his full conviction of his own incapacity for fupporting an argument could fcarcely prevent him from telling the declaimer, that the remedy was worfe than the difeafe.

Fitzofborne's

Fitzofborne's contempt for the difpofition and abilities of fir William betrayed him into an indifcretion which his mafterly addrefs could fcarcely repair. From his firft arrival at Powerfcourt he had ftudied the characters of the Evans's with jealous difcrimination ; and, as their talents and manners were alike undifguifed, he foon found, that they would prove moft formidable opponents to his iniquitous defigns. He was, therefore, peculiarly careful to conceal from them thofe nefarious principles which he fancied he had fufficiently enveloped to efcape the confufed apprehenfion of the good baronet. He was, however, completely miftaken. Sir William's ruminations on Edward's affertions difcovered confequences which were at firft unperceived ; and, his uneafinefs increafing, he determined to difclofe it to his good friend the rector, with a hope of being reaffured by his fuperior learning.

At the conclufion of an unfuccefsful rubber at backgammon, by way of apology for bad play, he frankly owned, that he had been thinking of fomething elfe all the time. " It is cer " tainly very wrong in me," faid he, " but I " almoft doubt of the truth of what Solomon " tells us, that there is nothing new under the " fun." He then repeated Fitzofborne's theory, and added, " Is it not a new way of punifhing " a man for ufing one wife ill, by giving him " leave to marry another ?"

Many years had elapfed fince Mr. Evans's knowledge of the great world had been folely derived from the limited information of books and newfpapers. The dafhing fpirits with whom he had been formerly acquainted fought celebrity by high phaetons, Pomona green

coats

coats, and Artois buckles; and feldom ventured
upon more profound difquifitions than what
were neceffary to determine the height which
the younger Veftris could jump, or the diftance
that Eclipfe could gain on a dray-horfe in a
courfe of five minutes. The elegant tutor was
now changed into the rural divine, and, in common with all lovers of literature, he rejoiced to
hear, that the frivolity of fafhionable manners
was yielding to a fpirit of deep refearch and
difcriminating curiofity. Suppofing that Philofophy *ftill* retained her character of being the
handmaid of Truth, he felt inclined to pardon
a few extravagancies in her admirers; and, be-
lieving the fountain pure, he repeated the popular couplet:

> A little draught intoxicates the brain,
> But drinking largely fobers us again.

Neither the general philanthropy of Mr. Evans's
character, nor the prepoffeffing impreffions which
lady Monteith's warm encomiums on Fitzofborne had made upon his mind, could induce
him to give a favourable interpretation to a
propofition that threatened to fever the grand
link which unites correct morals and focial happinefs. His candour could only point to one
conclufion, which was, that the natural imbecillity of his revered patron's underftanding
increafed with his years, and that the conclufion he had drawn from the arguments which
Edward had ufed, was directly contrary to
what the orator intended.

The anfwer which he returned to fir William
was of a temporizing kind. But, after revolving the converfation in his own mind, he
determined

determined to apply to that confidant to whom, since deprived of a ftill dearer friend, he had been accuftomed to intruft all his perplexities. He was concerned to find that Lucy's opinion of Mr. Fitzofborne was not in unifon with the fentiments of the countefs. She expreffed her diflike of the myfterious air which he generally affected ; and obferved, that Geraldine, who knew his difpofition thoroughly, apologized for the eccentricity of fome of his fentiments by urging his foreign education, and affirming that fhe knew he poffeffed the beft heart in the world. " Perhaps he does," continued Mifs Evans ; " but people who wifh well to any " caufe feldom attempt to break down the bul- " warks that defend it." Her alarmed father eagerly inquired, if fhe fufpected any thing deiftical in his principles.

" Thank God," returned Lucy, " none of " my acquaintance are deifts ; therefore I do " not know in what manner they would act. " But furely, my dear fir, when religious " truths are impreffed deeply upon a cultivated " mind, they muft give a tincture to our ordi- " nary converfation. Subjects which we " efteem facred are not dragged into table-talk " controverfy ; and the narratives of holy writ " are not degraded by being drawn into a lu- " dicrous parallel with the light events of the " paffing moment. But I am willing to allow " that I may be more fevere from being lefs " accuftomed to the freedom of fafhionable " manners ; for I obferve my Geraldine, who " poffeffes the piety and the purity of an angel, " is not fhocked at this fpecies of levity."

" Does not Mr. Fitzofborne appear to fhow " a very marked admiration of the countefs ?" inquired Mr. Evans.

" Every

" Every body muſt admire her," returned Lucy, evading a direct reply : " I do not mean " merely on account of her perſonal charms, " though ſhe is now lovelier than ever, but for " her patient ſweetneſs and her dignified reſig- " nation."

" When you uſe the term reſignation, my " dear," interrupted Mr. Evans, " you ſhould " confine it to ſeverer trials than thoſe which " your enchanting friend has yet been called " upon to endure. Though we have often " lamented the capricious inattention of her " lord's behaviour, it is only one of thoſe leſſer " conflicts, by which Providence mercifully " prepares us for the more excruciating ſtrug- " gles that we muſt all ſuſtain before we are " liberated from this world. You know whoſe " ſentiments I now repeat. The harmonious " voice which once gave them utterance is " ſilent ; yet the will of Heaven calls for cheer- " ful acquieſcence, and I obey."

Unwilling to depreſs her father at that moment, by repeating obſervations which might probably be merely the creatures of her own fancy, Miſs Evans dropped a tear to her mother's memory, and was ſilent.

CHAP.

CHAP. VII.

———Mark you this, Baſſanio ;
'The Devil can cite Scripture for his purpoſe :
An evil ſoul, producing holy witneſs,
Is like a villain with a ſmiling cheek ;
O, what a goodly outſide falſehood hath !

SHAKSPEARE.

MR. EVANS was not one of thoſe ſupine
paſtors who, contented with their own immediate ſecurity, forbear to warn their flock of
the inſidious approaches of the wolf. His
daughter's obſervations determined him to
watch Fitzoſborne with ſcrupulous attention ;
and, if any thing ſhould happen to confirm his
doubts, the hazard of being cenſured for imper-
tinent interference would not deter him from
ſtating to lady Monteith the danger of an intimacy with a man whoſe paſſions were not ſub-
jected by the reſtraints which religion impoſes.

Edward ſeemed rather to ſolicit than to ſhun
this ſcrutiny. Some caſual expreſſions from Sir
William, and the turn which Mr. Evans generally gave to the converſation, convinced him,
that his zeal to make proſelytes had thrown
him off his guard, and that in order to ſecure
one convert he muſt allay the ſuſpicions which
a deſire to gain many admirers had excited. He
ſaw in Mr. Evans a man poſſeſſed of a ſincere,
zealous, well-informed mind, occaſionally the
dupe of its own excellence, ſomewhat haſty in
its concluſions, and diſpoſed to receive a few
ſtrong expreſſions as a fair definition of character :

racter: to which was added, a confidence in its own attainments, not unfrequent in an educated perfon long eftranged from the invigorating collifion of congenial fociety. Edward adapted his behaviour to the rules which this difcovery pointed out, and he feized the opportunity which Mr. Evans had given, by leading the converfation to the finitenefs of human comprehenfion, to make what appeared like a candid difclofure of his fentiments.

"I perceive fir," faid he, "that you are anx-
"ious to difcover my opinions; and inftead of
"blaming, I highly admire the integrity of
"mind which fuch curiofity evinces. I will
"own, that during my refidence upon the
"Continent I was fomewhat tinctured with
"the fcepticifm fo prevalent there: and I will
"confefs too, that the converfation of the
"higher circles in my own country, and above
"all the manners of many of the clergy, have
"not tended to remove my doubts. While the
"church appears to be more affiduous to de-
"fend its emoluments, than to promote the
"falvation of its members, no wonder if we
"reject its meagre doctrines. The character
"of the gentleman and the divine are not often
"feen in unifon. If I had early poffeffed the
"opportunity of contemplating the happy mix-
"ture, religion would have appeared to me
"more attractive from the reflected beauty of
"its minifters; but, inftead of lamenting what
"is paft, let me, by propitiating your candour,
"improve my prefent happy acquaintance."

"Religion," faid Mr. Evans, returning Fitzofborne's bow, "cannot really fuffer by the mif-
"conduct of its officials in the opinion of any
"well difpofed, confiderate mind. Our at-
"tendance

" tendance at the altar does not remove us
" from human temptations ; and with refpect
" to the fault to which you allude, a too great
" pertinacity refpecting our temporal rights,
" candour will remember that our poffeffions
" are not hereditary. Moft of us have united
" ourfelves to fociety by the ftrong ties of huf-
" band and father ; and the ftudy of thofe di-
" vine precepts which were meant to enlarge
" the focial affections may, by the infirmity of
" human nature, which mixes error with our
" ' faireft aims,' fometimes extend to a culpa-
" ble folicitude for the fortunes of thofe dear
" connections, and abate the reliance which a
" chriftian ought to place in the direction and
" fupport of the friend of the friendlefs."

" I admit that your apology has weight,"
refumed Fitzofborne ; " but what will you fay
" of that avidity for field fports and love of
" diffipation which fo ftrongly characterife the
" divines of this age, and which you, fir, con-
" demn by your own example ?"

" I blame every particular inftance," replied
Mr. Evans, " without admitting the cenfure to
" be determinate againft the *whole* order. We
" are marked by our habits from the reft of
" fociety ; and the ' fox-hunting parfon,' or the
" infignificant ' Bob Jerome,' is pointed out to
" fatire, while the pale ftudent, who confumes
" his health over the midnight lamp in the moft
" important refearches, or the laborious in-
" ftructor of his village flock, are prevented
" by their obfcurity from counterpoifing the
" weight of public odium by their ufeful un-
" obtrufive virtues : but, granting the general
" conduct of the clergy to be as bad as their
" flanderers intimate, the fervice to which we

D " are

" are confecrated partakes not of our depra-
" vity."

" Perhaps not in minds endued with ftrong
" powers of reflection," returned Fitzofborne :
" but, as the chriftian fyftem feems beft adapt-
" ed for the lower orders of fociety, it is much
" to be lamented, that any thing fhould im-
" pede its progrefs where it has the beft chance
" of fuccefs. Perhaps the rules by which I
" would eftimate the conduct of its minifters
" are too ftrict, and though, unhappily, my
" own principles have inclined to deifm, I
" have candour enough to regret, that while
" law and phyfic are permitted to efcape un-
" contaminated by the knavery of pettifoggers
" or the ignorance of empirics, divinity im-
" pofes perfection upon its ftudents. But our
" converfation is likely to be interrupted. Per-
" mit me to fay that I fhall renew it with plea-
" fure. I am a novice at compliment, and
" fhall therefore only obferve in my abrupt
" manner, that if the caufe you fupport were
" always as ably defended both in the pulpit
" and in fociety, infidelity would be deprived
" of one of its moft powerful weapons."

Every one has his weak fide. Though the
cup of undifguifed flattery would have been rejected with difdain, yet when tempered by apparent moderation, and a wifh for conviction,
it became tolerably palatable. Mr. Evans, indeed, ftill felt the propriety of hinting the dangerous tendency of Fitzofborne's principles to
lady Monteith ; but he thought it juft to qua-
lify his cenfures with many expreffions of refpect for his character, and admiration of his
abilities. " I grieve for his perverted talents,"
faid he ; " and yet they encourage me to hope,
" that

" that the happy time will come, when they
" will be inftruments of reftoring him to a
" comfortable ftate of mind. Many people
" are driven into infidelity by the ftings of a
" burdened confcience; but I fhould *think* that
" is not Mr. Fitzofborne's excufe for fcepticifm.
" Yet the manners of the clergy can be no
" more than an oftenfible reafon."

Geraldine was not in a difpofition to doubt
Edward's virtues. Though fhe had been that
very morning the unhappy dupe of his cruel
duplicity, her agonized foul clung to him as
to the guardian angel who was to refcue her
out of an abyfs of forrow. She had difcovered
a letter from Mrs. Harley to her lord. It lay
open upon his dreffing-table, and the hated
name was fo confpicuoufly placed as neceffarily
to attract her eye. She could not refift her
defire to perufe it, and the fatal contents foon
convinced her, that the bufinefs which lord
Monteith had hinted would foon recal him to
London was nothing more than a wifh to renew that degrading connection. The difcovery
feemed to be perfectly accidental. She perceived
no preconcerted plan in the circumftance of her
having been fent into the room by Fitzofborne
to fetch a volume of Rouffeau, from which he
had juft mifquoted a well-known paffage. She
never confidered that he had free accefs to her
lord's apartments; and fhe could not know
that he had not only purloined the letter from
Monteith, but that he actually inftigated him
to the propofed journey, by thofe indirect
means of oppofition which he had found to be
the moft fuitable way of governing a 'head-
ftrong impetuous character.

D 2

Fitzofborne

Fitzofborne allowed her time to perufe the letter, and then followed her to the dreffing-room. She was leaning in a kind of ftupor over a chair, her eyes fixed on the portrait of her lord which hung over the chimney, with a fort of complaining fweetnefs in their expref-fion which language could ill defcribe. Ed-ward addreffed her with rhapfodical confufion. He faid the letter was a miftake. He affured her that Monteith's affections were ftill unquef-tionably her's. He execrated his conduct, and then befought her to be calm for her children's fake. At that interefting adjuration the ref-trained tears ftole in filence down her cheek; and her tears again elevated Fitzofborne's fym-pathifing tendernefs to frenfy. He called her " dear lovely excellence!" He wifhed ten thoufand plagues to overwhelm the narrow foul of the traitor who wanted difcernment to be juft to her merits; and he vowed that he could not look at fuch a ftriking imperfonification of fuffering meeknefs without wifhing to avenge her wrongs.

The countefs anfwered in a faint tone : " My " wrongs require no avenger. My lord fhould " be more careful of his correfpondence. Let " me entreat you to conceal the weaknefs into " which my curiofity has betrayed me."

" And is that the only proof I can give you " of my inviolable regard ?"

" What other proofs can a wife receive, con-" fiftent with her folemn duties ?"

" The ftricteft delicacy, the moft rigid pru-" dence, would allow an adopted brother to " take a more active part. Remember too, it " is ftill poffible, that the ties of efteem may " be fanctioned by thofe of kindred. Can I
" feek

" feek the recovery of lady Arabella's favour
" by worthier means than by trying to difen-
" gage her brother from a criminal attach-
" ment ?"

" O! name the means that may produce
" that blcffed end," exclaimed the impaffioned
Geraldine, with clafped hands, and wild em-
phatic looks : " refcue my Monteith from this
" dreadful thraldom ; reftore to me his valua-
" ble but eftranged heart, and I will pray for
" you, Fitzofborne—I will entreat of Heaven,
" that all your future days may be as happy as
" thofe I once enjoy'd."

Edward had no defire to be included in Geraldine's prayers. He was equally averfe to
hear of her attachment to her hufband, and of
her dependance on Heaven. The advice he
gave was of a fatiric nature. It was, to charge
her lord with his infidelity ; to humble him by
her fuperiority ; and to convince him by her
eloquence. Vice, he affirmed, muft fhrink from
the prefence of virtue. The funbeam of her
eye muft diffipate the clouds by which Monteith's reafon was enveloped. His recovered
judgment would compare innocence, grace,
and beauty, with proftitution, vanity, and caprice ; and a repentant hufband, awakened by
her reproofs to a fenfe of honour, would at her
feet abjure the infamous Harley, and all her
flagitious fifterhood.

Lady Monteith's perturbed mind ftill poffeffed
fufficient clearnefs to refift the adoption of fuch
a dangerous expedient, which, by inflaming
the violent paffions of her lord, was more likely
to make him caft off all the decorum which a
dread of difcovery impofed, than to check the
career of his vicious indulgence ; and her delicacy

cacy pointed out the imprudence of arming his pride in the caufe of a courtezan, when fhe hoped it might be made the happy inftrument of releafing him from a degrading connection. " I have," faid fhe, " prefcribed to myfelf but " two rules for my conduct in this unfortunate " affair ; and to thefe I will rigidly adhere. I " will never reproach lord Monteith, nor will I " ever divulge his indifcretions. Even my Lucy, " the partner of my foul, does not know that " the dejection which fhe muft obferve in me " proceeds from any other caufe than latent " indifpofition."

" There are certainly many reafons for " withholding fuch confidence from Mifs " Evans ; and when I confider your father's " age and increafing infirmities, I renounce a " plan which the refpectability of his character " once fuggefted to me, of acquainting him " with his fon-in-law's conduct, and urging " him to affume the tone highly becoming an " injured and affectionate parent."

" O ! for Heaven's fake ! reject that idea," exclaimed the terrified countefs. " Let not " the halcyon calm of his declining years be " clouded with a doubt of his child's happinefs. " How ungrateful, how impious fhould I be, " to draw from repofing age the pillow on " which it finks to reft, cheered by approving " confcience, and holding fweet communion " with that peaceful world for which it has " been long preparing."

" And are you not afraid that his paternal " folicitude will pervade your pious conceal- " ment ?" inquired Fitzofborne. " I have feen " him watch your varying looks, and caft glan-
" ces

" ces on lord Monteith ftrongly indicative of
" fufpicion."

" You alarm me. Surely I had better leave
" Powerfcourt immediately,.before thofe fuf-
" picions fhall be confirmed."

" That propofal, madam, indicates your cuf-
" tomary prudence, though it is hard at fuch a
" time to deprive yourfelf of the comforts of
" his tender affection, and the foothings of
" Mifs Evans's friendfhip. Whither will you
" direct your penfive fteps ?"

" Not to that cruel world, Fitzofborne,
" which has tarnifhed my reputation, and
" robbed me of my hufband's heart. I will go
" to Monteith, and embrace my dear little
" girls, from whom I have been ten months
" feparated. Their playful prattle will perhaps
" amufe me ; at leaft their undifcerning fim-
" plicity will not impofe upon me a painful
" reftraint, in order to efcape yet more infup-
" portable obfervations ; I fhall be allowed the
" free indulgence of tears, and my mind may
" poffibly recover ftrength from folitude."

" And is this the lot of the nobleft orna-
" ment of her age and country ?" exclaimed
Edward." " O lady Monteith ! are you ano-
" ther victim to the blind caprices of For-
" tune ?"

" I was the carver of my own fortune, and
" muft not complain of her caprices. I was
" juft to the impulfe of an early attachment,
" and I have no one to condemn. Even at
" this inftant complaint is filenced by pity.
" Lord Monteith cannot be happy. The re-
" collection of me muft obtrude upon his guilty
" dalliance. The imprudent woman, by whom
" he is fatally entangled,.can urge no claim to
" his

" his affections, to invalidate my prior right.
" I am the mother of his children, the faithful
" repofitory of his fecrets, the partner of his
" forrows. I have foothed his anxieties, com-
" pofed his ruffled temper, watched him in
" ficknefs.——O Fitzofborne ! words cannot
" exprefs how mnch this agonifing heart pre-
" ferred his intereft and his happinefs to my
" own."

Edward grafped her unconfcious hand, and
tremuloufly articulated, " Muft corroding for-
" row wafte the faireft pattern of all that is
" good and attractive ? Surely, Monteith !
" thou art the only man who could be unjuft to
" fuch excellence."

" My good friend," faid the countefs, roufed
to recollection by the ready tears which bathed
her hands, " fupprefs this keen fenfibility of
" my forrows. You fhall fee that I will en-
" dure them. For my children's fake, for the
" fake of all who love me, I will endeavour to
" exert myfelf: and to be amufed, I will vifit
" the good cottagers whom I once made happy ;
" I will retrace the groves I planted, and re-
" fume my accuftomed occupations ; though
" every employment, every purfuit, even life
" itfelf, is taftelefs now."

Fitzofborne dried his tears, and took a turn
acrofs the room to recover the philofophy which
he protefted had never before been fo feverely
tried. Could nothing be done, nothing be
thought of, to reftore the charming fufferer to
the peace which fhe fo highly merited ? Again
he addreffed the trembling mourner, who,
gazing on the portrait of her lord, feemed to
apoftrophize the beloved remembrance, and to
implore not merely compaffion but juftice, inattentive

tentive to the blandifhments of her feducer, unconfcious of the impropriety of that confidence
which her agitated foul beftowed, and only fufceptible of the fenfe of anguifh, or the feeble
hope of regaining an alienated heart.

"At length," faid Fitzofborne, after two or
three ineffectual endeavours to fpeak, "I have
"thought of two plans. They will, indeed, in-
"clude a little oblique conduct; but the end is
"too pure, too defirable to render objectionable
"the means of obtaining it. I know a young
"nobleman who wifhes to rival your lord in
"Mrs. Harley's favour. He is rich and extra-
"vagant, and I have fome influence over his
"mind. It is but fpiriting him to outbid your
"hufband, and the venal fair will foon forbid
"the vifits of her lefs liberal keeper. Or, I
"could feign a letter as from Mrs. Harley to
"this gentleman, which would awaken Mon-
"teith's jealoufy, and probably might have the
"fame effect of diffolving the connection. You
"ftart, madam. Confider that the infamy of
"the woman is confirmed, and how forcible
"are the claims which your innocent children
"have upon your exertions!"

"I muft not preferve their innocence by the
"forfeiture of my own. What right have I to
"aggravate the guilt of an unhappy woman, or
"to transfer to another family the calamity
"which weighs me down? Nor can I yield to
"fully my integrity by bafely framing a forged
"accufation, or to taint my reputation by ex-
"pofing it to the difgrace of a difhonourable
"difcovery."

"I lament when generofity becomes roman-
"tic, and I muft beg permiffion to urge my
"fchemes with what I think irrefiftible argu-

"ments,

" ments, if the faint hope which I have found-
" ed upon my influence over lord Monteith's
" mind fhould fail me. Unfortunately, he is
" fo bent upon going to town, that it will be
" ufelefs to oppofe his plan ; but I will accom-
" pany him, and exert all my limited abilities
" to diffolve this enchantment. No matter
" though I lofe his friendfhip ; his vicious pur-
" fuits have annihilated my efteem, and I fcorn
" to receive future favours from a man unjuft
" to you."

" Ah !" thought Geraldine, " what can break
" the adamantine chain which links him to my
" heart ! Should the hour ever arrive when af-
" fection ceafes to throb, will not duty continue
" to urge its refiftlefs claims ? But I cannot
" wonder, that a mind fo refined as Fitzof-
" borne's fhould call weaknefs vice, and difdain
" communion with one who gives licence to
" thofe rebel paffions, which his firmer fpirit
" holds in calm fubjection. O, that Monteith
" poffeffed his virtues ! But earth muft not re-
" femble heaven."

" You paufe, madam," faid Fitzofborne, in-
terrupting her train of thought. " Am I ftill fo
" unfortunate as not to be able to fuggeft any
" thing deferving of your approbation ?"

" My excellent friend !" refumed the Countefs, " follow the dictates of your own good
" heart. Whatever fcheme your knowledge of
" the world fuggefts, whatever diffuafive argu-
" ments your fuperior talents direct you to ufe,
" exert them in my caufe. But be careful to
" reftrain your zeal to reftore my ruined peace,
" left it fhould urge you to purfue thofe indirect
" paths which, even if fuccefsful, my principles
" muft conftantly difapprove."

" I

" I think," returned the fophifter, the code
" of laws which you dignify by your obedience
" permits the ferpent to be blended with the dove.
" Your innocence and your reputation cannot
" be injured by actions in which you do not
" participate; and if my confcience juftifies
" my proceedings, what have you to oppofe ? Be
" affured, that not even your intereft would
" prompt me to any ftep which I did not *think*
" highly warrantable; and here again I am
" countenanced by thofe doctrines which teach
" me that the motive conftitutes the act."

" Be fure," faid the countefs, " to examine
" your motives with fcrupulous care, left you
" fhould be deceived by a fpecious good."

" My motives," faid Fitzofborne, " have un-
" dergone the defired fcrutiny, and I will abide
" by the refult of my inquiry. But I have two
" favours to requeft of you. Do not, while with
" unremitting affiduity I ftake all my hopes,
" and brave every peril to reftore to you the
" happinefs you have loft—do not, deareft lady
" Monteith ! while I am far diftant from you,
" liften to any uncharitable fuggeftions that
" might tend to prejudice me in your efteem.
" Should any reflections be caft upon me for
" cherifhing fome peculiar notions, call to mind
" that noble candour which teaches us, that
" thofe principles cannot be wrong which
" prompt right actions. Permit me too the
" honour of your correfpondence; and if fuc-
" cefs fhould crown my hopes, if my once va-
" lued friend fhould return to Monteith wor-
" thy of you, allow me to partake your
" tranfports; and let the cloud of forrow and
" difappointment which now obfcures my
" youth, be brightened by the gladdering ray

of

" of your fociety. For it is only your unre-
" ferved friendfhip that can *now* render life de-
" firable."

The countefs promifed the required favours
with penetrating fincerity. She confirmed the
affurances of her permanent efteem by giving
him a miniature porfrait of herfelf, which had
been drawn with a view of being decorated with
brilliants, and prefented to lady Arabella on her
intended nuptials. Her opinion of Fitzofborne's
merits was wrought up to admiration; and the
refult of this interview convinced him, that he
had gained all the ground in her affections which
probability allowed him to expect. Her delicacy was no longer ftartled by his paffionate
manner: the warm intereft which he took in
her caufe no longer awakened the apprehenfion
of unwarrantable defigns. She had all the confidence in his integrity which he wifhed to infpire; and he relied upon her gratitude and
her generofity to divert every inference, and
filence every fuggeftion, that might be urged to
his disfavour.

The moment, therefore, was unpropitious
which Mr. Evans had chofen to alarm her fears,
by ftating his conviction, that the *fingularity* of
her friend's fentiments were more nearly allied
to deifm than their apparent moderation and
candour made her fufpect. I have already
mentioned the motives which induced Mr.
Evans to foften his intended cenfure; but Geraldine liftened with impatience even to the ex-
tenuated accufation. Not that fhe thought the
charge of deifm a light reproach, or that her
own conviction of the truth of revealed religion
was enfeebled; on the contrary, her prefent
dejected fpirits more ftrongly impelled her to

draw

draw water from the refreshing fountain of
eternal truth. But her prepossession in Edward's favour made her allow for a little clerical
zeal for orthodoxy, which might, she thought,
confound characters separated by many discri-
minating tenets: and, granting that Mr. Evans's
suspicions even in their widest latitude were
still well-founded, no danger could result from
her intimacy with a person to whom he allowed
the possession of so much talent and so much
moral principle.

Her reply, therefore, to Mr. Evans's observations commenced with a popular sentiment,
' that the faith could not be wrong, when the
' life was right.' ' I am afraid,' said she,
' many people, who profess themselves warm
' advocates for the doctrines of our religion,
' would be unwilling to have the reality of
' their own belief ascertained by this simple
' and compendious maxim. We cannot judge
' of another person's heart but through the
' medium of his actions; and even calumny
' itself casts no censure on Mr. Fitzosborne.
' Let us not then condemn him on account of
' some *singularity* of opinion; for opinion, my
' dear sir, you know, is free. We can only be
' affected by the actions of others, not by their
' sentiments.'

" Beware, my dearest lady Monteith," re-
" sumed Mr. Evans, " how you extend the
" apologies which may be urged in behalf of
" harmless singularity, to the vindication of
" of those perilous doctrines which not only
" corrupt the soil where they are suffered to
" spring, but also threaten the general destruc-
" tion of all that is dear and valuable to society.
" Do the virtues of even the moral deist stand

upon

" upon any firm ground ? Reason is his god ;
" and he may to-day, discover the footsteps of
" his deity in the paradoxes of Epicurus, and
" to-morrow in the fables of the Koran. The
" credulity of the infidel is proverbial, and his
" notions of right are as varying as his creed.
" He, my dear lady, is the corrupt tree from
" which, infallibility itself tells us, good fruit
" cannot spring. He is the polluted fountain
" whose waters must be bitter. As the mind
" thinks, the tongue speaks, and the man acts.
" The battery which he erects against the rock of
" faith is built on sand, liable to be undermined
" by every tide, and overthrown by every wind ;
" yet with restless malevolence he persists in
" his attack. Observe, madam, the system ever
" pursued by sceptics is *offensive* warfare; the
" liberty of private judgment does not content
" them. Pressing their pestiferous doctrines at
" every opportunity, they deny us the freedom
" which they claim for themselves, and never
" resort to the plea of moderation, but when
" closely pressed by arguments which they can-
" not otherwise avoid. But let them remem-
" ber, when either vanity or the desire of mak-
" ing converts induces them to unsettle the
" minds of others, opinion then becomes acti-
" on, and they are as answerable at the audit
" of God and their country for the principles
" which they promulgate, as for the deeds they
" commit.

" Have you not rather exaggerated Mr.
" Fitzosborne's errors ?" said the countess, in
a more decided tone than she was accustomed
to use to her reverend instructor. " I have
" often heard him expatiate upon serious sub-
" jects, but must own that I never discovered
" any

" any tendency to deifm. If I thought him an
" infidel, it would give me the livelieft con-
" cern; for, befide the efteem which his vir-
" tues infpire in my mind, I owe him indeli-
" ble gratitude for many uncommon marks of
" friendfhip."

" I have repeated the very words he uſed,
" madam. Be you the judge. Why he fhould
" affeƈt referve to you, and choofe to be un-
" neceffarily explicit to me, is fomewhat myf-
" terious. What you tell me of this young
" gentleman, and what I have myfelf obferved,
" ftrongly awakens my compaffion. He has
" defired to renew the fubjeƈt of our late con-
" verfation. I fhall return to it with pleafure,
" and efteem myfelf happy if my efforts can
" direƈt his abilities to their priftine intent,
" and reftore to his bofom that tranquillity
" which he cannot now enjoy." _

" You are always in charaƈter, my dear
" Mr. Evans, compaffionate and benevolent
" even to thofe whofe conduƈt you difapprove.
" I will endeavour to be a fellow-labourer in
" the fame good work; and though my know-
" ledge is too limited to convince Mr. Fitz-
" ofborne's judgment, I may expedite the con-
" viƈtion the defires by pointing fome perfua-
" five paffages to his heart."

" Ever-amiable lady Monteith!" returned
" the good man with pious earneftnefs, " be-
" ware how you enter the thorny paths of
" theological controverfy. I refpeƈt your fex
" too much to wifh them to hazard the mild
" luftre of benignity with which the god of
" nature has adorned them, to purfue that
" uncongenial fplendor which they can never
" obtain. Metaphyfical deduƈtions, and philo-
" logical

" logical learning, by which we defend our
" faith againft its affailants, require a fevere
" courfe of ftudy, and more intenfe thought
" than your habits, or perhaps the peculiar
" tendency of your intellectual powers, will
" afford. You will be entrapped into conclu-
" fions which nothing but fkill in the fubtilties
" of argument can elude ; confufed by objec-
" tions oftentaticufly multiplied ; the fallacy
" of which the Ithuriel fpear of biblical litera-
" ture would inftantly detect. By a dignified
" filence, or an indication of difpleafure, con-
" vince the bold difputant who obtrudes his
" crude notions of an invifible God on your
" ordinary converfation, that your refpect is
" too profound to enter lightly on the facred
" theme, and your conviction too fincere to
" need the adventitious aid of a vanquifhed
" opponent. Thefe fophifts, my dear madam,
" though they feek to embarrafs others, are
" themfelves well acquainted with the torments
" of doubt ; and it is only by the converts
" whom their falfe theory bewilders that they
" are kept from renouncing it themfelves. It
" is not to a zeal for truth, nor even to the
" mifgivings of confcience, that fcepticifm
" owes moft of its adherents, but to the pride
" of human reafon, and the love of fingularity.
" Permit them to difplay thefe qualities, and
" you grant them the triumph they defire."

Geraldine allowed the general truth of thefe
obfervations, but claimed an exemption in behalf of her friend. He was too placable and
gentle to love difpute, and too candid to repel
conviction. Mr. Evans determined to invefti-
gate the exiftence of thefe qualities at their
next converfation ; but the opportunity of ob-
serving

ferving them never occurred. Lord Monteith
fet off for London the following morning, and
Fitzofborne, by accompanying him, confirmed
the countefs in that lively fenfe of efteem and
gratitude which fhe thought fhe could no way
better exprefs than by exerting all her powers
to impart to his character whatever in her judgment it ftill wanted of perfection.

CHAP. VIII.

An elegant fufficiency, content,
Retirement, rural quiet, friendfhip, books,
Eafe and alternate labour, ufeful life,
Progreffive virtue, and approving heaven;
Thefe are the matchlefs joys of virtuous love.

THOMSON.

LADY MONTEITH's fortitude was fo feverely tried by her confcioufnefs of the motives
which occafioned her lord's hafty departure
for London, that fhe found it neceffary immediately to adopt Fitzofborne's advice of returning to Scotland, left the forrows of her afflicted
heart fhould fometimes difdain the difguife which
filial piety induced her to affume. Her parting
with her father was marked by circumftances of
peculiar tendernefs. I fhall not, however,
draw from them any ominous predictions. Sir
William's advanced age and increafing infirmities on the one hand, and his lovely daughter's
depreffed fpirits on the other, may account for
this

this acute fenfibility without afcribing to either the powers of prefcience.

The evening previous to Geraldine's departure, her penfive mind was fomewhat enlightened by a very agreeable converfation with Mifs Evans. " You know," faid that amiable girl, " I always had a caft of the whimfical about " me ; and probably if you had folicited my " company at Monteith, I might have raifed " an invincible hoft of objections ; but fince " you fay nothing upon the fubject, I am per- " verfe enough to determine to go back with " you to Scotland."

" My deareft Lucy," faid the Countefs, while her pale cheek kindled with the blufh of pleafure ; " may you always be thus delight- " fully perverfe ! Why I expreffed lefs folici- " tude for your company partly proceeded from " the nature of my own profpects, but prin- " cipally from what I fufpect to be yours."— " We fpinfters," replied Mifs Evans, paffing over her friend's allufion to the ftate of her own affairs with a ftifled figh, " are feldom hand- " fomely ufed by you married ladies, when " we choofe you for cur confidants. Yet, " though I am convinced that lord Monteith " will know all my fecret the very firft time " you write to him, I fee the fpirit of curiofity " fo very ftrongly imprinted upon your coun- " tenance, that I fhall indulge you with a fight " of two letters."

Perhaps fome of my *female* readers may happen to have a little of their great-grand-mother Eve's failing about them, as well as my heroine ; and to gratify it, though in a lefs degree, I fhall inform them, that thefe important papers were a love-letter, with the reply : and that the author

author of the former compofition was Henry
Powerfcourt. An attentive obfervation of Mifs
Evans's numerous excellencies had made him
for fome time her fincere admirer ; and, fince
not all the prudent delicacy of her character,
nor the diffidence of his own, could entirely
conceal from his obfervation the important
fecret of her preference, his high fenfe of
honour had long prompted him to a difcovery
of that reciprocal affection which her unaffum-
ing virtues had awakened in his heart. He was
reftrained by reflecting, that, as he had only
that heart to beftow, a declaration of his attachment might fubject her to all the inconve-
niencies which are incident to a tender engagement, when pecuniary circumftances prevent it
from being cemented by the marriage-bond.
His refpected patron, with fomewhat of the
imbecillity of age, and fomewhat of that tena-
city of power which ftrengthens our attachment
to the poffeffions in which our tenure daily
grows more precarious, had ftill delayed con-
firming to him the independence which he intended to bequeath. He contented himfelf with
liberally fupplying his prefent wants ; and as
he was perfuaded, that the young man was
very well as he was, and had no wifh to alter
his condition, he even brought himfelf to believe, that refigning to him the Merionethfhire
eftate would be giving him a vaft deal of trouble, which, as he feemed fonder of reading
than of bufinefs, he would certainly be as well
pleafed to avoid.

Panting for independence, yet difdaining to
acquire it by any means which he thought
irreconcileable with lady Monteith's interefts, or
with his deference and gratitude to her father,
Mr.

Mr. Powerscourt repeatedly resolved to pursue the desired blessing by the slow, but pleasant path of his own active exertions in some employment. Yet sir William's love of his kinsman's society increasing with his infirmities furnished a thousand objections to every profession or engagement which was successively proposed. The baronet at length precluded all further application by asking Henry, why he wanted to leave him? " Don't be uneasy," said he, " about your future prospects. De-" pend upon it, I shall provide for you." Thus compelled to refer the security of his own happiness to a distant and uncertain period, Mr. Powerscourt submitted with respectful silence to his benefactor's will. He contented himself with acquainting the amiable object of his affections with the peculiarity of his situation ; and he hoped her penetration would consider that as a sufficient reason for preventing his tongue from avowing the preference which his manner strongly expressed.

Though Henry's behaviour perfectly agrees with my ideas of honour, I am afraid some sister of the quill, better versed in the new code which has been introduced into the court of Cupid, will detect a thousand gross misdemeanours, of which the above Henry Powerscourt has been guilty. They may prove, according to the letter of these *recent* acts, that his behaviour to Miss Evans ought to have been more rude, capricious, and inattentive, in proportion as he discovered her preference, and felt the increase of his own. Very likely the new method of argument may prove, that this would have been the most honourable way of proceeding.

I shall

I fhall ftill continue obftinately difpofed to deny that it is the moft natural.

Gifted with that intuitive knowledge which the votaries of the purblind god individually poffefs, Lucy read her lover's fentiments in his eyes, and allowed the propriety of his conduct. Yet, when fhe looked forward to the expected events of her future life, gratitude, efteem, and veneration, generally excited a pious tear at the idea, that her own anxieties muft not expect a final termination until the neighbourhood was deprived of the bleffings it had long received from the unfparing benevolence of fir William Powerfcourt.

Affairs were in this fituation, when lady Monteith arrived from London. She had juft opportunity to make a few agreeable difcoveries, when the party were deprived of Mr. Powerfcourt's company. He was fummoned to attend the fick bed of his father, whofe expectations, in refpect to the marriage of his fon, had been quite as unfavourable to Henry's defigns, as the protracted bounty of fir William. Young Powerfcourt being unqueftionably the fineft gentleman the good old yeoman had ever feen, there arofe a neceffity of his matching well; and as no lady in all the land could refufe him, there was no reafon why he fhould take up with a parfon's daughter. Indeed old Mr. Powerfcourt had already felected his daughter-in-law; his bold ambition having directed him to no lefs a perfonage than madam Hetty ap Owen ap Thomas, his own landlady, and lady of the manor befide. But as the juvenile attractions of youth, beauty, and fweetnefs, were lefs vifible in the preferred fair, than the folid advantages of large property and high blood,

blood, the father was a more ardent admirer
than the fon : and, though the path of the latter
was very much fmoothed by the encomiums
which the former beftowed upon ' fon Hal,'
and an enumeration of what his coufin fir
William intended to do for him, which were
repeated every time he went to pay his rent :
nay, though mifs Hetty herfelf always diftinguifhed the bow of young Powerfcourt by a
lower curtefy, as fhe walked up the aifle to her
own pew on a Sunday, and even once honoured him fo far as to afk him to dine with her
and the curate, Henry continued inviolably
conftant to his Lucy's

  ' Dimpled fmile, and damafk cheek,
  And eye of gloffy blue.

He was relieved from a perfecution which
was urged with fuch well-meant but miftaken
earneftnefs as at length made it painful, by the
death of his father. His regret for that event
was foftened by receiving a letter from fir
William a few days afterwards, inclofing the
title deeds of the Merionethfhire eftate, and
containing an affurance, that fince he wifhed to
marry, he fhould have a houfe built 'for him
within a mile or two of Powerfcourt manor.

As, in common with all Arcadian writers, I
prefume the village ruftic is too happily engaged
with his flocks and his fhepherdefs to attend to
the affairs of his neighbour ; and being perfuaded that the love of news and the fpirit of
interference of which I have formerly feen
fome traces at Danbury are merely local difeafes ; I fuppofe the acceffion to Mr. Powerfcourt's fortune continued to be a profound
                                fecret

fecret in the parifh where his father refided :
at leaft I cannot conceive that any whifper,
which the taylor, or the fchoolmafter, or the
barber, might circulate, could, through the medium of the curate, be diffufed in the atmof-
phere of mifs Hetty's beft parlour ; or that any
one, by adding a unit to the rent-roll which fir
William had refigned, could be the occafion of
the extraordinary and even oppreffive civilities
with which the diftinguifhed lady whom I have
juft named loaded Mr. Henry Powerfcourt.
Her houfe was at his fervice ; her carriage was
at his fervice ; her fervants were at his fervice ;
nay the world even faid, that fhe more than
hinted an offer of herfelf. This latter report I
difbelieve, becaufe it went fomewhat further
than what the proverbial hofpitality of her
country can account for. But if fhe had any
latenta views, they foon received a complete
mortification. Henry's firft ftep, after the arrival of the welcome gift, was to exprefs his
gratitude to the donor ; his next, to requeft,
that mifs Evans would render independence
more valuable by fharing it with him.

‘ And now, my Geraldine," faid Lucy to
the countefs, fcarcely allowing her time to
finifh the letter which had introduced this long
digreffion, ‘ I call for your felicitations. Henry,
‘ you fee, ingenuoufly avows the early attach-
‘ ment which made you the firft miftrefs of his
‘ heart. I have not that extreme refinement
‘ which can only be content with a primary
‘ affection. It is fufficient for me, that after
‘ long obfervation he owns a preference which
‘ he is too noble to affect, and too upright to
‘ withdraw. Secure in his honour and his
‘ virtue, not even your attractions will excite
‘ fufpicion ;

‘ fufpicion ; and though the tempered expec-
‘ tations of four-and-twenty abate much of the
‘ fanguine enthufiafm of nineteen, neither ex-
‘ perience nor reflection teach me to doubt of
‘ the general happinefs of my future lot with
‘ fuch a partner as my long-loved Henry·’

Lucy’s head now reclined upon the fhoulder
of the countefs, to conceal at once her blufhes
and her tears. “ But,” added the fweet girl
after a moment’s paufe, “ you exprefs neither
“ furprize nor pleafure at the wonders which I
“ am revealing.”

The reader, who remembers the connubial
forrows which clouded the countefs’s mind, will
not wonder, that, though free from envy, her
Lucy’s brighter hopes occafioned a painful com-
parifon ; and we cannot be furprifed at events
which ourfelves have directed. It was natural
for Mifs Evans to *wonder* why fir William, who
had fo long delayed the promifed gift, fhould beftow it juft at that time ; and why he, who had
been generally hoftile to marriage, and decided-
ly averfe to Henry’s forming any engagement
which threatened to deprive him of his fociety,
fhould even fuggeft a plan for his immediate eftablifhment. But lady Monteith poffeffed the clue
that could unravel the fecrets of the labyrinth.
Her obfervations on her coufin’s manner had
convinced her, that he was no longer infenfible
of her friend’s worth, and fhe affiduoufly employed all her intereft with her father to expedite his intended donation, to the delay of which
fhe rightly attributed the prevention of a defirable union. She had once intended to apply
to the known munificence of her lord ; but her
illnefs, and the painful events which had followed and preceded it, prevented that defign, and
interrupted

and interrupted her negociation with her father.
She renewed it with increafed earneftnefs upon
the death of the elder Mr. Powerfcourt; and
at length, by the difcovery of her Lucy's fecret,
won his cheerful acquiefcence. ' I never
thought, my dear,' faid the good man, ' that
' thofe young people had a liking for each other.
' I am fure, if they had told me fo, I fhould
' have given my confent immediately. Why
' did they keep me in the dark ? My god-daugh-
' ter is a very difcreet girl; and you know I
' can fix them fo near me that I may fee Henry
' every day, which, as it is fitting you fhould
' give up moft of your time to your hufband and
' children, is, let me tell you, a great comfort
' to me. I always was afraid, that Henry would
' take it in his head to be in love with fome of
' your London ladies, who would not like to
' play a game of cribbage to divert an old man
' now and then; and I thought Lucy never in-
' tended to marry, not hearing of her having
' any lover, which for fuch a pretty modeft girl
' was rather extraordinary. Well, I muft fay,
' it is very odd that they fhould happen to like
' each other, for things don't often happen as
' we wifh they fhould.'

Though fir William's conftitutional habits
gave a flownefs to his deliberations, nothing
could be more rapid than his execution of any
plan in which he knew the happinefs of a fellow-
creature to be involved. He immediately fent
for his fteward and his attorney. The writings
were forted out, the deed of gift drawn up, the
letter written, and the meffenger difpatched, before he could commit himfelf to his pillow with
the hope of enjoying a comfortable revifion of
the proceedings of the paft day. Lady Monteith

VOL. II.   E   could

could fcarcely reftrain him from telling his little
god-daughter, as he called her, after dinner,
that he liked her choice very well, and that, if
Geraldine had told him fooner how fhe had fixed her affections, fhe fhould not have been kept
in fufpenfe. The countefs was defirous of enjoying the refined pleafure of fecretly difpenfing
good; and fhe wifhed, that an explicit avowal
on the part of Henry fhould precede the detection of Lucy's love.

The avowal was made in terms equally honorable, to his own ingenuous integrity, and aufpicious to her future happinefs. And while a
tear ftole down Geraldine's cheek at her coufin's
impreffive recollection of the event which conftrained him to fubdue an attachment that
' grew with his growth' and entwined itfelf with
all the ftrong impreffions that ardent youth receives, fhe faw with pleafure the fucceeding paragraph point out the merits of his mature
choice with clear difcrimination, and generoufly
prevent the confufion of maiden delicacy, by
carefully avoiding that apparent certainty of acceptance which his knowledge of the ftate of her
heart might have prompted him to affume.

Mifs Evans's reply announced the paternal
fanction which her lover had folicited, and fhe
added, with all the frank fincerity of her character, a confeffion of the efteem and gratitude
(I am almoft afraid fhe faid *tendernefs* too)
which his long-known worth had infpired. The
laws by which we veftal fifters were accuftomed
to conduct our affairs of courtfhip were much
more auftere and remorfelefs, and better calculated to keep up the dignity of the fex than thofe
which the prefent race of beauties adopt.

Then

Then love could live on flender bounties,
Then lovers gallop'd o'er two counties,
The ball's fair partner to behold,
And humbly hope fhe caught no cold.

One year generally elapfed before the fuitor could prefume to expect a direct reply; and it was not till after feven years punctual attendance, or the actual drawing up of the marriage fettlements, that the lady's acknowledgment of reciprocal efteem could be juftified. Some hufbands, my cotemporaries, have declared, that the trepidations of doubt and anxiety fcarcely fubfided till thofe of the modern couple generally begin; I mean, when the fair one promifes at the altar to be her good man's unalienable property 'till death do them part.' But though I difapprove of the renunciation of this decorous feverity in moſt inſtances, I am inclined to permit a little latitude when the lover acts with the integrity of a Henry Powerfcourt, and the lady poſſeſſes the unaffected prudence of a Lucy Evans. To terminate my diffufe account of this correfpondence, Lucy repreffed her lover's hopes of a fpeedy union by ſtating her previous refolution of fpending the following autumn in Scotland.

"No, my love," faid the countefs, whofe attention appeared to be roufed by the conclufion of her friend's epiſtle, "I will not allow you
"to make fuch a facrifice. Dearly as I prize
"your fociety, you fhall be juft to prior claims.
"I fhall not be wretched, I mean dull, without
"you. I will fit under my favourite beeches,
"and meditate on that fair portrait of connu-
"bial happinefs which you and your Henry
E 2   will

" will prefent. He has been long depreffed
" in his fortunes and croffed in his hopes. How
" fhall I rejoice in the idea of his being at laft
" poffeffed of the independence that he fo well
" deferves, and of the happinefs which his dif-
" paffionate judgment beft approves ! You too,
" my Lucy, rich in every domeftic excellence !
" my heart rejoices at the profpect of your
" virtues expanding in a larger fphere ; of
" your fortitude and quiet heroifm receiving
" its merited reward. I will not be the means
" of delaying this aufpicious union a fingle
" hour."

" But as my fwain fays nothing upon the
" fcore of an early day, or fond impatience, am
" I to give him a hint that I expect fuch flou-
" rifhes ? No indeed ; I think I have been quite
" frank enough already, and fet him more at
" eafe than any lover (I mean except himfelf)
" ought to be. His father's death is very re-
" cent ; and I know his fenfe of propriety will
" prevent him from propofing marriage at pre-
" fent. Let me then, by fhowing that I do
" not expect it, convince him that I can imi-
" tate the virtues I revere. What ! but one
" faint fmile, Geraldine, at that declaration ?
" I expected to have heard fome pretty allufion
" to Sir Charles Grandifon, or to the ' Phœ-
" nix, that fole bird." Cannot you recollect
" fome little fhade in Henry's character ? his
" purple coat, for inftance, which diverted you
" fo much two years ago. But perhaps you
" truft to time to abate the romance of my fen-
" timents, or mentally quote the anfwer to
" your own conundrum, ' why marriage is
" like a microfcope ?'—' becaufe it difcovers
" little blemifhes.'

" It

" It is happy," faid the countefs, " when " there are only little blemifhes to difcover. I " will no longer refufe your fociety, my dear " playful friend ; but I accept it upon one con- " dition, that I may put a poftfcript to your " letter to Henry."

" If you will promife to fay nothing as com- " ing from me."

The countefs gave her word to the contrary, and then added the following lines :

' I have confented to take your dearer felf ' to Scotland, in hopes that the ftrong attrac- ' tion will compel you to give us the additional ' pleafure of your company. I would tell you ' how I rejoice at your propofals to my Lucy, ' but words are fo inadequate to my feelings ' that I muft refer you to your knowledge of ' my character to eftimate the fincerity of my ' tranfports. May you be as happy as your ' mutual virtues deferve, bleffed with health, ' peace, and every worldly comfort ! There *is* ' an event (O how my filial heart abjures the ' impending evil !) which will enable me to ' give my valued friend ftronger marks of ef- ' teem and gratitude than ineffectual wifhes, by ' fulfilling a promife ever facred to

' GERALDINE MONTEITH.'

CHAP.

CHAP. IX.

——Is aught fo fair
In all the dewy landfcapes of the fpring,
In the bright eye of Hefper, or the morn,
In nature's faireft forms, is aught fo fair
As virtuous friendfhip?

AKENSIDE.

No event happened immediately after my
Heroine's return to Scotland that deferves to be
recorded. Though Mifs Evans's conviction that
fome concealed forrow preyed upon her amiable
friend's mind, was the fecret caufe of her accompanying her, fhe rightly judged that it was
of a fpecies which would receive no diminution
from participation, and therefore forbore to intrude upon the fanctity of woe. She contented
herfelf with employing the ftores of her well-
cultivated mind, and the emanations of her
fportive fancy, to alleviate the dejection which
admitted not of cure. Her anxious defire to
amufe her penfive companion fometimes made
her cheerfulnefs more redundant than agreed
with her natural character. But lady Monteith's perfuafion, that the funfhine of her
profpects gave a more feftal gaiety to her fpirits,
prevented her from perceiving that her Lucy's
vivacity was more fymptomatic of affiduous,
anxious friendfhip, than expreffive of the calm
fatisfaction of heartfelt happinefs.

The countefs fometimes drew a parallel between her friend's fituation and her own, and
her

her he: ... at the chilling contraſt. How
brigat ... ... of ... purified by eſteem!
How ... luſtre of equal minds, humble
but ... ... ſimilar taſtes, and
mod... ... blank were her own
view... ... ... uncontrolled poſſeſſion of an
exten... ... ... pomp and ſuperiority
of ... ... d-capped mountains
crowned with ... ls of pine, lakes beſtudded
with verdant iſlands, and fringed with odori-
ferous ſhrubs, could now afford her any pleaſure. The ſpacious manſion, the numerous eſtabliſhment, ſeemed but mementos of their
abſent Lord. Even the ſociety of her lovely
children could not give the expected conſola-
tion. They ſpoke and looked like their faithleſs
father, and the tear of anguiſh mingled with
the ſmile of maternal rapture.

The correſpondence of Fitzoſborne afforded
no ſatisfactory intelligence. If one letter announced a plan which it was hoped might detach him from Mrs. Harley, the next epiſtle
proclaimed its failure, and only detailed ſome
mutilated converſations which implied a more
total alienation of his lordſhip's affections than
the writer thought it was prudent to communicate. Her tearful eyes fixed upon theſe particulars, and paſſed over with cold and vacant
gaze the compliments which Edward addreſſed
to her perſon, mind, and conduct. She ſcarcely
obſerved even the ſympathy that he expreſſed
for her ſufferings ; and the advice he gave her
to detach her affections from a man who he
feared would never again return her tenderneſs,
was rejected with a conviction that it was im-
practicable.

The

The frequency of lady Monteith's receiving letters in a male character very diffimilar to her lord's, at length excited Mifs Evans's curiofity; and it even rofe to anxiety upon perceiving, that they were always referved for a private. perufal. Her attention, thus cafually fixed, was continually revived by fome frefh myftery which every poft-day revealed. The countefs feemed almoft fretfully impatient till the mail arrived; and if any company were prefent at the founding of the horn, fhe always made fome excufe to leave the room. More than once Lucy perceived her felect the letter of this favoured correfpondent, and retire to read it, while even her lord's lay unopened. Yet they appeared rather to increafe her melancholy than to relieve it; and conftantly, after having fhut herfelf in her own apartment to anfwer them, her face bore unequivocal marks of having been bathed in tears.

Difdaining to fatisfy her doubts by indirect means, and unable to purfue any plan of raillery or playful artifice on what fhe feared was a very ferious fubject, Lucy determined to give her friend an impreffive hint of a very apparent impropriety; but unfortunately the interference of the Evans's was always fo ill-timed as rather to affift than to fruftrate Fitzofborne's diabolical views. In reply to a letter in which the countefs, like the artlefs placable Defdemona, had profeffed that it was impoffible for her affections ever to change their object, Edward announced the welcome tidings of her lord's fpeedy return. The merit of this reformation was, however, wholly owing to his friendly monitor's contrivance. He had cut out that part of Geraldine's letter which contained thofe affecting expreffions

of

of inviolable attachment, and pretending, that it was addreſſed to one of her London correſ-pondents, with whom he was intimate, he had ſhewn it to lord Monteith, and ſo ſtrongly worked up his feelings of compunction and ſhame, that a rupture with Mrs. Harley was the conſequence. Fitzoſborne regretted, that he was not likely to witneſs the reconciliation which he had ſo anxiouſly laboured to promote; but the Miniſter had juſt given an abſolute pro-miſe in his favour; and his long experience of courtly forgetfulneſs convinced him of the poſi-tive neceſſity of reviving recollection by conſtant attendance. He however added, that if his friend ſhould not be in a deſirable ſtate of mind when he left London, he would renounce all his hopes of an eſtabliſhment rather than riſk the ſtability of recent reſolutions by leaving him, during his long journey, to the ſuggeſtions of his wayward fancy.

An exclamation, or rather ſhriek of ſurprize and tranſport, which followed the peruſal of this letter, drew Miſs Evans into the counteſs's chamber. She found her friend ſunk upon her knees, her hands and eyes lifted up as in a ſtrong tranſport of devotion, while the paleneſs of her countenance indicated immediate danger of fainting. Lucy flew to aſſiſt her. 'No,' ſaid lady Monteith, gently rejecting the proffered ſalts, 'I am not ill.—A ſudden ſurprife has 'overwhelmed me—leave me to myſelf a little '—I ſhall ſoon be compoſed.' Miſs Evans ſilently withdrew.

Contrary to the uſual hoſpital'ty of Monteith caſtle, the friends ſat down *tête-à-tête* to dinner. The noble hoſteſs was recovered from her firſt emotion; but her manner indicated that ſome important

important event demanded all her thoughts, which reluctantly submitted to pay a scanty attention to passing objects. The servants were no sooner withdrawn, than unable any longer to restrain her full-fraught heart, she told her friend that they should soon have a welcome addition to their party in the company of lord Monteith, and perhaps Mr. Fitzosborne also.

'I sincerely rejoice in my lord's return,' said Miss Evans; 'but I thought his friend was fully 'occupied either in attending the Minister's le-'vee, or in discharging the duties of the office 'which you told me his lordship's interest would 'procure him.'

'He will sacrifice every thing to the desire of 'proving his sincere attachment to me,' said lady Monteith, too much engrossed by the lively passion of gratitude to attend to the caution which she had hitherto used upon the subject of her correspondence with Edward.

Alarmed at these expressions, Miss Evans persevered in a curiosity which she would have reprobated upon any other occasion; and Geraldine, drawn by her interrogatories to be more explicit than she at first designed, at length confided the whole story of her latent sorrows. She spoke the present feelings of her heart; and though she supposed it still attuned to gentle complacency and forgiving sweetness, distress had for some time prevented her from engaging in her customary duty of self-examination; and the indignant sensations of slighted beauty, and offended desert, gave an air of resentment to her narrative of her husband's perfidy, which the limited merit of his reluctant return and irresolute repentance could not subdue. She hastened from this painful subject to the more pleasing theme of Fitzosborne's discernment, zeal,

zeal, and fidelity; his refined delicacy, correct judgment, and all the capacious powers of his exalted foul.

‘ Poffibly he may mean well,’ obferved Mifs Evans, after having, with marked attention, twice read Fitzofborne’s letter. Surprifed at a fuggeftion which feemed deficient of her ufual candour, lady Monteith replied, that the integrity could not be doubtful which fpoke by the moft noble actions. ‘ What,’ faid fhe, ‘ but ‘ difinterefted virtue could thus direct his unwea- ‘ ried affiduity to attempt the reftoration of my ‘ domeftic happinefs ?’

“ There is a myftery in this bufinefs,” conti- nued Lucy, “ which I cannot penetrate. It is to “ me aftonifhing, that lord Monteith, after hav- “ ing been feveral years your happy hufband, “ fhould, unfolicited and felf-feduced, abandon “ you for a woman, whofe weak pretenfions to “ his notice muft arife from fome faint tranfcript “ of that intelligent beauty which animates your “ countenance, or fome contemptible imitation “ of the playful wit which irradiates your con- “ verfation.”

“ My dear fecluded friend,” replied the coun- tefs, “ knows nothing of the corrupt manners of “ the world; of the eclat which general opinion “ attaches to novelty, or of the celebrity which is “ oftener fhared by eccentricity and a bold defi- “ ance of decorum, than awarded to real de- “ fert.”

“ True,” faid Lucy ; “ happily both for my “ temper and my heart, I am ignorant of the “ manners you defcribe. But how could lord “ Monteith fee this Mrs. Harley ? A woman “ of her defcription muft be a ftranger to the “ parties he would frequent; I mean, while he “ continued

" continued unfeduced by the allurements of
" vice."

Lady Monteith obferved, that though women
of character never vifited courtezans; yet unlefs
they were very low, or very audacious, the latter always appeared in public places; and if a
certain degree of fafhion was annexed to them,
either on account of their own wit and elegance,
or for the rank or talents of their admirers, gentlemen felt themfelves not difgraced by being feen
in their parties. It was, therefore, very poffible
for her lord to fee Mrs. Harley fufficiently to be
allured by her perfon and converfation, without
his frequenting any fcenes unbecoming his rank
or injurious to his reputation.

Lucy fighed at the relaxed manners which
feemed to ufher in the triumphs of relaxed principles. But her fufpicions of fome nefarious
preceedings on the part of Fitzofborne were not
yet entirely removed. " I muft not then," faid
fhe, " fuppofe my lord quite changed; but ftill
" I know you are the fame. Your feeling heart
" will not allow you to eftimate the degree of re-
" gard which you fhould bear to the hufband of
" your youth and the father of your children by
" the cold plea of defert. Your forgivenefs
" would outftep his folicitations; and every
" time you fpoke or wrote to him, the fentiments
" of your full-fraught heart would give a digni-
" fied tendernefs to your expreffions, remote
" from reproach, and better calculated to awaken
" compunction. How came it, my love, that
" this fuffering gentlenefs, exerted at Powerf-
" court, or the affectionate letters that you have
" written to him fince you have been here, have
" had no effect; but that the mighty good fhould
" at length be accomplifhed by the fkilful contri-
" vance

" vance and artful interpofition of Mr. Fitzof-
" borne? Has he a greater influence over your
" hufband than you could acquire? You, who
" are fo much interefted to exert the refiftlefs
" power of your many invincible charms! How
" diffimilar muft. lord Monteith's character be.
" from what it appears!"

Geraldine pleaded, that the people are differ-
ently difpofed at different times; and that fimilar
actions and fentiments frequently fail of producing
correfpondent effects; and fhe accounted for the
inefficacy of her pen by owning, that fhe had only written fhort and in fome fort formal letters to
her lord fince her return to Scotland. " No
" longer able," faid fhe, " to pour forth my
" whole heart, I was glad of fome extraneous
" fubject which would occupy the vacant page."

" And how did you then hope to reclaim
" him?" inquired Lucy: " I fhould think that
" if he perceived any coldnefs in your manner he
" would turn that difcovery into an apology for
" his behaviour."

" I could not help the conftruction he might
" put upon my letters. Sorrow cannot be dif-
" fufe, unlefs where it may unbofom its woes."

" Did you not write at large to Mr. Fitzof-
" borne?

" I did. He knew my fecret, and in his in-
" terpofition was my only hope."

" Do women of fafhion, my Geraldine, coun-
" tenance one another in the cuftom of having
" male confidants as well as male attendants?"

" There is a little pique," thought the countefs in that obfervation; " but friendfhip warm
" as my Lucy's is very fufceptible, and I will not
" refent her well-meant acrimony."

" Be

" Be affured," faid fhe, clafping Mifs Evans's
hand with a fmile of tender fweetnefs, "that ac-
" cident alone gave him poffeffion of what pru-
" dence taught me to conceal from you." She
then related the principal particulars of what
paffed in lord Monteith's dreffing-room at Powerfcourt: but though all her communications
were intended to place Fitzofborne in a fairer
point of view, the fufpicious Lucy only difcovered increafing myftery, if not abfolute duplicity.

· " It is plain," faid fhe, in reply to lady Monteith's narrative, " that Fitzofborne early knew
" of your lord's inconftancy.   It is plain too,
" that he has all along been affured that he pof-
" feffes a confiderable influence over his mind.
" Your admirable conduct, my Geraldine, has
" convinced the world, that, though your huf-
" band's paffions are hafty and impetuous, they
" may be directed by gentle management.   Is it
" not wonderful then, that all Mr. Fitzofborne's
" boafted penetration, judgment, and felf-com-
" mand, fhould not have ftruck at the root of
" this fatal connection before it was confirmed
" by habit; or that it fhould continue fo long,
" after he had fet all his acknowledged abilities to
" work for its annihilation, when he had him to
" himfelf too, with uninterrupted power to act
" as he thought moft expedient ?"

" But he has fucceeded at laft," obferved the
countefs, rather fretted than convinced by the
evident drift of her friend's converfation.

" He has: but how ? By means incompatible
" with the frank ingenuoufnefs of your character,
" and which muft either fubject you to the ap-
" prehenfion of your lord's difcovery of a preme-
" ditated fraud, or force you to confefs that, de-
                                  " fpairing

" fpairing of your own influence, you have ap-
" plied to a knight-errant for affiftance.   Only
" confider too, how inadequate are the means, if
" the victory were indeed fo difficult.   Did lord
" Monteith doubt your affection, your conftancy,
" your forgivenefs ? Who infpired thofe doubts ?
" Or how came it, that your champion's elo-
" quence could not difpel them ? But I perceive
" I diftrefs you, my Geraldine.   Pity, love, and
" admiration for you, are the predominant feel-
" ings of my foul, which exults in your bright--
" ening profpects.   See, for once I tranfgrefs
" againft my ufual abftemioufnefs : this glafs of
" Champagne is, to the fpeedy and happy return
" of the agreeable lord Monteith. You pledge me,
" I know, in that fentiment.   I have not, how-
" ever, quite finifhed it.   Obferve what follows :
" —But no Fitzofborne with him."

The countefs, fmiling, wiped a ftarting tear.
" I perceive," thought fhe, " whence Lucy's pre-
" judices againft this amiable man arife.   Her
" father fufpects him of infidelity.   It is a pity,
" indeed, that he does not add the luftre of piety
" to his acknowledged virtues; but it is more un-
" fortunate, when religion gives its champions a
" tincture of bigotry and cenforioufnefs."   Her
children, entering the room at that moment, made
the images of Fitzofborne and his opponents
yield to the tender recollection of their returning
father.

That much defired event fpeedily took place,
and received an additional recommendation from
its happening fooner than even lady Monteith's
calculations judged to be poffible.   Her lord met
her with a glow of tendernefs, which quickly
made her trembling agitation yield to the moft
delightful compofure, while Lucy's fympathetic

bofom

bosom swelled with grateful rapture. She turned
her head aside to utter a prayer for the continu-
ance of this renewed affection, and perceived that
all her wishes were not fulfilled. Fitzosborne
was of the party. He made her a most profound
bow. An abrupt curtesy was her return, as she
glided by him to her own apartment.

  " It is but suspicion," said she to herself, striv-
ing to calm her agitated thoughts; " and I am
" certainly very wrong in acting upon it as if it
" were certainty. I think I see invidious guile in
" every feature of his countenance. Yet suppo-
" sing my conjecture right, is it prudent for me
" to put him upon his guard, by showing him
" that I dislike him? I shall be better able to
" warn my friend of his depravity, by at least ap-
" pearing to receive that impression which he
" chooses to give me of his character."

  Miss Evans's natural sincerity, and the ardour of
her attachment to the countess, prevented her from
pursuing the line of conduct which she had prescribed. As her strong sense and extensive reading enabled her easily to detect the fallacious sophisms which
Fitzosborne easily passed upon his more partial or
less discerning auditors; so her frank ingenuousness,
undisguised by the habits of polished life, heightened by her early imprinted reverence for sacred
truths, and her anxious apprehensions for the security of her beloved Geraldine, against whom
she saw that the infernal artillery was chiefly directed, scarcely allowed her to confine her indignation within the bounds which her unaffected
propriety of manners would otherwise have observed. But violence generally defeats its own
intentions. The horror she conceived against
Fitzosborne's supposed designs induced her to view
his every word and action with suspicion: and
                                              her

her eagerness to convict him not unfrequently
produced a false accusation, of which lady Monteith's anxiety to clear the wounded honour of
her friend conftantly took advantage.

The refult, therefore, of this vigilant fcrutiny
was not what Lucy hoped it would be. Geraldine,
inftead of being convinced that fhe harboured a
bofom-traitor, faw in the friend of her early youth
another inftance of the ufual effects of a fecluded
way of life, pertinacity of opinion and aufterity
of manners.

The reconciliation of the earl and his countefs,
though apparently cordial, was not attended with
that tranquil confidence which preceded the difaftrous period of his lordfhip's enormities. He
feemed to feel degraded by the virtues of his wife.
He difcovered reproach in her obfervations, and
feverity in her conduct. No longer able to flatter himfelf with the hopes that his faults were not
trumpeted to the winds, he fometimes conftrued
her behaviour into contempt and indifference;
and though the exquifite anguifh which that idea
caufed might have told him that a tranfient infatuation cannot difplace rooted regard, he always
fancied that he could retort fcorn with fcorn; and
as his decifions and actions followed each other
with rapid pace, he foon determined to relinquifh
that tendernefs of manner which compunction
had impofed on his firft return, and which, he
thought, had too much the air of felf-accufation
to fuit the dignity of a hufband's character. She,
on the other hand, though affured by Fitzofborne
that the breach with Mrs. Harley was irreconcileable, could not reprefs her fears, left a heart
which once had wondered might be again in-
thralled. It was plain that Fitzofborne had the
fame apprehenfion. His vifit to Monteith proved,
that,

that, to ufe his own words, " his friend was not
" in fuch a defirable ftate of mind as to permit his
" dependance upon the ftability of recent refolu-
" tions." Thus aggravated, Geraldine's dread
of eftranging her hufband by her behaviour, or
giving him an excufe for future infidelity, far exceeded the bounds which affection alone would have
prefcribed ; and her manner had an air of reftraint which the increafing gloom of her lord's
did not relieve.

Befide the accufations of confcience, Monteith's foul ftruggled with other forrows. His
initiation into the myfteries of the gaming-houfes
had been attended by fevere loffes ; and while
the extravagance of a mercenary courtezan had
been fupplied with the fums appropriated to his
tradefmen, he had fatisfied his debts of honour by
granting annuities upon his eftate to that fet of
harpies who glory in the wealth which they have
acquired by adminiftering to the vices of mankind. For the firft time fince his marriage, the
earl was informed by his fteward, that the yearly
expenditure would greatly exceed his rent—roll.
Impatient of enduring the blame of any fault
which he could transfer to another, he determined
to place this defalcation to the fums which lady
Monteith had expended in the improvement of
the adjacent country, and in fome frefh erections
at James-town, with which fhe had amufed herfelf during his abfence. He read her a long lec-
ture of œconomy ; reprobated her turn for ex-
penfive alterations ; and affirmed, that it would
be the means of compelling him to leave the feat of
his anceftors. Thefe reproofs were new, ill-
difguifed by the pretence of providing for his fon's
education, and ill-timed : for, relying upon his
wonted liberality, Geraldine had not only endeavoured

voured to occupy her mind by some expensive
erections in the park, but had also set on foot
some new charitable institutions which her benevolent heart could not abandon without feeling
the most lively regret. Forgetting, or perhaps
wanting fortitude to use the guiding clue by
which she had formerly been accustomed to influence his opinions, she attempted to remon-
strate, but was soon silenced by a reply which her
enfeebled spirits could not support. She retired
in tears.

The reader will not believe 'that Fitzosborne
had been sincere in his wishes of effecting an
entire reconciliation. It answered his purpose
to bring the earl back, freed from his connexion
with Mrs. Harley; he had performed that un-
dertaking, and taught the countess that she owed
him an indelible debt of gratitude. He now
generally left his lordship to that misery which
must be the natural effect of a perturbed conscience and perplexed circumstances upon a mind
which wanted wisdom to plan and fortitude to
persevere in a system of œconomical retrench-
ment, or to efface error by sincere repentance.
He saw with pleasure the gay, careless, generous
earl of Monteith, become gloomy, absent, mo-
rose, and penurious. He saw too, that the bottle was constantly applied to, not, as formerly, to
be an auxiliary to mirth, but as an opiate to silence care. Affection could no longer bind the
heart of Geraldine to such a partner. Continual
provocation must weaken the claims of duty;
and there needed nothing more than that himself
should exhibit the full effect of contrast, by a dis-
play of the virtues most opposite to Monteith's
vices, and to proceed in his design of enfeebling
the power of religious principles, to render the

unsuspecting countess his easy prey. Her opposition to what she thought the extreme rigidity
of some of Miss Evans's opinions, and her tacit
acquiescence to several of his tenets, convinced
him, that he had made a considerable progress.
He continued silent upon the subject of her lord's
conduct. An air of pity and respect, mingled
with the uniform attention of his manner, spoke
a language far plainer than words.

CHAP. X.

I hate when Vice can bolt her arguments,
And Virtue has no tongue to check her pride.
                                    MILTON.

I HAVE already observed, that miss Evans's
impetuosity was of disservice to the noble cause
which she conscientiously espoused; and Fitzosborne, certain that her zeal would defeat her
intentions, passed her in silence, as an enemy
whom he could only render formidable by appearing to fear. But the cause of principle was
now defended by the arrival of another champion.
Mr. Powerscourt availed himself of the countess's
invitation to chide his Lucy for a tyrannical ex-
ercise of female prerogative, in compelling him
to take a journey of two hundred miles to whisper a love-tale which might have been more
agreeably told in a little woodbine bower which
she had erected, in strict conformity to the rules
prescribed by her favourite poet Mason, in the
parsonage garden at Powerscourt. Henry had
named it after the Nerina of that elegant bard,
                                    and

and decorated it with the following infcription
and motto :

> I only begg'd a little woodbine bower ;
> Nerina's bower, where I might fit and weep. .
> 　　　　MASON'S ENGLISH GARDEN.

Wind, fragrant woodbine ! round Nerina's bower :
　　Clematis, deepen the umbrageous fhade ;
And, mingling with the jas'mine's penfile flower,
　　Fulfil the wifhes of the mourning maid.

Here oft, when evening finks in foft repofe,
　　Shall ·Mafon's numbers wake the flumbering
　　　　'grove ;
Here, gentle Lucy fhall recite the woes
　　Of orphan beauty and unhappy love.

As tafteful fympathy enjoys the theme,
　　Fancy, the local landfcape fhall extend ;
Bid Grecian fanes in dim perfpective beam,
　　And Gothic arches mid the pine trees bend.

Ye fportive fays, ye fine etherial forms,
　　Nymphs of the fun-beam, fylphids of the breeze ;
Defend their foliage from untimely ftorms,
　　From blafting mildew fave thefe votive trees.

Here, on this verdant turf, the tuneful queen
　　With attic grace her deathlefs fong renews ;
And native virtues confecrate the fcene,
　　Sacred to Lucy's tafte, and Mafon's mufe.

The chidings of a fincere lover are rarely formidable ; and Mifs Evans had an excufe to plead,
which would have difarmed a fiercer refentment
than ever glowed upon any occafion in Henry's
breaft. In the fame moment he forgave her
flight, applauded her motives, and promifed to
　　　　　　　　　　　　　　　　　affift

affift her defigns. " I knew Fitzofborne while
" I was in Italy," faid he ; " our acquaintance
" was but flight, yet I difcovered enough to be
" convinced that he muft be a dangerous inmate
" in any family."

But though Powerfcourt poffeffed fufficient
penetration to read the character of a mafked villain, Edward's profound difcernment had for
once led him to form an erroneous conclufion.
The fociety in which he had met Henry was compofed of perfons whom the latter defpifed for
their folly, or detefted for their impiety ; and
convinced, that even the argumentative powers
of the unrivalled Crichton would be in vain exerted againft wilful error, he determined, by not
treating them with a difpute, to fuffer them to
enjoy their fading poppy-garlands uncontefted.
Fitzofborne had concluded, that the reafon of his
countryman's filence was his having nothing to
fay ; and he hailed the arrival of an antagonift at
Monteith, whofe fpeedy defeat would add to the
already-exalted reputation which his fcientific abilities had acquired among the rural efquires, feu-
dal lairds, and officers in quarters, who frequent-
ed the earl of Monteith's table.

When Geraldine acquainted her friend with
her coufin's expected arrival, his ftile of com-
mendation expreffed his idea of his character.
" O, Harry Powerfcourt ! I was acquainted
" with him abroad. A very honeft, downright
" foul, with true Englifh notions ; he feemed
" always afraid of mixing with ftrangers. I
" fhall be very happy to fee him again, for I en-
" joyed his fincerity."

" He is an exception then to the general ob-
" fervation ; for he is moft honoured by thofe
" who beft know him," faid the countefs. " We
" efteem

" efteem him a good fcholar, and a very fenfible
" intelligent companion."

" A great deal, my dear madam, depends up-
" on our confining ourfelves to the ftrict defini-
" tion of words, or elfe our intentions are am-
" biguous. I perceive that by my neglect of
" this rule, you have miftaken mine. Mr.
" Powerfcourt has indifputably a very good *plain*
" underftanding, and I dare fay he is an excel-
" lent claffical fcholar. But pardon me if I fay
" he has never ftepped out of the beaten track,
" nor attended to what I fhould call the concate-
" nation of deductions, or confecutive effect of
" given poftulates; and from this want of ar-
" rangement in his mental faculties, it follows,
" of courfe, that he takes things as they are,
" without examining from what caufes the di-
" feafes in the moral and natural world originate,
" or how they may be remedied."

The countefs underftood as much of this
fpeech as the fpeaker intended fhe fhould; and
fhe could only lament her early inattention to
logical ftudies, which might have convinced her,
as they had done Fitzofborne, that creation wanted to be new-modelled; and that the prefent age
had more wifdom than all the preceding ones
taken collectively.

The intended combatants now ftood, like Homer's heroes, " panting for the fight," and impatient for the fignal of engagement. Though
the defire of victory alone would not have induced Powerfcourt "to unlock his lips in fuch un-
" hallowed air," the prefervation of Geraldine
from the fnares of a feducer infpired him with a
zeal warm even as that which Lucy Evans poffeffed. But being tempered by fuperior judgment, he determined to appear, as if he rather
adopted

adopted an opinion from his obfervation of Fitzofborne's behaviour, than came with a predeter-
mined refolution of difliking what he was expected to admire.

Aware that it is much eafier to affail the opinions of others, than to bring forward a well-
digefted fyftem of your own, Fitzofborne determined to commence the attack. An opportunity
foon offered for him to point fome of thofe contemptible but blafphemous farcafms which pafs
for wit, againft the Old Teftament, which infidelity is now pleafed to term an indefenfible
outwork of the popular theology. A fcandalous
tale of a married nobleman had found its way into a public paper; Fitzofborne pointed it out to
Monteith by a fignificant glance, while he, with
the pleafure common to offenders on difcovering
a companion in guilt, honoured the wretched jeft
with which the paragraph concluded with a hearty
laugh.

" What has entertained you, my lord," inquired the countefs. " May we not partake of
" your mirth ?" Monteith haftily replied, that it
would not amufe her; and Edward, toffing the
paper among the other publications of the day,
fagacioufly obferved, that the conduct of the
prefent age correfponded more with the practices
recorded by the Jewifh claffics than with the precepts of their auftere lawgiver. " The offences,"
continued he, " which feem to give eclat to
" thofe heroes who are recorded in the fongs of
" their bards, are in their legiflative code punifh-
" able with death, at leaft if we fuppofe thefe
" narrations literal. But we muft allow, that
" the beft critics, confidering the allegorifing
" temper of thofe people, are led to believe, that
" the whole compafs of their literature is fabu-
" lous

"lous, and by no means poſſeſſing that claim "of high antiquity to which it pretends."

Henry's heart throbbed with indignation; but he determined to wait his opportunity of inter- poſing when his audacious adverſary was thrown off his guard. Warm with affectionate zeal for thoſe truths from which her father had ſo often drawn inſtructive moral leſſons, and the moſt auguſt views of ſuperintending Providence gra- dually unfolding its amazing deſigns, Miſs Evans determined immediately to reply. "It cannot," thought ſhe, "be any dereliction of female mo- "deſty and delicacy to ſhow an infidel that "women may be courageous in a ſacred cauſe. "Even my father's avowed opinion, that we "ought to withdraw from controverſial topics, "would change with the exigency of the preſent "caſe, which calls me to repel the attacks of "profligacy and impiety united for the deſtruc- "tion of my unſuſpecting friend."

Determined by theſe reflections, ſhe addreſſed Fitzoſborne: "How long, ſir, have theſe ſaga- "cious critics ſucceeded in convincing the world "that their ſtile of reaſoning was juſt? My "father has devoted his whole life to the attain- "ment of ſacred learning; and I have heard him "ſay, that the attempts of ſceptics ſerved but to "confirm the ſtability of that heaven-erected "edifice which they ſought to undermine."

"The honour of an argument with Miſs "Evans," returned Edward bowing, "is too "great a novelty for me to decline embracing it; "and I cannot but lament that I have not been "previouſly prepared for the conteſt, by having "obtained a knowledge of the arguments by "which the ſuperior judgment of Mr. Evans was "decided. I am myſelf a ſincere friend to reli-

" gion, anxious for its *real* rights, and jealous
" of its *true* honour; and as fuch I have been
" tempted to wifh that fome untenable points
" were fairly given up, and that the profound
" theologifts of the prefent day would felect thofe
" paffages which bear ftronger marks of infpira-
" tion.   I confefs that I have often felt mortified
" at feeing the abilities of the order exerted in
" the defence of thofe parts of the fyftem which
" were more prudently abandoned by candid dif-
" putants."

" And I," faid Lucy, " have been mortified
" too, when I have feen religion degraded by a
" mock defence."

Mr. Powerfcourt exulted in the blufh of honeft
indignation which glowed on his Lucy's cheek,
and enjoyed the temporary confufion of her adverfary. Fitzofborne foon recovered; but, too
much piqued to preferve the ufual politenefs of
his manners, he begged Mifs Evans to have the
goodnefs to repeat her father's obfervations. They
would, he was fure, be entitled to refpect; perhaps might operate to his conviction. Were
they drawn from his perfect acquaintance with
the Greek and Hebrew languages, or had he ftudied Syriac literature?

" I do not know," faid Lucy, fenfible that this
attack was defigned to expofe her.

" From chronology, natural philofophy, or hif-
" tory? But I believe, madam, you are yourfelf
" miftrefs of thofe fciences."

Mifs Evans's colour heightened with every interrogatory. There was a large party prefent,
and fhe felt the cruelty of thus holding her out
to general ridicule. She blamed her own temerity in having attacked a *Proteus* who could hide
his native deformity in a thoufand forms.

Henry

Henry felt her embarraſſment too ſtrongly not to relieve it. " Do not diſtreſs yourſelf, Miſs " Evans," ſaid he, " by endeavouring to recol- " lect your father's expreſſions. I had the hap- " pineſs of being educated under his auſpices, and " I know the value of his opinion too well to " withhold it from thoſe who deſire information."

" You were of Oxford, I think, ſir," ſaid Fitzoſborne, diſconcerted by the determined coolneſs of Henry's manner. " Several of my " friends muſt have been your cotemporaries." He then enumerated a long liſt, in which he took care to include the moſt conſpicuous young men of the age.

" My time," ſaid Henry, " was chiefly de- " voted to ſtudy, and I formed few connections. " Suppoſing myſelf deſtined for orders, I appli- " ed cloſely to the Greek and Hebrew languages, " and I made ſome progreſs in the Syriac. I at- " tended all the lectures on natural philoſophy, " and am not unacquainted with hiſtory and " chronology." His enumeration of the very topics on which Fitzoſborne had queſtioned Lucy was rendered more ſignificant by the modulation of his voice.

Fitzoſborne bowed, and expreſſed an earneſt wiſh to cultivate his acquaintance. The bow was returned. " I thought, ſir," added Henry, " that you were ſolicitous to receive a little infor- " mation reſpecting thoſe arguments which in- " duced Mr. Evans to affirm, that inveſtigation " had proved of inconceivable uſe in eſtabliſhing " the authenticity of the Old Teſtament."

" I ſhall eſteem it a particular favour if you " would inform me," replied Fitzoſborne. " Can " you give me your company in the library for " that purpoſe to-morrow morning ? The ladies

" wil

" will thank us for adjourning the debate for
" the prefent."

" I fhould conceive, fir," faid Powerfcourt,
" that the ladies are interefted in the authenticity
" of their bibles; and when any doubts are ftart-
" ed, explanations fhould follow of courfe.   By
" your calling forth a *lady* to debate thefe points,
" you muft certainly join in my opinion, that the
" caufe of infpiration is perfectly fafe in the hands
" of that fex, who are accuftomed to argue from
" the feelings of an unvitiated heart, rather than
" from the cold deductions of the underftand-
" ing."

" No one," refumed the evafive Fitzofborne,
" can have a greater refpect for female excel-
" lence than myfelf; and before you profefs
" yourfelf the champion of fentiment, as oppof-
" ed to argumentative deductions, you fhould
" foften the afperity which appears in your man-
" ner, by remembering that I never attacked the
" fair."

" Not in a direct way, I believe," faid Henry
in a moft animated voice, and at the fame time
leading the eye of his antagonift to the countefs,
who fat netting near them, feemingly engroffed
by fome country vifitors, but really attentive to
this converfation.

Edward felt ftruck as by an electrical fhock.
Habitual referve could not prevent a fudden crim-
fon from flufhing his face; and his quickly withdrawn eye told a truth which he would willingly
have concealed; namely, that he underftood
Powerfcourt's allufion.

Unable to purfue a theme where difcovery me-
naced every word, and precluded from the fub-
terfuge which availed him in his former difpute
with Mr. Evans (I mean a reference of the argument

ment to some future time, which it depended
upon himself to procrastinate,) Fitzosborne must
either have waited for Henry's attack on deistical
principles, or have renewed his own charge against
the authenticity of the scriptures. He chose the
latter. He began to lead back the conversation
by some flourishing compliments on the peculiar
suitability of religion to the female character;
and the impression which every thing supernatu-
ral and elevated always made upon the delicate
organs of their imaginations. His zeal to correct the sacred text—(he used the term correct
upon the present occasion, in preference to his
usual expressions of reform or improve)—proceeded from a sincere persuasion of the merits
of several parts of the received canon, and a
wish to expunge from it whatever might corrupt the delicacy of female readers, or harden
their exquisite sensibility of the narration of some
acts of more than savage brutality.

   'The simple manners and unrefined language
'of the earlier ages,' replied Henry, 'are re-
'corded by their faithful historians in characters
'of undisguised veracity. Our ideas of decorum
'vary with the customs of the time and country;
'but vice and virtue are stationary. It may be a
'subject of regret, that translators who render
'authors of very remote antiquity should think
'themselves compelled to give a verbal transcript
'of passages which might be safely paraphrased;
'yet, with respect to the bible, I observe, that
'some of those interpreters who profess to avoid
'the faults which many years observation have
'discovered in our present copy, have substituted
'a sort of gay licentiousness in the place of the
'objectional grossness, much more offensive to
'the purity of the heart. Respecting your se-
                'cond

' cond obfervation, as I do not recollect any in-
' ftance in which the vindictive fpirit of the Jews
' is pointed out to the imitation of fucceeding ages,
' I fhould fuppofe their hiftory might be ftudied
' even in a critical or hiftorical point of view as
' an authentic monument of ages but for infpira-
' tion wholly obliterated, with lefs danger of ren-
' dering the feelings obdurate, than the page of
' Homer, or even the epic labours of that cham-
' pion of antichriftian liberality, Voltaire."

' You forget," faid Fitzofborne triumphantly,
' the merit annexed to the extirpation of the
' Canaanites; and the extinction of Amalek. Such
' pretended injunctions from the beneficent Pa-
·' rent of the univerfe are with me a conclufive
' proof againft the *entire* infpiration of the Old
' Teftament."

' I read in thofe commands," replied Powerfcourt, ' an inconteftable mark of Divinity. I
' recollect the ftate of fociety at that time, and I
' venerate the merciful feverity which imprinted
' upon the minds of a fmall portion of mankind
' a renewed abhorrence of that cruel and degrad-
' ing idolatry prohibited by one of the firft com-
' mands which was imparted to the father of the
' Poftdiluvian world. Surely, *you*, fir, forget the
' maxim of a poet whofe mifdirected mufe is of-
' ten quoted by our prefent deifts to eftablifh
' principles from which he would have fhrunk
' with horror. If

' —— The great firft caufe
" Acts not by partial but by general laws;

' he is not bound by thofe rules of conduct which
' determine the equity of the actions of imperfect,
' fhort-fighted, perifhable man. He, in whofe
' hands are the iffues of life and death, cannot
' be

' be called upon by his creatures to anfwer for the
' operations of any of his inftruments of punifh-
' ment, be they famine, peftilence, or war.   To
' fulfil fome vaft defign, perfected perhaps cen-
' turies after its formation, the Jewifh babe may
' bleed at Bethlehem, or the Calabrian infant be
' ingulphed with its parents by the defolating
' earthquake, without impeding the juftice of the
' Creator, with whom a thoufand years are but
' as a day. We finite creatures, ftanding upon
' a little fpeck of time, cannot comprehend the
' plans of infinitude, which extend to eternity.
' Admit a future ftate, and every idea of particu-
' lar feverity vanifhes.   He who exifts for ever
' can recompence the unoffending children of the
' idolatrous worfhippers of Moloch with an hap-
' py immortality.   He who knows the heart can
' crown with perpetual blifs the confcientious
' affertors of a declining perfuation, whom the
' more peftilent fanaticifm of infidelity immolat-
' ed upon the banks of the Loire.   The giver of
' eternal life can reward the patience he exercifes,
' and amply repay the premature privation of
' temporal exiftence.'

' The company liftened with profound attention,
roufed by the folemn energy with which Mr.
Powerfcourt delivered thefe fentiments.   Mifs
Evans enjoyed the unaffected applaufe which appeared on every countenance. That of the lovely
countefs was lighted up by a moft exhilarating
fmile, and her exulting heart whifpered; ' Ed-
' ward fought conviction ; furely he cannot refift
' the heavenly energy of Henry's heartfelt expref-
' fions.'   The converfation was not continued
on this fubject.

Eager to know if Fitzofborne's opinion of
Powerfcourt had been changed by this difpute,
Geraldine

Geraldine feized the earlieft opportunity of afking him, if fhe had over-rated her kinfman's
merits.

'Not in the leaft,' was the reply. 'He is
'certainly very eloquent, and he poffeffes fome
'command of temper, a virtue rarely found
'among your keen difputants. But I need not,
'lady Monteith, explain to your fagacity the ex-
'act point in which I could have preffed him,
'if politenefs would have permitted me to have
'continued the argument. His whole reference
'is to infinitude and eternity, terms of which we
'can form no clear ideas. He gives no pofi-
'tive proof, no mathematical demonftration of
'the infpiration which he tries to infer from con-
'tefted pofitions; and till this is given by *our*
'fchoolmen, deifm may always reply, that in-
'attention to thofe duties which are merely pre-
'fcribed by revelation, admits of fome excufe, if
'we confider the extreme doubt which attaches
'to thefe fubjects; for, if our prefent code of
'religion may be true, it may alfo be falfe.'

'But is there not a great difficulty, if not a
'total impoffibility, of giving the fatisfactory
'proofs which you fay are required?'

'There, madam,' faid Edward, 'is unhap-
'pily the ftrong hold of fcepticifm, of which all
'the powers of orthodoxy have not been able to
'difpoffefs it. It is pleaded, and certainly with
'an air of reafon, that if divine intelligence real-
'ly dictated what we call revelation, it would
'carry with it inconteftable proofs of its origin
'by filencing every objection, and enforcing
'conviction upon every mind.'

Cowardly lady Monteith! why, reftrained
by a fear of offending determined depravity, forbear affirming, that the gift of reafon was never
intended.

intended to fuperfede the practice of chriftian graces? It was intended to confirm and affure that faith which fhall one day be changed into certainty, to animate that hope which her boafted power could never clearly difcover without divine guidance. Why fear to drive the mean diffimulator from the affected decency of deifm into the bold audacity of atheifm, by afking, how animated duft and afhes can prefume to queftion the power which called it into exiftence, demanding, ' Why ' haft thou made me what I am?' How intelligence confeffedly finite can charge the counfels of that mind which pervades infinitude and extends through eternity, with inconfiftency in prefcribing a rule of action to probationary beings, without at the fame time compelling obfervance? Why forbear to inquire how his favourite freewill can confift with fuch a fcheme of government? Nay, bid him not ftop at the moral world; but fay, why earth is not heaven, and man an incorporeal effence, fuch as we believe the bleffed inhabitants of that better region. Reftrained by the growing attachment which, though confined within the ftricteft bounds that the fpecious affectation of Platonic affection could impofe, and unacknowledged even to herfelf, certainly made Fitzofborne's approbation of confequence to her peace, lady Monteith forbore to oppofe where fhe dreaded to offend; and fhe contented herfelf with wifhing the mind of the moft amiable of men to be relieved from thofe doubts which his converfations fometimes transfufed into her own bofom.

CHAP. XI.

Why, I can fmile, and murder while I fmile;
And cry, ' Content' to that which grieves my heart;
And wet my cheek with artificial tears;
And frame my face to all occafions.

SHAKESPEARE.

THE difpute which occupied the preceding
Chapter was not the only inftance of the triumph of manly fenfe and found principle over
fophiftry, declamation, and hypocrify. Confcious of his advantage, Mr. Powerfcourt at
every opportunity purfued infidelity into its re-
treats of falfehood. He expofed the credulity.
of difbelief, the inconfiftency of fcepticifm,.
and the inconclufive futility of every argument
which dared to fet up Nature in oppofition to
its Author.

It was not with a hope of effecting any
change in Fitzofborne that Henry thus continued to dare him to the ' keen encounter of their
' wits;' he knew from inconteftable authority,
' that thofe who love darknefs rather than light,
' becaufe their deeds are evil,' muft conftantly
refift the elucidating ray of truth. It was the
fituation of the Monteiths which urged him to
this continual warfare. He plainly faw the
predilection of the countefs, and the infatuation
of her lord; and he vainly wifhed for that
' warning voice' which might aroufe them to a
confcioufnefs of their danger. He was not
without

without hope too, that Edward's pride, mortified by repeated defeats, might provoke him to
quit a refidence which continual oppofition
muft render difagreeable ; and, ftimulated by
the enterprizing warmth of fincere friendfhip,
he fcarcely calculated the chance of being called out by a man, who, on fome previous occafions, had proved himfelf to be

Jealous of honour, fudden and quick in quarrel ;
Seeking the bubble reputation.
Even in the cannon's mouth.

But the patience and humility which Edward
exercifed upon this occafion was as wonderful
as his perfeverance. Let not the reader con-
clude that I give him credit for thofe virtues ;
for it cannot be fuppofed that he would adopt
qualities which he efteemed to be weak imper-
fections. He ufed them only as the means
which were fanctified by the propofed end.
Taught by his recent defeat to abftain from
attack, he contented himfelf with barely attempt-
ing a defence, when Powerfcourt preffed him
with fome powerful inference ; always taking
care that fomething in his expreffion, look, or
manner, fhould convey to the quick apprehenfion of Geraldine a hint of unfair treatment ;
an infinuation of his love of peace ; and a complaint that his adverfary began the debate, and
that it was unjuft to feek to deprive him of his
own opinions, when he did not moleft others
in the quiet enjoyment of their peculiar notions.

Lady Monteith loved fociety, and few people were better calculated than herfelf to enjoy

ant.

and impart the namelefs delights of converfation. Whether we define it, according to the
ideas of the Swan of Twickenham, to be ' the
' feaft of reafon and the flow of foul;' or,
perfonifying its exhilarating graces, defcribe it
in the likenefs of Milton's Euphrofyne, ' buck-
' fome, blithe, and debonaire,' yet ftill the
affociate of ' unreproved pleafure;' in whichever
fhape the goddefs prefides, the irritating fpirit
of contradiction, and the fcowling genius of
continual argument, muft be profcribed admiffion, or the fweets of the mental banquet will
be foured by fermentation. The relaxed mind
cannot repofe upon the bofom of confidence,
and pour forth all its choiceft ftores, when
every expreffion roufes the clamour of oppofition. The dimpled fmile of fportive mirth is
too timid to encounter the auftere afpect of de-
clamatory inveftigation.

Such were the reflections of Geraldine,
who, driven by conjugal infelicity to feek
amufement out of herfelf, had fondly hoped
that the moft refined focial pleafures would refult from the friends of her early youth meeting
with the accomplifhed intelligent Fitzofborne.
She had anticipated the delights of literary converfation, the corufcations of playful wit; and,
while fhe enjoyed with fincere pleafure the
profpect of her Lucy's happinefs, fhe determined to divert herfelf with the little aukward-
neffes which the prefence of a beloved object
generally gives to the manner of a young woman poffeffed of a delicate fufceptible mind.
Inftead of thefe expected luxuries, the demon
of Difpute took poffeffion of the dining-room
and the faloon; accompanied their walks and
rides, their fifhing parties and mountain tours;
and,

and, inftead of leaving the mind of the countefs at liberty to entertain her guefts with fomething enchantingly whimfical, or negligently
elegant, her anxiety was perpetually exercifed
to reprefs every topic of difcourfe which threatened contention.

Perhaps Geraldine overcharged this defcription. She was alfo miftaken in fixing the
whole blame of this controverfial fpirit upon
Henry. More accuftomed to Edward's ftyle of
converfation, and lefs aware of its tendency,
he could at any time drop the gage of defiance
without arrefting her attention, till the reply of
his antagonift called her to divert the rifing
ftorm. Her infenfibility of her own danger,
and confequent ignorance of the confcientious
motives which urged Mr. Powerfcourt to vio-
late the prefcribed rules of good breeding ftrict-
ly adhered to in polifhed fociety, precluded
her from framing any excufes in his juftification. That eternal gratitude which fhe had
promifed to preferve for the generous friend
who had facrificed his own happinefs to her's,
imperceptibly abated, as the conviction that
fhe had founded her hopes of connubial felicity
on a wrong bafis gathered ftrength. On the
other hand, the recent fervices of Fitzofborne,
and the marked contraft between him and her
lord, hourly made a deeper impreffion; and
her difapprobation of what fhe thought cavalier
behaviour increafed her indifference for the
fociety of Lucy and her lover. Real efteem
could not be weakened; but affection fenfibly
declined, at leaft fo far as to make her wifh them
married and happily fettled at Powerfcourt.

Geraldine's eftrangement from her once-
loved friends could not be attributed to Mr.
Fitz-

Fitzofborne's *fuggeftions*. However poignantly his feelings might be wounded, he was too generous to complain ; and refpect for the relation of his fair friend withheld him from anfwering his perfecutor as moft gentlemen would do. As fome of his own notions had a tendency to democracy, he could not confiftently hint the humble fituation of Henry's father, as a reafon why his fon was unfit to mix with men of rank. Befide, he recollected that he had paffed through the purifying ordeal of a college education, which always confumes every particle of plebeian infection ; and that he could not caft an oblique cenfure on his origin without involving the reputation of the high-feated Powerfcourt anceftry. He therefore never uttered a farcafm of the kind ; nay he even once attempted to foften Geraldine's difpleafure, who confeffed herfelf to be a little hurt at her coufin's behaviour, by obferving, that Mr. Powerfcourt's early connections might not have led him into very polifhed fociety, and that habit was an irrefiftible enemy to that amenity of manners which marked the gentleman.

But though thus cautious with refpect to the countefs, the daring genius of Fitzofborne winged a bolder flight with her credulous lord. He too retained but a faint remembrance of the merit of the felf-denying, accommodating rival, who had refigned the girl he loved to his happier vows. He forgot the dejection and fubfequent illnefs which fpoke the anguifh of the facrifice ; and no longer finding, that the poffeffion of that bleffing which the generous. Henry reluctantly refigned had confirmed his own happinefs, he was prepared to look upon him as he would upon any other gueft, and to regulate

regulate his behaviour to him, not by a sense
of gratitude or esteem, but by the present
amusement he received from his conversation.
I have sufficiently explained lord Monteith's
character for my readers to anticipate my confession, that his powers of discrimination were
very limited. In fact, hating controversy,
which he not unaptly called quarrelling, if he
could not contrive, by playing with his dogs or
his children, to make sufficient noise to prevent
himself from hearing the dispute, he rang the
bell for his horses and took a ride.

He had pursued this method twice before the
hint was understood, a sufficient excuse for
the total loss of patience which followed.—
Deceived by his own impetuosity, and some in-
sinuations of Fitzosborne, he mistook the part
which the countess acted upon these occasions,
which was generally that of a mediatrix; for,
though inclination led her to join with Edward,
especially when he more nicely affected the
plausible, yet if Henry, by pressing his arguments
close, surprised his opponent in the avowal of
some bold tenets, Geraldine could not refrain
from expressing her approbation of the champion of steady principle. Lord Monteith once entered the room, when every tongue was loud in
declaiming against some positions which Fitzosborne had just attempted to maintain on the subject of education. They were, that as it is presumptuous to assert, that obedience to parents is
any thing more than the preference of reason
enforced by affection, the child ought to lead
its own studies, and the parent or instructor follow; for youth should enjoy perfect liberty,
and be led to knowledge not by authority, but
by inclination. His lordship had no disposition

to

to give himfelf the trouble of underftanding the debate. He heard.fomething of the cruelty of debarring innocent infants of the liberty with which nature had endowed them, and he faw every one united in condemning Fitzofborne. He was an advocate for children enjoying them-felves, and he never either reftrained or corrected his own, except when they interrupted his par-ticular purfuits. He was,-befide,.ftrongly im-pelled to fupport Fitzofborne, who was now be-come abfolutely neceffary to him in the double capacity of a flatterer and an advifer.

The earl took a chair; obtained the lead in converfation; and foon made himfelf mafter of the field by filencing all oppofition. He caft a look of triumph round him. ' What,' faid he to Geraldine, ' have you not one word left ' to defend your opinion ? You.was haranguing ' very learnedly, and laying down a fyftem of ' management which you meant to adopt—with ' James, I fuppofe; but as I may not converfe ' with you upon this fubject again, I would ad-' vife you to give it up, for I fhall never allow , it. You have broke the fpirit of the poor ' -girls already by your leffons and your punifh-ments; and I.fhall educate the boy according. ' to my own plan.'

The countefs anfwered by an acquiefcent fmile; but his lordfhip had talked himfelf into a fit of indignation,. which fome domeftic per-plexities fecretly increafed. He arofe, and, gi--ving his chair rather a whirl than a pufh, ftalked out of the room.

Every one who has witneffed little conjugal rencontres knows, that it is the bufinefs of by-ftanders to take no notice of the paffing fcene, but to exert the happieft addrefs to divert the at-tention.

tention of the parties engaged to fome new fubject. Geraldine's ftarting tears were repreffed
by Lucy's obferving, that an uncommonly beautiful butterfly refted upon the chimney-piece;
and at the fame inftant Henry called her to re-
mark the characteriftic ftyle of excellence which
diftinguifhed Titian's paintings. Fitzofborne was
loft in dejected filence. He however rofe, as if
to examine the picture which Henry had pointed
out; and fancying his attention engroffed by
the butterfly hunt, which Mifs Evans enliven-
ed by a hundred humorous obfervations, he
whifpered to the ftill-agitated countefs, as he
paffed her; 'Dear fuffering meeknefs! fhall I
' follow him, and try to calm his favage frenzy?'
fhe faintly articulated, 'Yes,' and her champion inftantly withdrew. A thought that moment
ftruck the countefs, that his interpofition might
add to the paffion which quiet felf-reflection
would beft fubdue. The colours of nature or
of Titian could no longer give a tranfitory diverfion to the pangs of thought. The hitherto reftrained tears burft from her eyes, and fhe haftily flew after Fitzofborne.

'That man is a villain,' faid Henry to his
Lucy, who was now the only perfon remaining
with him in the room.

'I never doubted it,' faid fhe, relinquifhing
the juft-vanquifhed butterfly. 'But have you
' any frefh proofs?' Powerfcourt repeated the
whifper which he had diftinctly overhard.

'O my lovely, enchanting Geraldine, how
' perilous is thy fituation!' exclaimed Mifs
Evans; 'between a hufband infenfible of thy
' virtues, and a pretended friend who is deter-
' mined to undermine them!'

'And

‘ And how fatally infenfible of her danger!’
continued Powerfcourt.

‘ Are there no means to fave her ?’

‘ I have tried what to my judgment appeared to
‘ be the moft probable, and I have purfued them
‘ beyond the bounds which regard for the deco-
‘ rum of my own character would have impofed.
‘ I have clearly detected his principles, and, I
‘ fometimes hope, armed the countefs againft
‘ their feductive poifons. But I cannot remove
‘ him from Monteith. He endures my perfe-
‘ cution with a patience which convinces me
‘ that he will not be provoked to retreat; and I
‘ have no influence either with the earl or Ge-
‘ raldine. What can prevent her from every
‘ day, nay every hour, perceiving the ftrong
‘ contraft between his foft, infinuating, polifhed
‘ manner, and the inconfiftent, uninformed—I
‘ had almoft faid—cruel, deportment of her
‘ much-altered lord ? You fee, Edward himfelf
‘ draws the parallel.’

‘ And our beloved friend feels it,’ added Lucy.
‘ Can there be a ftronger proof of his defigns
‘ than the whifper which you juft overheard ?’

‘ Yes,’ replied Powerfcourt, ‘ there is a ftron-
‘ ger. She is lovely and attractive as fancy
‘ ever feigned. And what fhall induce that
‘ man to refift the power of her charms, who
‘ has filenced the reftraints of confcience, who
‘ fears no future retribution, and who has fuffi-
‘ cient cunning to elude the pecuniary punifh-
‘ ments which our laws award to his licentious
‘ crimes ? Hourly expofed to the blaze of Ge-
‘ raldine’s perfections, indulged by a credulous
‘ hufband with every opportunity for feducing
‘ her honour, he muft feel the fafcination of
‘ her beauty and her merit. Nay, his attentions
‘ prove,

' prove, even to cafual obfervers, that he does
' feel them. My right hand neighbour at the
' earl's laſt public dinner, aſked me, ' Who is
' this Mr. Fitzoſborne ?' I told him, an admirer
' of lady Arabella Macdonald. ' I am very
' glad to hear that,' faid the blunt enquirer ;
' for we country people fancied he made love
' to the countefs.'

Lucy determined to tell her friend this ſtory,
and Powerſcourt approved the fuggeſtion. ' Be
' careful, however,' faid he ; ' alarm her deli-
' cacy, but not her pride. Convince her, that
' it is only *ſtrangers* that can doubt her recti-
' tude ; that fhe owes the immediate difmiſſion
' of Fitzoſborne to the judgment of the world,
' not to the opinions of thofe friends who know
' her worth, and who deem it almoſt impoſſible
' that fhe fhould fall.'

' And fo it is,' faid Miſs Evans with energy.
' I defy all the traitor's arts to allure her to wil-
' ful guilt. She cannot feel any real predilec-
' tion in his favour.'

' Ah, Lucy,' interrupted Henry, ' we foon
' ceafe from the perfecuting attentions which
' we find *difpleafe* the object of our purfuit.'—
Lucy afked him whether he learned that maxim
of her or Geraldine ; and the converfation
changed to a more agreeable topic.

In the mean time lady Monteith had overtaken
Fitzoſborne, and, finding her perfuafions to induce him to abandon his defign of reproving her
lord for his petulance ineffectual, fhe extorted
from him an engagement, that he would act
with the gentleſt caution. This agreement,
like the promifes of the weïrd fifter to the guilty
Thane of Cawdor, was ' kept to the ear, but
' broken to the fenfe.' The caution was exercifed

rifed for his own fecurity, and the gentlenefs
was the refined covering of fimulation.

He had that day made himfelf mafter of a
fecret, the difcovery of which would, he knew,
point the whole torrent of the earl's fretful impatience againft the countefs and Mr. Powerfcourt. I have frequently ftated, that lord Monteith's natural character ftrongly partook of generofity and benevolence. Thefe noble fenfa-
tions, blunted by felfifhnefs and inconfideration,
were now effectually chilled by the embarraff-
ments attendant on perplexed circumftances ;
and his irritable temper was continually fretted
by the reprefentations of his agents, and the folicitations of his creditors. It was to fome har-
raffing occurrences of this nature, that his late
behaviour to the countefs muft be afcribed ; and
the moment he left the room, his fenfe of her
meek fufferance added to his torment. He
flung himfelf upon the bank of the canal which
wound round the managerie, and was beginning
to yield to that tranquillity of mind which the
warbling birds, the waving trees, and the calm
fplendour of a mild autumnal fun, infpired,
when Fitzofborne feated himfelf by his fide.

‘ When do you cut a communication between
‘ this canal and the lake ?’ inquired he. The
earl only anfwered by a profound figh.

‘ You told me,’ refumed his tormentor, ‘ that
‘ you had fuch a defign. You alfo mentioned
‘ your intention of levelling a fmall eminence
‘ which intercepts your view of the Grampian
‘ hills.’

Stung by the recollection of thofe plans of
princely magnificence by which he had once
intended to embellifh the feat of his anceftors,

lord

lord Monteith could only anfwer by execrating the dice-box.

'My good friend,' faid Fitzofborne, 'why
'perfift in teazing yourfelf with ufelefs recol-
'lections of paft misfortunes? Let us look for-
'ward to the future. You have noble expec-
'tations. Sir William Powerfcourt cannot in
'the courfe of nature live long.—But I be-
'lieve I fhould not have entered upon that
'painful fubject.'

Lord Monteith, who at that inftant felt the mifery of ftraitened circumftances too ftrongly to regard with forrow the death of an old man who would leave him a handfome fortune, in-quired, why he fhould think it fuch a painful event? 'There is a great deal of whimfical
'goodnefs about the old baronet,' added he;
'but people cannot live for ever.'

'I did not fufpect you of the puerility of
'grieving for his death," faid Edward fmiling.
'I allude to the awkward circumftances in
'which you will be placed at his demife.'

'Is coming into the poffeffion of five thoufand
'a-year an awkward circumftance?'

'No; but I think I fhould not like to be the
'mere fteward of my wife and children. I
'fhould rather like to have the expenditure di-
'rected by myfelf.'

'And who elfe will direct it?' inquired the earl, raifing himfelf from the ground.

'Poffibly you have fome influence over the
'part which is fettled upon your daughter or
'your unborn fon; but the two thoufand a-year
'which the countefs difpofes of will be totally
'diverted from your purfe.'

'Why, what does fhe mean to do with it?'

'Are

' Are you really ignorant of her defigns then?
' I muft have been mifinformed.' Repeated
entreaties drew from Fitzofborne what he now
termed a mere guefs of his own, arifing from
the peculiar warmth of the countefs in. her
friendfhips ; namely, that it was intended to
increafe the opulence of Mr. Powerfcourt and
his bride. Then, looking attentively on the
earl, he inquired what ' bloody paffion fhook
' his very frame ;" and he entreated him not
to be difcompofed at his idle fuppofitions; at
leaft, to pafs the matter in filence till it was
better confirmed. My lord promifed ; but his
behaviour to Mr. Powerfcourt became, in confequence, fo ftrikingly inhofpitable, that the latter foon found himfelf compelled to leave a
family, in which, independent of his attachment to his Lucy, the livelieft feelings of his
heart were now centered.

Inftead of obtruding his keen fenfe of Monteith's extraordinary behaviour upon the obfervation of the countefs, he contrived to give his
departure the air of choice ; and he declined
with an air of regret rather than pique Geraldine's faint invitation to fpend another week
with them. He had, however, entrufted Mifs
Evans with his real fentiments. ' I am con-
' vinced,' faid he, ' that the earl is but the pup-
' pet of the treacherous Fitzofborne on this
' occafion. There are fome mafterly but dia-
' bolical machinations on foot which I cannot
' develope. My continuing here can be of no
' fervice ; indeed it is impoffible, confidering
' the treatment which I hourly experience. No
' effort of mine could fhake the confidence
' which this credulous tool of fubtle villainy
' repofes in the betrayer of his peace. Be
                                        ' you,

'you, therefore, my Lucy, the Guardian angel,
'and watch over your much-endangered, too
'confident friend. I know your zeal and your
'unfhaken fidelity; but I fear you will be called
'upon for exertions which will put your forti-
'tude to 'the feverest trial. Endure the altered
'looks of your Geraldine; even brave her re-
'fentment. Remember, that fhe is now la-
'bouring under the impulfe of a fatal delufion,
'and that her returning reafon muft blefs the
'hand which fnatches her from deftruction.'

'I know, Henry,' replied Lucy, 'that I fhall
'continually want your directing judgment.
'O that we had her fafe at Powerfcourt ! How
'would we join to pour the balm of friendfhip
'on her wounded foul !'

'Cannot you,' faid Henry, 'plead a little
'pardonable caprice, and fay you have made
'a refolution not to confirm my happinefs till
'the dear companion of our youth is prefent,
'to fee your father knit the folemn bond which
'will make you for ever mine ?"

'I know not," cried Lucy, giving her hand
to her lover with a faint fmile, 'what folly
'I would not affect to fave my Geraldine.'

C H A P. XII.

Is all the counfel that we two have fhar'd,
The fifter's vows, the hours that we have fpent,
When we have chid the tardy footed time
For parting us ; O and is all forgot ?
All fchool-days friendfhip, childhood innocence ?—
And will you rend our ancient love afunder ?

                              SHAKESPEARE.

IT is a general obfervation, that ceremony increafes as affection declines. Confcious of the
unkindnefs wnich we blufh to avow, we poorly
attempt to difguife our inconftancy by a parade
of words, without confidering that we betray
our hypocrify by a fcrupulous regard to thofe
minutiæ, to which, while our hearts glowed
with real regard, we were too much occupied
to attend.

In proportion as lady Monteith felt the pleafure fhe took in Mifs Evans's fociety really diminifh, fhe was more obfervant in her hofpitable attentions, not with a view to deceive,
but from the more generous motive of wifhing
to avoid giving pain. Though fhe would not
have felt any uneafinefs to have feen her accompany Henry back to Caernarvonfhire, fhe
expreffed a lively fenfe of her Lucy's goodnefs
in remaining. She was ever fearful at dinner
that her friend was not taken good care of;
and though Mifs Evans had made repeated
vifits to Monteith, it now firft occurred to the
countefs, that there was an impropriety in
                                        lodging

lodging her in one of the turret chambers, though the primary reason for doing so had been, that it was the nearest to her own.

Lucy experienced all the trials which Henry had predicted ; but she recollected, that she had determined to endure them. " Let the worst
' come,' said she, ' that my fears predict, her
' heart can never be vitiated. The moment
' the seducer pulls off the mask, she will detect
' him ; and as the delusion vanishes, her sus-
' ceptible heart will recal those *real* friends
' who strove to snatch her from destruction.'

Vice is never secure, even when triumphant. Let earth and hell conspire to favour its designs, nothing is so mean, nothing so cowardly as guilt. The removal of Powerscourt was a grand point gained ; but the watchful, fearless, determined Lucy remained ; and though Fitz-osborne perceived her influence hourly decline, he felt her presence to be an impediment to his concluding machinations. He could not banish her, as he had done Henry, by the agency of the earl ; for the whim of the moment always predominated with that nobleman. The incon-veniences which he fancied he suffered from a controversial propensity, produced his resolu-tion of driving his guest from Monteith ; and though the suspicion, that Henry was intended to inherit a large portion of sir William's estate gave that determination immediate action, it was considered separately as a circumstance which lord Monteith's generosity would have entirely disregarded in a less embarrassed state of his own affairs. He well knew that Miss Evans was intended to share in his lady's libe-rality ; but she was less objectionable to him, on the important account of her never attempt-

ing

ing a formal argument. He detefted long harangues ; but a piquant retort was his delight, and fhe was peculiarly happy at repartee. Her fprightly unaffected manner, and comparative ignorance of fafhionable life, amufed him : and fhe had long borne him a degree of affection as being the hufband of her friend. She efteemed his good qualities ; and her concern for the delufion under which 'he laboured induced her to be even more than ufually attentive to his humour, and indulgent to his follies.

But though Fitzofborne was thus compelled to leave Monteith out of his counfel, and Lucy refufed to read a wifh for her removal in the fickly funfhine of her Geraldine's languid fmiles, he refolved, that other means fhould expedite her departure. A project was therefore contrived. The evening before its completion, lord Monteith had devoted to his increafing love for Bacchanalian indulgences. The hour was late, but madeira and burgundy preferved their attractions. The joyous party had fent excufes to the countefs for not joining her in the faloon ; and Geraldine, after fupporting a languid evening with her two friends, (for Fitzofborne had early pleaded indifpofition as a reafon for leaving the noify Anacreontics,) retired to her own apartment.

She was here encountered by her favourite attendant, who with much reluctance, and many affurances that fhe would not have taken fuch a liberty, but that fhe really had already advanced all her own money to the diftreffed parties, prefented a petition from the workmen who had been employed in laying the foundation of the amphitheatre which was begun in the park. They were now reduced

to

to the laſt diſtreſs, not only by an unexpected
diſmiſſion from their employment, but by the
non-payment of wages already due.   Maria
declared, that her father and brothers were of
the number; and the many anecdotes of authentic ſuffering which ſhe recited, and traced
to this culpable remiſſneſs, ſwelled the feeling
heart of Geraldine with indignation and pity.
‘ My lord,’ ſaid ſhe, ‘ promiſed to pay all the
‘ bills immediately, as ſome compenſation for
‘ the diſappointment I cauſed the workmen, by
‘ giving up the deſign before they had finiſhed
‘ the work they had contracted to execute.   It
‘ muſt be the ſteward’s fault. Is he up ? I will
‘ ſpeak to him immediately.’
    ‘ There was a light in his office when your
‘ ladyſhip rang the bell.’
    ‘ Deſire him to come up ſtairs.   But no ;
‘ he is very old and infirm ; I will go to him.’
    The reſult of the converſation was not at all
to the counteſs’s ſatisfaction.   She found that
the delay was wholly attributable to her lord,
who had inſiſted that the appropriated ſums
ſhould be tranſmitted where the claims were
leſs juſt, but more clamorous.   The ſteward
mentioned many other circumſtances which
increaſed her agitation, and he anſwered her
earneſt ſolicitations that theſe bills might be
immediately diſcharged, by pleading that it
was totally impoſſible to advance what was not
in his poſſeſſion.
    Geraldine returned towards her own apart-
ment, ruminating on what meaſures ſhe could
purſue, and determining privately to diſpoſe of
ſome of her mother’s jewels, rather than that
the helpleſs babes of the labourer ſhould want
bread.   While ſhe was croſſing the gallery

leading from the ſtair-caſe, the loud but indiſ-
tinct noiſe of catches and glees inarticulately
ſung, and interrupted by applauding clamours,
or reproving oaths, iſſued from the banquetting
room. She ſtopped for a moment, and fancied
that ſhe heard Monteith's voice. ' Has he
' then,' ſaid ſhe, ' loſt all the feelings of hu-
' manity, as well as all ſenſe of refined plea-
' ſure ? Compaſſion, nay juſtice demands, that
' the waſte of riot ſhould have been appropri-
' ated to nobler ends.'

Her eye then glanced towards the library,
which was at the end of a ſuite of rooms oppoſite to where ſhe ſtood. The door was open,
and ſhe ſaw Fitzoſborne ſit with a book in his
hand in a poſture of fixed attention. She never
felt the power of contraſt ſo ſtrong before ; and
a momentary impulſe almoſt tempted her to
tear from her finger the witneſs of that bond
which had ſealed her miſery.

Still Fitzoſborne continued to read, and Geraldine, leaning over the baluſtrade, ſtill alternately looked and liſtened. ' O ſplendid wretch-
' edneſs !' ſaid ſhe, gazing on the marble
figures which decorated the ſtair-caſe, and the
richly carved roof, now rendered more conſpicuous by the coloured lamps which hung from
every pediment ; ' the lonely villager, whom
' we abridge in his ſcanty enjoyments, curſes
' this parade of luxury ; and the curſes of the
' injured will one day come into judgment
' againſt their proud oppreſſors.''

Still indulging her melancholy feelings, the
counteſs contemplated the compoſure of Fitzoſborne's looks. ' All muſt be right,' ſaid ſhe,
' in his boſom. He is neither tortured by re-
' morſe nor fear ; and can what I have heard
                                        'of

' of the fceptic's wretched ftate be juft? Per-
' haps at this moment I fhould feel fome con-
' folation in thinking, that the great Author of
' the univerfe is too much engroffed by his own
' perfections to take cognizance of things be-
' low; for then I need not fear his avenging
' the wrongs of indigence." At that inftant
the cries of her little fon in the nurfery threw
her thoughts into a different train. ' Ah! my
' poor babes,' refumed fhe, ' whatever is my
' own lot, a mother muft, for your fakes, hope
' that there is a *fpecial* Providence to protect
' your helplefs infancy.'

Fitzofborne now rofe, and, advancing towards her, interrupted her mufings. ' For
' Heaven's fake, deareft lady Monteith! what
' keeps you up at this late hour?'—' My for-
' rows,' replied the countefs, burfting into
tears.

' I hoped,' returned Edward, affectionately
preffing her hand, ' that they were hufhed in
' oblivion. Permit me to lead you from the
' hearing of thefe offenfive revellers. It is too
' fhocking to refined delicacy like yours.'

Geraldine inquired where they fhould go?
and Fitzofborne propofed the garden. ' The
' Comus of this place will not lead his band of
' waffailers there,' faid he. ' The meaner or-
' gans of thefe fatyrs are only capable of en-
' joying the groffeft animal gratifications. Par-
' don my allufion. I have juft been enraptured
' by the fublime bard's defcription of revel jol-
' lity. How different is the brutal vociferation
' which we hear from thefe rapturous ideas:

' Eraid your locks with rofy twine,
' Dropping odours, dropping wine,

' Rigour

' Rigour now is gone to bed,
' And Advice with ſcrup'lous head.
' By dimpled brook, and fountain brim,
' The Wood-Nymphs deckt with daiſies trim,
' Their merry wakes and paſtimes keep :
' What hath night to do with ſleep ?'

His further quotation was here interrupted by
the appearance of Miſs Evans, who, declaring
the evening was much too beautiful to think of
going to bed, propoſed joining them in their
excurſion into the garden. They took a ſhort
and ſilent turn under the colonade, and then
retired to their apartments.

The counteſs very ſoon after perceived that
Miſs Evans was at her chamber-door. ' I am
' haunted, my dear Geraldine," ſaid ſhe, ' by
' ſome very diſagreeable company ; my own
' thoughts I mean. Will you allow me to loſe
' them for one hour by converſing with you ?'
Lady Monteith deſired her maid to retire, and
the two friends ſat for a few moments gazing
at each other in expreſſive ſilence.

Miſs Evans firſt ſpoke : ' There was a time,
' my Geraldine, when our full-fraught hearts
' never wanted a ſubject for converſation. That
' confidence is paſt, I ſee ; yet I will neither
' lament nor complain. But for your own,
' for your dear children's ſake, let not any re-
' cently-diſcovered fault in me induce you to
' ſlight the important diſcoveries that I can re-
' veal. My anxiety for your little boy, who is
' not quite well, brought me this night to wit-
' neſs a fuller confirmation of Fitzoſborne's
' villany.'

' What villany ?' inquired Geraldine with
an unaltered countenance.

' He

‘ He placed himſelf purpoſely in the library,
‘ that you might ſee him.’

‘ What then ?’

‘ I firmly believe too, that the banqueting-
‘ room door was ſet open by his order, that
‘ you might hear the confuſion ”

‘ And was not lord Monteith moſt to blame
‘ to cauſe that confuſion ?’

‘ I do not vindicate my lord. O, my ſainted
‘ mother ! if I could but breathe the energy
‘ of thy diſcerning ſpirit into my dear unſuſ-
‘ picious friend——’

‘ I never knew that Mrs. Evans thought ſuſ-
‘ picion a virtue.’

‘ She never would have ſuffered an audacious
‘ man to have offended her ears with reflec-
‘ tions on my father’s conduct. Though mild,
‘ and patient of reproofs to herſelf, her quick
‘ ſuſceptibility of his honour——’

‘ You ſurely do not recollect,’ interrupted
lady Monteith, ‘ that the compariſon you have
‘ ſtarted is moſt exquiſitely painful to me. I
‘ will only ſay, that the regularity of your fa-
‘ ther’s conduct diſproved ſlander. Do *you*
‘ draw the inference.’ The tears which at that
inſtant ſtreamed from her eyes avowed her tortured heart.

‘ My ſweeteſt Geraldine ! can I witneſs thoſe
‘ tears, and not wiſh to relieve thy ſorrows ?’

‘ Then ſeek not to deprive me of my only
‘ friend.’

‘ Your *only* friend ! How is your ſtyle of
‘ of expreſſion changed ! What then am I ?
‘ what is Henry Powerſcourt ?’

‘ Both ſtrangely altered by unjuſt ſuſpici-
‘ ons.’

s ‘Our

' Our fufpicions are not pointed at you. We
' know that you are pure, and guiltlefs of the
' fmalleft *intentional* fault. We grieve to fee
' your candour betrayed, your unfufpecting in-
' nocence infnared, your reputation blafted."

' My reputation blafted, Mifs Evans? Are
' you not cruel in referring to a flanderous
' tale, invented by envy and falfehood, which
' you once told me my conduct fufficiently dif-
' proved ?'

' No! no! my heart is a ftranger to defigned
' cruelty to any one, and leaft of all to you.
' It is not to the attacks of malignity, it is to
' the conclufions of guilelefs fimplicity, that I
' refer.' She then repeated the obfervations
which were addreffed to Mr. Powerfcourt at
the public dinner.

' Muft I then,' aid the countefs, ' clear my
' character to the world by throwing treble
' odium upon my lord's? or, muft I renounce
' the only companion who feems ftudious to
' fweeten the bitter cup of anguifh which I
' now drain to the dregs? Am I to publifh the
' obligations which I owe to Fitzofborne? obli-
' gations which would juftify me in every one's
' opinion; or fit a lone, folitary, flighted being
' in this magnificent prifon?'

Lucy now melted into tears. ' Does your
' palace, your bower of blifs, as you once ftyled
' it, now receive that appellation? O! what
' has wrought this dreadful change? It is not
' quite a twelvemonth fince your own dear
' hand-writing to me traced thefe ftrong ex-
' preffions. ' I enjoy as much happinefs as
' experience teaches us to expect in this un-
' certain world. I poffefs my hufband's affec-
' tionate confidence, the efteem of my friends,
                                        ' the

‘ the love of my dependants. With what heart-
‘ felt tranfport, my Lucy, do I tell you, that
‘ lord Monteith feems every hour more firmly at-
‘ tached to me and his children. You know his
‘ manner is fingular. It once gave me pain, but
‘ reflection has reconciled me to it, and I difcover,
‘ even in his eccentricities, indubitable marks of
‘ an excellent heart.’ Do not wring your hands,
‘ my love ! I do not recite this paffage to awaken
‘ your poignant feelings, but to convince your
‘ judgment.’

Mifs Evans paufed ; the countefs was unable to
fpeak, and fhe proceeded.

‘ Can all this ruin originate from chance ?
‘ Can your lord withdraw his affection, his con-
‘ fidence, nay even treat you with feverity, with-
‘ out fome tempter ? Truft me, my Geraldine,
‘ if Fitzofborne were indeed your friend, the in-
‘ fluence which he fo eminently poffeffes over
‘ your impetuous lord muft be apparent and
‘ produce the moft oppofite behaviour.’

‘ In what,’ faid Geraldine, recovering herfelf,
‘ do you perceive this influence ? does lord Mon-
‘ teith ever coincide with Fitzofborne’s fenti-
‘ ments ?’

‘ Rather fay, does he ever oppofe them ? Fitz-
‘ ofborne is too fubtle to let me ever hear his *real*
‘ fentiments ; but I read them reflected in the
‘ undifguifed countenance of your lord. His eye
‘ continually watches his artful favourite, a
‘ proof that he feels his influence. He is not on-
‘ ly warm and uniform in his approbation of
‘ Fitzofborne, but his behaviour is marked by a
‘ degree of refpect and deference which I never
‘ obferved him to fhew to any one elfe, except to
‘ you in thofe happy days when you reigned the
‘ undifputed fovereign of his heart. You,

who

' who knew the gentle clue by which he was
' imperceptibly led to comply with your wishes,
' must know, that the delicate management
' which his temper requires can only be visible
' to others by its effect.'

' For what purpose should Edward wish for
' this ascendancy over lord Monteith ?" inquired
' the countess.

' In my opinion for the most diabolical pur-
' pose—to alienate his heart from you, and to in-
' duce him to treat you with such unkindness, as
' may subvert, in your mind, those sentiments of
' affection and esteem which, next to the princi-
' ples of duty and honour, form the strongest
' guards of female purity. Nay, hear me one
' moment more. Every audacious whisper which
' he utters against your husband, every look of
' artificial tenderness by which he dares to re-
' commend *himself*, are employed to batter down
' the same defence, while his atheistical insinua-
' tions tend to repress the compunctions of con-
' science, and to weaken that principle of reli-
' gion upon which your safety principally de-
' pends."

' Before you draw such harsh conclusions,
' Miss Evans,' said the offended countess, ' you
' should describe what parts of my conduct will,
' in your opinion, expose me to the indignity of a
' licentious address. I must also add, that as your
' judgment of Mr. Fitzosborne seems to be too
' decided to be the mere result of suspicion, I
' have a right to bid you *prove*, that he feels for
' me a bolder sentiment than pity or esteem. If
' he is what you describe, instead of being the
' ornament of society, he is its disgrace.'

' Do recollect,' replied Lucy, ' that I give
' him credit for the deepest contrivance, the most
                                      ' profound

' profound artifice.. I am not in his confidence.
' The only pofitive proofs which I can bring
' againft him are, your prefent wretchednefs, his
' influence both over lord Monteith and yourfelf,
' and his avowed infidelity.'

' You and Mr. Powerfcourt have ever given
' that harfh name to a fingularity of opinion
' which your candid father only *fufpected* of lean-
' ing to deifm. All doubt with you appears to
' be a crime, and a diffent from your notions on
' fome important but myfterious point fubjects
' your ill-fated opponent to the moft confirmed
' imputation of the blackeft guilt, even though
' his whole previous conduct evinces a courfe of
' almoft unfinning rectitude and exemplary vir-
' tue.

' O my Geraldine ! I will urge you but this
' once more. Is is from himfelf that you hear of
' this unfinning rectitude and fhining virtue ?
' His character is comparatively unknown in his
' country. Abroad it was efteemed to be far
' from immaculate. His conftant affociates were
' men of loofe principles and profligate man-
' ners.'

' It is from Henry Powerfcourt that you learned
' this catalogue of vices ?" inquired Geraldine
with a refentful air.

' It is,' returned Lucy. ' It is from that
' Henry Powerfcourt whom we both fo tenderly
' efteem ; the dear companion of our early happy
' years, thofe years of confidence, tranquillity,
' and mutual affection. O lady Monteith ! how
' exquifitely painful is that reflection now. Hear
' me yet on my bended knees ; hear my folemn
' requeft. Mine is no difplay of officious zeal,
' no falfe colouring of a hollow heart. If I have
' erred, it is from a miftaken judgment ; and
' punifh

' punifh me as that crime deferves. Yet, my
' ever beloved friend! do not let your confidence
' in your own difcernment lead you into danger.
' It is not becaufe I fufpect your virtue that I
' thus impreffively warn you; but it is becaufe I
' confider you to be furrounded with fnares which,
' without divine protection, no mortal can ef-
' cape; and to that protection I commend you in
' my moft earneft prayers."

Vanquifhed by this affectionate appeal, Geraldine raifed her Lucy, and folded her in her
arms. The reconciliation was as fincere as it
was affecting. The countefs protefted, that
though fhe could not adopt her opinions of a man
whom fhe had ftudied with unremitting attention,
fhe yet gave entire credit to the fincerity of her
motives; and Mifs Evans hoped, that the communication, which had fomewhat relieved her
burdened mind, would not be entirely forgotten
in the hours of calm reflection. They then parted, after mutually engaging to name this affecting fubject no more.

Mifs Evans's thoughts were diverted the next
morning to a fubject yet more poignantly diftreffing, and which, as the mafter-forrow, fwal-
lowed up every other care. A letter from her
father's houfe-keeper announced, that he was
alarmingly ill, and requefted her immediate prefence at Powerfcourt. This letter flung her into
fuch violent emotions, that fhe had not felf-com-
mand fufficient to reflect upon fome very extraordinary circumftances which accompanied it.
The ftyle and the writing were greatly fuperior
to Mrs. Mary's ufual performances. This was,
indeed, accounted for in the poftfcript, which
ftated, that being afhamed of her *poor fcrawl*, fhe
had got the clerk to copy it, and to rectify the
spelling.

spelling. The excuse was more conspicuous than
the writing; for Mrs. Mary and the clerk were
not upon good terms, and it seemed extraordinary,
that a faithful confidential servant should think of
such minute explanations when a beloved master
lay in the utmost danger, and requiring all her
active services. Where too was Henry? Was
it not natural for him to write to his Lucy? and
how improbable, that he should permit another
pen to transcribe his message that he wished her
to return instantly! The alarm which the letter
excited prevented the consideration of these con-
tradictory particulars. Miss Evans was in the
chaise on her return to Caernarvonshire in half
an hour after it arrived; nor was it till her anxiety for her father was relieved by finding that the
whole narrative was an infamous imposition, that
she began to be surprised at her own want of penetration in not *immediately* discovering it to be
so. A statement of this fact, which seemed to
convey some fresh indications of Fitzosborne's
guilt, was immediately dispatched to Monteith,
and Henry Powerscourt undertook to be the
courier. His generous heart braved every indignity and every danger; nor could even his Lucy's
apprehensive terrors dissuade him from defying
the resentment of a man whom she believed to
be capable of adding murder to his other crimes.
The preservation of his once-fondly loved, and
still-tenderly esteemed Geraldine, overpowered
all regard for his own personal safety. But his
generous intentions were frustrated by the events
which had happened at Monteith previous to his
arrival.

CHAP.

CHAP. XIII.

O much deceiv'd, much failing, haplefs Eve !
Of thy prefum'd return ! event perverfe !
Thou never from that hour in paradife
Found'ft either fweet repaft or found repofe ;
Such ambufh, laid among fweet flowers and fhades,
Waited with hellifh rancour imminent :
To intercept thy way, or fend thee back :
Defpoil'd of innocence, of faith, of blifs !

MILTON.

THE diftrefs of Mifs Evans for her father's
fuppofed illnefs had given a temporary diverfion
to lady Monteith's ideas ; but they foon recurred
to the contemplation of her own forrows. The
affecting fcene of the preceding evening, by reviving all her former tendernefs, gave that importance to her friend's judgment of which it had
been for fome time deprived ; and while fhe recollected the impreffive earneftnefs and indifputable
fincerity with which it was delivered, fhe deemed
it at leaft entitled to attention ; and fhe determined to fcrutinize the principles on which fhe
had founded her opinion of Fitzofborre.

She firft reverted to the high eftimation in
which his character was held by the world. Every one fpoke of him as a moft extraordinary man ;
and his inviolable integrity was confirmed by
his behaviour on the difcovery of lady Arabella's
attachment to him. Nay, ftrange as it might
feem, fhe often thought that he ftill cherifhed her
idea in his heart. She knew that he had preferved
her

her picture, and he had juſt rejected the propoſal of an advantageous alliance with the rich
heireſs of an Iſlandic chieftain.   This conſtancy,
though from the diſcordance of their character
ſcarcely attributable to the caprices of love, proved
the ſolidity of his virtue, and ſecured herſelf from
even a poſſibility of being the object of his licentious paſſion.   His ſpeculative notions on ſome
points were indeed reprehenſible; but then they
were merely ſpeculations; and ſhe ſtill thought
Mr. Evans's notions, which tended to confine
opinion, were deficient in liberality, and founded
on a tyrannical deſire of ſubjugating the free independent mind.   All her own obſervations
tended to convince her, that Henry and Lucy
exaggerated his errors.   No direct charge was
brought againſt *him*, even ſuppoſing his companions to have been as profligate as they were deſcribed.   A twelvemonth's intimacy was ſome
ground whereon to judge of characters; and ſhe
could not help affirming, that the innocence of
his conduct was a proof of the inoffenſiveneſs of
his principles.

The change in lord Monteith could not, even
by Lucy's own confeſſion, be *clearly* traced to his
influence.   The ſuſpicion that he was acceſſary
to his lordſhip's faults only aroſe from the probability of his having ſome ſecret ſeducer, and the
influence which Fitzoſborne ſeemed to have over
him.   For her own part ſhe was doubtful of the
exiſtence of a ſeducer, and could not perceive any
certain proof of that ſuppoſed influence.

His marked attentions to herſelf formed the
next accuſation.   But Lucy knew nothing of
the manners of the great world, or the free-
doms which cuſtom had rendered general.   The
univerſal homage, which even *appropriated* beauty

ty required, and the familiar intercourse to which the cenforious did not affix the leaft fhadow of impropriety, would fhock her friend's notions, formed in the depth of retirement, and rather founded on the idea of what was prudent, than on the confideration of what is practicable.

Her thoughts then fell into a train of reflection upon the incidents of her early years, the peaceful fhades of Powerfcourt, the joyous hours of playful gaiety, the endearing recollection of tender confidence, and interefting fimplicity, all rendered ftill more exquifite by the vivid glow of youthful hope, which fpread a more fafcinating fplendour round the prefent fcene, by the promife of more brilliant future enjoyments. Fallacious promife! falfified prediction! " Is there," faid fhe, cafting her eyes from the proud heights of Monteith caftle on the fubject vale; " is there in ' all this wide domain a wretch more miferable ' than me?"

She ftarted at that recollection. ' Yes, there ' are. *There* exifts pining penury; *there* defti- ' tute ficknefs fuffers, and wafting infancy de- ' clines; not only deprived of the affiftance ' which former experience prompted them to ex- ' pect from their lord, but even refufed what juf- ' tice determines to be their own. O Fitzofborne! ' how ftrongly do fuch fituations demonftrate the ' truth of your opinion, that the prefent order of ' things requires the bold hand of fome intelli- ' gent reformer!"

Leaving lady Monteith's conclufion to dif-prove itfelf, I proceed with my narrative. She walked to the cabinet which ftood in her dreffing-room, and, opening the cafket which contained her mother's jewels, fhe determined to divert them from the fervice of oftentation and vanity to

the

the nobler purpofes of benevolence and integrity.
She looked over, without a figh, the various ar-
ticles of ornament; but her mother's picture, fet
round with diamonds, excited a ftrong repug-
nance. It had been prefented to one of her fifters, and reftored to the Powerfcourt family, on
the death of its owner. Lady Monteith attentively contemplated the features. 'Thou art at
'reft,' faid fhe; 'would I were fo too. Thou
'didft endure fevere bodily fuffering; mine are
'the fharper tortures of the mind. The neglect
'of an eftranged hufband never rived thy heart!'

She then began a letter to a friend at Edinburgh, whom fhe wifhed to employ as an agent
in this bufinefs. The difficulty of affigning a
motive for this action, and the fufpicious fecrefy
that fhe was forced to require, made her incapable of executing it to her fatisfaction, though
fhe made repeated attempts. 'It will certainly
'be difcovered,' faid fhe. 'If it fhould come to
'my father's knowledge, it might difpleafe, it
'muft diftrefs him. To whom but him fhould
'I apply for affiftance? Ah! hard neceffity! that
'I alone cannot folicit the bounty of his ever
'liberal hand!"

Tear after tear flowed down her cheek, when
the found of Fitzofborne's foot upon the ftairs
roufed her from the ftupor of grief. 'He fhall
'not fee me in this diforder. Lucy fhall not re-
'proach me with having a *male* confidant.' She
haftily fnatched up her papers, and retired to her
own chamber. Her expedition was too much
the effect of agitation to admit of exactnefs, and
fhe left behind her a part of a letter which, with
her jewels lying upon the table, were fufficient to
inform Fitzofborne of the nature of her recent occupation. He immediately inclofed bank-notes for
four

four hundred pounds, which feemed to be the required fum, and addreffed to lady Monteith a few refpectful lines, in which he entreated her to permit him to enjoy a luxury feldom annexed to humble fortunes, by appropriating what was to him an incumbrance to thofe noble offices, to which he durft affirm fhe had deftined the value of her jewels. He then fealed the note and retired.

Lady Monteith only waited to hear him quit the room to leave her retreat. She read the paper, which was addreffed to her, and though fhe fteadily determined to reject the inclofed prefent, fhe felt enraptured at the generofity which proffered the gift, and at the delicacy which fo infinuatingly fued for its acceptance. The reader will not partake in her feelings, when informed, that juftice would have *ordered* the reftitution of this property to the Monteith family, it being only a *part* of a larger fum which had been tranfmitted to Fitzofborne by a right honourable *rook* of his acquaintance, as a douceur for the favour of being permitted to have the principal plucking of the fineft *pigeon* that had been for many years brought to market.

Ignorant of the nature of the ' accurfed fpoil,' the countefs remained fteady in her refolution of returning it. In vain did Edward attempt to relift her determination. ' My pecuniary difficul-
' ties,' faid fhe, ' are not fo diftreffing as to per-
' mit me to fequefter the flender portion of a
' younger brother.'

' Recollect,' replied Fitzofborne, ' that the
' influence of lord Monteith has permitted me to
' extend my hopes beyond the narrow fphere of
' a younger brother's enjoyments, and do not
' check the impulfe of gratitude.'

' Then

' Then to lord Monteith be the recompenſe
' made.'

' And why not to his charming wife? I ſhould
' admire this lovely pride. did I not ſuſpect that
' it was united to a degree of ſuſpicion, unworthy
' of your purity and my own honour. Can I no
' way convince you of my ſincere diſintereſted
' friendſhip? Can I make no offers which will
' not be diſdainfully refuſed?'

' Yes, certainly you may,' replied the counteſs; ' and I will depute you, inſtead of my
' Edinburgh friend, to diſpoſe of theſe jewels.
' Faſhion varies ſo much, and people in the
' country dreſs ſo plain, that I ſcarcely ever want
' ſuch ornaments. Beſide, lord Monteith was
' remarkably liberal on my marriage. They re-
' ally are not of the ſmalleſt uſe to me.'

' I willingly undertake the commiſſion,' returned Fitzoſborne; ' but it may be ſome time be-
' fore I can find a purchaſer; and why ſhould this
' money lie uſeleſs in my ſecretary? Are the objects
' of your bounty (for I know it is not extrava-
' gance, but generoſity, which limits your re-
' ſources) to languiſh to an uncertain period?
' Why may I not advance it by way of loan?
' Indeed, lady Monteith! you are too ſcrupu-
' lous.'

' I believe,' ſaid ſhe recollecting herſelf, ' I
' am. I will accept your offer. The jewels
' will, I am confident, diſcharge the debt; and
' pray never expect me to redeem them.'

This buſineſs being adjuſted, a momentary
pauſe enſued. ' We exceedingly regret,'' ob-
' ſerved Fitzoſborne, the loſs of our cheerful
' companion Miſs Evans. I hope ſhe will find
' her father better.' The counteſs ſincerely
joined in that wiſh.

' She

' She was the life of our party,' continued Edward. ' My lord is quite miferable at her go-
' ing. He declares that he never met with a
' woman whofe manner fo much entertained
' him; all vivacity and fpirit; and certainly fhe
' was affiduoufly attentive and obliging to his
' lordfhip.

' She is generally obliging to every one,' replied the countefs. ' But I think you fometimes
' experienced rather a fevere bon mot.'

' O, I don't doubt that my impertinence de-
' ferved it; and it was of no confequence to
' me, fo fhe kept lord Monteith in good hu-
' mour.'

Fitzofborne's remarks were never without
meaning; and the moft candid tempers, when
roufed to fufpicion, are ever the moft watchful.
' Does he', thought the perplexed Geraldine,
' mean to infinuate that fhe was improperly at-
' tentive to my lord? She is deftitute of vanity,
' and infinitely fuperior to every finifter defign.
' If fhe was more pointed in her civilities, it
' muft have been from her conviction that I
' failed in paying him due obfervance; and fhe
' ftrove to fupply my deficiency. Alas! even
' my bofom-friend condemns me. Even my
' Lucy will not allow how difficult it is for an in-
' jured heart to be at once affectionate and fin-
' cere, to difguife the bitter feeling which un-
' kindnefs calls forth, under a forced fmile that
' has loft the power of pleafing.'

This inference was exactly what Edward
wifhed her to draw. He had for fome time attempted to revive the flame of jealoufy in lady
Monteith's bofom; but it was not in the chafte
fimplicity of Mifs Evans's manner that he hoped
to find materials to feed the fire. It was fufficient
for

for him, that Geraldine ſhould think her friend
cenforious and partial; another objeċt had long
fince been fixed upon to effeċt the confummati-
on of Fitzofborne's treacherous devices.

Among lord Monteith's tenants was a young
woman, the daughter of a farmer, highly gra-
ced by the charms of natural beauty, and not
leſs diſtinguiſhed by a levity of manner, and a
faſhionable arrangement of dreſs, extremely diffimilar to the plain attire and fober demeanour
of the neighbours in her rank of life. Theſe
circumſtances, though perhaps only the reſult of
folly and inconfideration, or at the worſt unfufpicious vanity, the uncommon beauty of the girl
forced into attention; and even at the caſtle,
when better fubjeċts were exhauſted, the perfon,
the finery, and the flirtations of Pattie Thompfon formed an occafional theme for converfation.
Geraldine had been frequently diverted by her
awkward, yet not difgufting imitation of her
own dreſs and manners; and on Fitzofborne's
firſt arrival at Monteith, ſhe pointed her out as
a figure very likely to attraċt general attention
if feen in Grofvenor-fquare or Hyde-park. Edward gazed a few moments, gave an exclamation
of furprize, and then whifpered her, that ſhe
was the exaċt likenefs of Mrs. Harley.

From that moment the countefs turned her
eyes from the blooming Pattie with an involuntary ſhudder of horror; and when ſhe invited
the rural laſſes to a dance in the caſtle in honour
of one of her daughter's birth-days, ſhe was
fecretly pleafed that Farmer Thompfon's daughter could not be of the party. Even her vifits
at the old man's houfe were lefs frequent than
thofe which ſhe made to her other neighbours.
She felt herfelf wrong, and ſhe determined to
make

make a painful effort to be right. She set out accordingly, and had nearly reached the dwelling, when she saw lord Monteith walking hastily towards it by another road. The discovery was of itself sufficiently agitating, but Fitzosborne, as usual, pointed the dart more directly to her peace of mind by the sudden exclamation of ‘ Good Heaven !’ He left her instantly, flew to the earl, and, seizing him by the arm, with a degree of violent gesticulation, walked back with him to the castle.

The visit of the countess was short, and her manner was ungracious. She returned home, and, pleading that the walk had overcome her, she continued confined to her chamber the remainder of the day. However poignant her feelings, she never disclosed them even to her Lucy, who was then at Monteith. But she had continued to brood over this really accidental circumstance in secret till the time of which I am now treating. If it should here be objected to my narrative, that chance had too considerable a share in the success of Fitzosborne to give probability to the similar designs of another villain, let inexperience and self-confidence remember, that a determined seducer, admitted to an equal degree of intimacy, will always find in the domestic events of every family equal opportunities of expediting his views. The most subtile genius cannot preconcert every operation. It is in the directing skill by which incidental circumstances are made to conduce to one great design, that the power of superior ability is most eminently visible.

Fitzosborne, now conceiving the mine to be fully delved, determined on the immediate explosion. He was conscious that a discovery was impending;

impending; and when he confidered the magnitude and the intricacy of his plots, he felt aftonifhed at his own good fortune in having fo long efcaped detection. To trifle with danger was now folly.

My readers have doubtlefs afcribed to him the letter which hurried Mifs Evans to Caernarvonfhire, as they will eafily conceive that her prefence was an infuperable obftacle to the completion of his iniquity. I muft now inform them, that by repeated bribes he had feduced the fidelity of lord Monteith's butler, and the groom who generally accompanied him on horfeback. They regularly gave him information of every event that happened in the family. His appearance in the library, and the opening of the banqueting-room door on the night lady Monteith went down ftairs to fpeak to the fteward, were not accidental. The watchfulnefs of Mifs Evans checked the audacious hopes which he had that evening dared to form from the extreme diftrefs which refentment had enkindled in lady Monteith's mind againft the degrading conduct of her lord. But Mifs Evans was now far diftant; the faithful confcientious fteward had fet out for Edinburgh to tranfact fome money affairs; and lord Monteith was wholly engroffed by the fhooting feafon, which had juft commenced.

The third morning after Mifs Evans's departure, my lord was abfent at breakfaft; but that was not uncommon. Fitzofborne read fome of Wieland's works to the countefs, commented on the beautiful defcriptions, and then propofed a walk. They went through the plantations to the lake. On the road fhe enlarged, with affecting fimplicity, on the pleafure which fhe
once

once enjoyed in adding a finifhing grace to the richnefs of that ftriking fcenery; and a tear ftole down her cheek, as fhe pointed out parts which her lord had *ufed* to commend. Fitzofborne's replies were calculated to confirm her apprehenfion that fhe muft now turn her mind to different objects; for that the pleafures of connubial efteem and confidence were loft for ever. On their way home they paffed near Farmer Thompfon's. Fitzofborne propofed calling, but the countefs, pleading wearinefs, declined going out of her way, and refted upon a ftile, while Edward went, as he faid, to pleafe himfelf with the fight of a pretty girl. He returned thoughtful and difconcerted, and obferved gravely that fhe was not at home.

Dinner was ferved foon after their return, but no one could find lord Monteith. ' This is ve-
' ry extraordinary,' faid the countefs. ' He
' ufed to be remarkably punctual. Who went
' with him ?'

' My lord took no fervant,' was the butler's reply.

Geraldine felt alarmed: ' Sure no accident
' has happened. Call my lord's groom.' He was queftioned refpecting the fafety of his horfe, and the countefs was now informed that he was not gone out upon any of his own horfes.

' Search the woods immediately. Some
' dreadful event muft have detained him. He
' never would go far from home on foot, and
' unattended. Had he a gun with him ?' The groom now owned in fome confufion, that his mafter had fet off early that morning in a hired chaife and four.

' Do none of you know which road he took ?' The fervants were divided in their opinions.
The

The greater part faid, he went towards the moors, but the butler and the groom declared that they faw the chaife turn round by the lodges in the park, as if it was going to Farmer Thompfon's, and then, after having ftopped for a moment, proceeded towards Edinburgh.

Geraldine now trembled with undefined diftrefs. ' Did you,' faid fhe to Fitzofborne, ' know nothing of this journey?'

He ordered the fervants to retire, and then faid, ' He confides none of *thefe* fecrets to me. , I only know that his affairs are defperate; but ' before I mention my further fufpicions, allow ' me to afcertain their validity. I will juft run ' to Farmer Thompfon's. For heaven's fake! ' be compofed. I will foon be back. Shall I ' fend your children to you?''

' No! no! fly! fly!' was all fhe could articulate.

He foon returned, and the tale he told corroborated in every particular the butler's account. Pattie Thompfon was feen in a chaife with a gentleman, wrapped in a riding-coat, at fix o'clock that morning. The countefs fainted.

The tiger who fports with the victim that he holds in his fangs, is not fufpected to feel compaffion; nor did the tender epithets which Fitzofborne addreffed to the object of his more favage cruelty indicate a relenting heart. He wifhed, indeed, to recal her fenfes; but it was only that fhe might feel the torments of guilt added to thofe of mifery.

No fooner did he perceive returning life faintly flufh upon her cheek, and her fcarcely-opened eyes fixed upon him with a look at once expreffive of confidence and defpair, than he de-

VOL. II.   H   termined

termined to confirm that defpair, and to abufe
that confidence.

'Where fhall I go? What fhall I do?' inquired the diftreffed Geraldine.

'I know not what to advife. You cannot
'ftay at Monteith. The creditors will certainly
'hear of the earl's departure.——'

'Cannot ftay!—why?'

'An execution will be immediately ferved.'

'O my helplefs, houfelcfs babes!—where
'fhall I fhelter *them*?"

'Surely your propereft afylum will be with
'your father.'

'True. O! let me fly to Powerfcourt.'

'Yet confider his years and infirmities. Will
'there not be fome danger in pouring upon
'him, while unprepared, the whole weight of
'your calamities; of afflicting him with your
'diftrefs before you have learnt fortitude to
'endure it. Cannot you be for a little time at
'the Evans's?

'My Lucy is already finking with her own
'forrow. Ought I to increafe it?'

'Permit me then, ever loved and refpected
'lady Monteith, to propofe another afylum. I
'have a fifter, a woman of the moft unblemifh-
'ed character, who will efteem it an honour to
'protect you. Allow me to conduct you and
'your children to her. She lives in Lanca-
'fhire.'

'No! Fitzofborne. I muft not take refuge
'with *your* friends.'

'I can name no other fanctuary, unlefs it be
'lady Arabella Macdonald's houfe. And furely
'calumny itfelf muft approve of your taking
'refuge there.'

'I can-

'‘ I cannot apply for protection to lady Ara-
‘ bella. She will be fevere, and make me feel
‘ the pang of dependance.'

‘ You are then unacquainted with the influ-
‘ ence which I have happily regained over her
‘ fentiments. But I recollect, that, engroffed
‘ by your forrows I have omitted to announce
‘ my own brightening profpects.'

He then drew from his pocket a letter which
ftrongly refembled the writing, and ftill more
the ftyle, of lady Arabella. It was addreffed to
the Honourable Edward Fitzofborne.

  ‘ SIR,

 ‘ I really do feel fo exceffively difconcerted,
‘ that I hardly know in what ftyle to begin. For
‘ one hates to own onefelf wrong, and yet I
‘ think I ought to tell you that I have been un-
‘ der fome little miftake : and not chufing to
‘ be upon bad terms with a gentleman fo vaftly
‘ well fpoken of, and received, every where, I
‘ juft add, that I fhall be very glad to fee you at
‘ my parties when you come to London. I
‘ hope this conceffion will fatisfy lord Mon-
‘ teith, to whom and his fweet Geraldine I beg
‘ my tender regards, and remain, fir, with fin-
‘ cere efteem,

  ‘ Your very obedient fervant,

   ‘ ARABELLA MACDONALD.'

 ‘ Shall I then throw myfelf at her feet ? and
‘ afk her to protect me and my children ; to
‘ fave us from want ; to foften the pangs of
‘ perfidy at leaft, till I can gently prepare my
‘ father ?' inquired the afflicted Geraldine.

   H 2   ‘ I would

' I would advife, that you fhould not only do
' fo, but that you fhould fet off immediately. A
' thought has juft ftruck me. You may over-
' take lord Monteith. He has certainly taken
' the road to London.'

' What? with that unfortunate girl.? O,
' Fitzofborne! a wife is bound by indiffoluble
' ties, and muft fuffer with him; but how could
' he be fo cruel, fo felfifh, to involve a ftranger
' in his calamities? She was innocent, happy,
' bleffed with humble competence.'

' Your candour has mifled you. I have cer-
' tain proof that a criminal connection has fub-
' fifted fome time between them. She proba-
' bly propofes to accompany lord Monteith
' abroad.'

' Abroad! Is he going abroad? What! ab-
' folutely defert me and my little ones without
' one preparatory word? Leave me too in all
' thefe complicated circumftances of grief and
' diftrefs? Oh! hold my brain, or let me
' lofe reflection in inftant madnefs. Unparal-
' lelled! unpardonable cruelty!'

' It is indeed unpardonable. Monteith, the
' execrable Monteith, is unworthy of you.'

' May the anguifh which I fuffer, Fitzofborne,
' warn you of the danger of a precipitate choice!
' Let not your eye miflead your judgment, nor
' your fancy cheat you with the femblance of
' non-exifting virtues.'

' My heart, moft charming moralift, is for
' ever fixed where my judgment has difcovered
' the moft unqueftionable excellence. Yet do
' not droop beneath your forrow. The tyrant
' laws of cuftom will not for ever bind you to
' the mean defpicable feducer of a fimple ruftic,
the

' the depraved affociate of a hireling profti-
' tute.'

' True. But my children. O! for their fakes
' what would I not fubmit to? I would ftill en--
' dure his contempt. I would kneel, and hum-
' bly fupplicate to be the partner in all *their*
' father's fortunes.'

Fitzofborne paufed. 'No injuries, I fee, can
' compel her to a willing elopement. It is well;
' I have a refource. I know that I poffefs her
' affections; and women always pardon where
' they love.'

' If fuch be your refolution,' faid he to the
half-frantic Geraldine, " let me inftantly order
' your carriage, that you may fet off in purfuit
' of him. Every moment's delay increafes the
' difficulty of overtaking him.'

' True. I will be gone. You are my better
' angel, Fitzofborne. Order my carriage, while
' I fetch my little ones. They fhall kneel with
' me to their faithlefs father.'

' Deareft lady Monteith,' returned Fitzofborne, infernal triumph fparkling in his eyes,
' how diftrefs affects your ftrong intellects! At
' this late hour, their feafon of reft, would you
' expofe their delicate frames to the danger of a
' rapid purfuit? Confider, that all your hopes
' of overtaking lord Monteith depend upon your
' fpeed. If you are fuccefsful, your own
' charms, and your deep diftrefs, muft poffefs
' fufficient eloquence; and if you are fo unfor-
' tunate as to mifs him, will it be acting with
' proper decorum to lady Arabella to obtrude
' your family upon her without previous prepa-
' ration?'

' Am I then to leave them here, the fport of
' mercilefs creditors?'

' Reft

'Reft affured, madam, that however barbar-
' ous our laws may be, in that particular, the
' execution of them is happily conducted with
' urbanity, at leaft to people of your rank. But,
' to foften my apprehenfion on their account,
' I will take care to efcort them wherever you
' pleafe to order, when you are placed in ho-
' norable protection. Their nurfes are very
' careful of them ; they are too young to know
' forrow by anticipation ; and any tale will ac-
' count for your abfence.'

'Is the carriage ready ? where is Maria ?'

'She and my fervant are packing up a few
' neceffary changes of linen. They can follow
' us in another chaife.' .

'Us, Fitzofborne ? You do not mean to go
' with me ?'

'On that head I muft be firm. Humanity
' will not fuffer me to let you undertake fuch a
' journey by yourfelf in circumftances of fuch
' peculiar diftrefs. Befide, if you fhould over-
' take Monteith upon the road, who knows but
' that his violence, aggravated by detected guilt,
' may make you want a protector.'

'What bloody fcenes are you revolving ?
' Loft, unhappy Geraldine ! Better perifh here
' than want a protector againft thy hufband.'

'He has abjured the feelings annexed to that
' title. Though I renounce the name of his
' friend, and cancel all ties of gratitude, yet for
' your fake you fhall fee me calm and difpaffio-
' nate, nay even patient of infult. But you forget
' how we wafte thefe precious moments.'

'Ah, true.' She ftept towards the door ;
and then, fuddenly ftopping, exclaimed, ' Where
' are my children ? I muft fee them once more ?'

'Would

' Would you wake them from their sleep?'
' cried Fitzofborne, who dreaded the event of
fuch an interview. ' Would you fill their inno-
' cent minds with forrow at feeing your dif-
' trefs?'

' Sleep on, my innocent, peaceful children;
' and never may ye know what your mother
' fuffers!' She then turned her eyes upon
Fitzofborne. The expreffion in his countenance
excited a momentary alarm. She withdrew
her hand from his impaffioned grafp, and fear-
fully uttered: ' Something ftill. whifpers me,
' that I ought not to go: at leaft, not with you.'

' Whence this cruel diftruft of your adopted
' brother, the contracted hufband of your Ara-
' bella?' returned the re-collected diffembler.
' Dear lady Monteith! Will thefe ftarts of too
' fufceptible delicacy never ceafe, even if you
' fhould fee that engagement fulfilled?'

' Then remember,' replied fhe, in an impreffive voice, ' that my diftraction enfeebles my
' judgment. My brain feems on fire. If the
' ftep you advife fhould widen the breach be-
' tween me and my lord, on you be all the
' blame.'

' May it reft upon me for ever!' He uttered
this terrible imprecation as he led his victim to
the chariot. He ftopped a moment, under pretence of giving his valet inftructions for their
route, while Geraldine, clafping her trembling
hands exclaimed, ' Adieu, Monteith! perhaps
eternally adieu!' The fervants crowded into the
corridor with looks of confternation and diftrefs. Fitzofborne called aloud, that the other
carriage fhould follow as foon as poffible, and
join them at the next poft-town. Then throwing himfelf into the chariot, the horfes fet off
full fpeed on the Edinburgh road.

CHAP.

CHAP. XIV.

Axylus, hofpitable, rich, and good,
In fair Arifba's walls (his native place)
He held his feat ; the friend of human race.
Faſt by the road, his ever-open door
Oblig'd the wealthy, and reliev'd the poor.
Breathlefs the good man fell.

POPE'S HOMER.

MARIA ſtood in the great hall ready to attend
her lady, her eyes ſwelled with tears, and her
heart throbbing with ſorrow at the idea of her
beloved miſtreſs's diſtreſs, when ſhe was joined
by the old houſekeeper.

'Pray, Mrs. Maria,' ſaid the good woman,
'can you tell me what is the matter with her
'ladyſhip ? It is ſo odd to ſet out for London
'at eight o'clock at night, and ſo late in Sep-
'tember too. Thank God! there is a very
'good moon to be ſure, and the roads are very
'ſafe, and I wiſh you all well there with all my
'heart. But poor ſoul muſt be faint, for ſhe
'has not ate one mouthful of dinner, though I
'ſent up two courſes as nicely diſhed as ever I
'did in my life. She has had nothing within
'her lips, the footmen ſay, but one glaſs of
'ſome ſort of cordial which Mr. Fitzoſborne
'mixed up and gave her.'

'My maſter did not touch one morſel neither,'
obſerved Fitzoſborne's ſervant, who now joined
them.

'Your

‘ Your mafter, Mr. Pomade, does not do
‘ many things which other people think they
‘ ought to do. He never goes to church, nor
‘ fays his prayers; and yet he pretends to be
‘ very good. So, if he can be good without
‘ going to church, or faying his prayers, he
‘ may live without eating for what I know.’

‘ You are rather fevere, Mrs. Annifeed.
‘ My mafter, madam, I muft inform you, is
‘ one of the moft generous, free, good-tem-
‘ pered gentlemen in the world.’

‘ Very likely; I only know that my lord
‘ and lady were as happy as kings and queens
‘ before he came.’

‘ I wifh,’ faid the weeping Maria, ‘ that our
‘ chaife was ready.’

‘ Go, Sandy,’ faid Pomade to one of the
grooms, ‘ do juft have the goodnefs for once
‘ to be expeditious; and if you will do me the
‘ honour of a call in town, a bottle of burgun-
‘ dy is at your fervice: but, à-propos, my dear
‘ Mifs Maria, fuppofe I have the happinefs of
‘ juft drinking one glafs of wine with you be-
‘ fore we fet out on our immenfe long expedi-
‘ tion.’

The houfekeeper now beckoned Maria into
the fpice-room. ‘ Do as you pleafe, child,’
‘ faid the fagacious matron; ‘ but if I was you,
‘ I would not go to London with that random
‘ fop. You and I will get into the chaife, and
‘ fay nothing to him, but go by ourfelves after
‘ our dear miftrefs.’

‘ But he has received directions what inns
‘ we are to ftop at on the road.’

‘ Never mind. With God’s blefling, we
‘ fhall find her as well without him as with him,
‘ I dare fay. Ah Maria! Maria! there is no

H 3. ‘ good

' good abroad, I fear. Heaven preferve her
' ladyſhip is all I ſay.'

One of the ſtable-boys now entered to ſay,
that, as my lord's groom was putting the horſes
into the travelling poſtchaiſe, one of them had
turned reſtive, and had kicked the ſhafts all to
pieces.

' Then harneſs out my lord's,' exclaimed
Maria.'

' That's impoſſible; for the coachman is
' gone with it to Stirling to be mended.'

' Then I will have the coach.'

' What? ſend the new coach twelve miles
' in the night? No! Maſter Sandy dare not
' do that, I know Why, the coachman would
' have us both turned off directly.'

' Then pray, William, let me have the
' curricle.'

' No,' ſaid the houſekeeper; ' I won't have
' my bones broke in the curricle; but I can
' ride double very well. Have the two ſaddle
' horſes got ready directly.'

A ſhout of ridicule was now raiſed againſt
the houſekeeper by Mr. Pomade, who came
to condole with Maria upon his misfortune in
not having the pleaſure of travelling with her
that evening. ' We muſt defer our expedition,
' my dear,' ſaid he, ' till morning's early ray;
' and I proteſt, but for the loſs of your charm-
' ing company, I ſhould be glad; for I find the
' thick mountain fog very pernicious to my
' lungs, which ſuffered extremely in croſſing
' the Alps when I came out of Italy. Mr.
' Fitzoſborne has too much friendſhip for me to
' be diſpleaſed at my not expoſing myſelf to
' the night air.'

' I will.

'I will follow my lady,' said Maria, 'if I go
'on foot.'

'You will be very likely to be sure to over-
'take her, who has set out an hour before you
'in a chariot and four. No! come, as it is
'utterly impossible for us to proceed, let us
'embrace my good friend the butler's proposal,
'and have a little festival. He has promised
'us plenty of excellent champagne; and I re-
'quest Miss Maria's hand for the ball. Nay!
'my dear creature, why do you cry so? Lady
'Monteith will be vastly well taken care of, I
'dare say. 'Pon my soul! I shall begin to be
'scandalous, if you take on so, and say, that
'though her ladyship looks like an angel, she
'is a devil of a termagant.'

'I don't know what your master looks like;
'but I could tell you what he is, if I chose it,'
'said the house-keeper: 'but it is not my
'way to be uncivil to any body.' Her moderation, however, continued no longer than till
she heard that the riding-horses were all loose
in the Park, and that the groom had fatigued
himself to no purpose in endeavouring to catch
them. She now poured upon Fitzosborne a
thousand execrations; and, without paying the
least attention to the excuses, which strove to
persuade her that these misfortunes were merely
the effect of chance, her passion and Maria's
tears became so troublesome, that the butler,
to pacify them, promised to walk to the next
post-town, and to order a hired chaise immediately.

He did walk, but it was only to the watch-
tower, where he, Mr. Pomade, and the perfidious groom, spent a riotous evening, exulting
in the triumph of wickedness, and anticipating
their

their promifed reward, while the reft of the family exhibited a fcene of diftraction.

The morning rofe, but not to bring confolation. The obftacles to Maria's following her lady multiplied every hour. Indeed, that faithful girl was now incapable of taking the journey. She had been in ftrong hyfterics moft part of the night; and the venerable houfekeeper, though fhe alternately blamed, pitied, and commended her affectionate fellow-fervant, had now fo exhaufted her own feeble ftrength, that fhe was unequal to any further exertion.

About two o'clock a carriage drove into the caftle-yard, and was welcomed by the univerfal fhout of, ' Thank God ! it is either my lord or ' my lady.' It was neither. Henry Powerfcourt arrived, but unhappily one day too late to fave the honour, and ultimately the life of Geraldine.

' Where is lady Monteith ?' was his firft inquiry. ' Gone.'—' Whither ?' No one knew.—' With whom ?"—Mr. Fitzofborne.'

Henry reeled againft the portal, clapped his hand to his forehead, and was fpeechlefs.

The fervants crowded round him. A burft of tears relieved his manly forrow. He then inquired, ' Where is my lord ?'—' Gone too.' —' What, in purfuit of the countefs ?'—No ! they believed her ladyfhip was gone after him.

' This is villany of a deeper caft,' refumed Henry. ' She is the victim of fraud, not of ' perfuafion.'

The houfekeeper was by this time got into the hall, eager to afk his opinion, or to receive his inftructions. And the pale trembling Maria, hearing that Mr. Powerfcourt knew
what

what was become of her lady, had dragged her
feeble frame to hear the defired tidings.

‘ Heaven blefs you! my good fir,’ faid the
houfekeeper. ‘ If you had but come a little
‘ fooner, it would not have been fo.’ Henry
now inquired the particulars, which were recounted as intelligibly as twenty different voices
could detail them. In one point they all agreed,
that their lady feemed in the greateft diftrefs.

‘ Ah, betrayed innocent !” exclaimed Henry.
‘ And is my lord’s journey a fecret too ?’

‘ A moft profound one, fir,’ faid the butler.

‘ He went, you fay, in a hired chaife and
‘ four, at fix o’clock yefterday morning, the
‘ road toward the Moors ?’

‘ I do, fir.’ replied the groom.

‘ Nay now, Sandy,’ faid one of the footmen,
‘ that is little better than a lie ; I faid fo, and
‘ you told my lady, when fhe feemed fo fright-
‘ ened about him, that you faw the chaife turn
‘ by the lodges in the park, and then ftop, and
‘ go back again toward Edinburgh.’

‘ Did not you think fo too, Mr. Thomas ?’
faid the groom, addreffing the butler.

‘ Why, my eyes might deceive me, but Mr.
‘ Pomade thought the fame.’

‘ Who is Mr. Pomade ?’

‘ Mr. Fitzofborne’s fervant.’

‘ Call him. He may poffibly throw fome
‘ light on this inexplicable bufinefs.’

‘ He went off to London at four o’clock this
‘ morning,’ anfwered the groom.

“ How ?”—‘ On horfeback.’

‘ Another lie,’ exclaimed the houfekeeper.
‘ O, there are fome wicked doings, and it will
‘ all come out. The very ftones in the ftreet
‘ will fpeak when there has been a murder.

‘ His

' His mafter has got no horfes, and you told
' us that you could not catch any of my lord's,
' if we would give you a thoufand pounds.'

' Do I,' faid Powerfcourt, ' fee around me
' fo many ftout healthy men, fed by lord Mon-
' teith's bounty; and would none of them walk
' to —— to order a chaife, that this young
' woman might have accompanied her mif-
' trefs ?'

A general murmur announced that they
would all have willingly walked to Johnny
Groat's houfe to ferve their lord or their lady,
but the butler had undertaken that office.

' And why did he not perform it then ?' faid
Powerfcourt. ' I ftopped at that town my-
' felf two hours ago, and I am confident, not
' only that there are chaifes to be procured,
' but alfo that no meffenger from Monteith had
' been to order one.'

The butler attempted an excufe; but the
groom, falling upon his knees, faid, he would
confefs all. Mr. Fitzofborne had long defigned
to run away with his lady when he had an opportunity. His lordfhip received a note on the
evening before her departure, after his lady
was gone to bed, giving him an invitation to
go to fhoot fome moor-game on the neighbour-
ing mountains with fome gentlemen of his
acquaintance; and, propofing to fet off foon in
the morning, he left a note for his lady, telling
her where he was gone. He confeffed too,
that he had told Mr. Fitzofborne this, and alfo
that he was gone in a hired chaife on account
of the bad roads, and without any attendants,
for gentlemen did not like to have any more
with them on the mountains than were abfolutely neceffary. That Fitzofborne then took
the

the note from him, and bade him fay, if he was
queftioned, that he went round by Farmer
Thompfon's, and then turned toward Edinburgh.

Influenced by a fudden ftart of indignation.
Henry ordered both the groom and the butler
into cuftody, without confidering that the
blackeft crimes will fometimes evade the punifhment of *human* laws. He now paufed a moment to confider how he fhould act, when the
head nurfe thus interrupted his mufings:

‘ Won't you fee the pretty little dears, fir?
‘ Alas-a-day! what is to become of them?
‘ They have been afking for their mamma all
‘ the morning. Lady Bell and lady Lucy have
‘ fat and learned the leffons fhe gave them
‘ yefterday, like two angels; and they fay that
‘ they know fhe will call them good girls, and
‘ kifs them, when fhe comes: and that dear
‘ beautiful little creature Geraldine has made
‘ up a nofegay for mam-mam. She can hardly
‘ talk, you know. Dear fweet fouls! to have
‘ their mother taken from them. So young
‘ too! Do, good fir, juft go and fee them.
‘ My little lord is vaftly grown, even fince you
‘ went away, and crows, and is fo merry!’

Henry fuffered himfelf to be led to the nurfery. The fcene overpowered his fortitude.
‘ O, coufin Harry!’ echoed the two elder,
‘ we are fo glad you are come again.’—‘ Do,’
continued Arabella, ‘ tell mamma we are ready
‘ with our books. Is not fhe well, that fhe
‘ has not been to fee us this morning? nurfe
‘ does cry fo, and fhe won't tell us why.’

‘ Were all thy drops of blood lives, Fitz-
‘ ofborne!’ exclaimed Henry, ‘ thy crimes de-
‘ mand the forfeiture of all. Villain! mon-
‘ ftrous

‘ ſtrous infernal villain ! to ſacrifice to ſenſual
‘ paſſion the peace, the welfare, the reputation
‘ of innocents like theſe !’

‘ My dear little ladies,’ cried the nurſe to
the terrified children, ‘ naughty Mr. Fitzoſ-
‘ borne has. took your mamma away ; but if
‘ you will be very good, and not cry, this good
‘ gentleman will fetch her back again.’

‘ Yes, indeed, I will be very good,’ ſaid the
ſobbing lady Arabella, ‘ and not cry, if I can
‘ help it. Pray, Lucy, don’t hold couſin-
‘ Harry’s coat ; conſider you will hinder him ;
‘ and when you find mamma, couſin, tell her,
‘ ſhe ſhall not ſee us cry when ſhe comes home
‘ again.’

Henry caught the children alternately in his
arms, and while his heart yearned at their miſ-
fortune, he commended their deſerted innocence to the common Parent of the orphan and.
the diſtreſſed. He at length tore himſelf from.
the affecting ſcene.

He now debated which way to ſhape his-
courſe : whether to ſet off in purſuit of the
counteſs, or to communicate the intelligence of.
her abſence to lord Monteith, and to conſult
with him what meaſures ſhould be adopted..
Every circumſtance proved that ſhe had been
rather entrapped than ſeduced. A hope ſtruck.
him, that his reſcue might come in time to ſave.
her from diſhonour, and he ſet out rapidly in:
ſearch of her.

He ſtopped at all the poſt inns on. the route.
to Edinburgh ; but his minute inquiries obtained no ſatisfaction. In that city he renewed his-
ſcrutiny; and when his failing hopes had almoſt.
deſerted him, he obtained what he thought a.
guiding clue. It proved evaſive. Still, however,

ever, convinced in his own mind, that London would be the place of Fitzofborne's deftination, as being beft fuited for the purpofes of concealment, he continued to travel towards the fouth, till he accidently faw a tenant of fir Willam Powerfcourt's at an inn door, where he was changing horfes. Anxiety for his Lucy induced him to inquire after her welfare. The honeft ruftic mournfully fhook his head. ' Ah! ' fir,' faid he, ' all is well at the parfonage ; but ' very bad news at the manor-houfe. Our ' good old mafter has heard that the lady coun' tefs his daughter ran away with a fine London ' 'fquire ; and it has thrown the gout into his ' ftomach, and they doubt he won't get over ' it. There's not a dry eye within ten miles of ' him by this time. I told all the folks I met ' as I came along, and they all began to pray ' for him, and to drink to his getting well. ' And they do fo curfe my lady countefs. For ' my part, fir, I can't curfe her ; for I don't ' think it true ; do you ? She was the prettieft, ' decenteft young lady I ever faw in my life, ' when fhe was with us ; but they do fay this ' London 'fquire was an eternal great rogue.'

Henry lifted up his eyes to heaven, as if requiring the tardy lightning to blaft Fitzofborne's complicated guilt. He now turned his courfe weftward, and arrived at Powerfcourt late the enfuing day, worn down by fatigue and anxiety. He had, however, the fatisfaction to hear, that fir William was ftill alive, and he learnt the following particulars from Mr. Evens.

The news of lady Monteith's elopement had travelled to Powerfcourt with inconceivable celerity. A dependent of the earl's, more grateful than judicious in his intentions, had

perfuaded

perfuaded himfelf, that a mighty noife was made about nothing at all; for that the lady was only gone to ftay a little with her father, as his wife would fometimes do, when he had a word or two with her. He determined therefore to ride poft to Caernarvonfhire, not doubting that he fhould bring news back of her being fafe and well. His uncouth manner, and confufed extravagant account rather amufed than alarmed the fervants, and it was accidentally communicated to fir William. Nothing refpecting his darling child was uninterefting to him. He ordered the " bonnie Scot" into his prefence; and though he gave little credence to the improbable narrative, he heard with concern, that lord Monteith's affairs were in a bad ftate, and that he and his lady were thought not to be quite fo happy as they were.

Sir William paffed a reftlefs miferable night, and the next morning appeared ferioufly ill. He rofe, however, with the determination of going himfelf into Scotland, when an exprefs arrived from lord Monteith, which proclaimed his own difgrace in terms of the moft rafh feverity; and haftened the crifis of fir William's diforder. He was immediately feized with fpafms in his ftomach, and, though fomewhat relieved by medical aid, he ftill remained fpeechlefs, and in a very alarming ftate.

' He is perfectly fenfible,' continued Mr. Evans, ' and his countenance is inconceivably ' interefting. I never faw fo much meek for-' row filently expreffed. I am confident, that ' his frame of mind is fuch as his life would ' warrant us to expect, and that he bleffes the ' Power that corrects him. I have juft been at ' prayers by his bed-fide. He preffed my hand

when

‘ when I had finifhed ; looked at the portrait
‘ of his daughter, which hung at his bed's feet,
‘ then on me ; and laftly raifed his eyes to
‘ Heaven. I underftood that he commended
‘ her to me. The ligature, as Sterne obferves,
‘ fine as it is, fhall never be broken. When
‘ the world forfakes her, I will receive and
‘ cherifh the mourner. She may be frail and
‘ criminal ; fhe cannot be wholly abandoned.”

Lucy now, having heard of Henry's return,
rufhed into the room with inquiries refpecting
her friend. She liftened with breathlefs eagernefs to the narrative which he related. ‘ ’Tis
‘ as I faid,’ exclaimed fhe, clafping her hands :
‘ I knew that her pure elevated mind could
‘ never yield confent to an adulterous elope-
‘ ment. O Henry ! do follow her to London
‘ —the traitor has certainly concealed her
‘ there ;—refcue her from him ;—fear not his
‘ oppofition—guilt like his muft be cowardly :
‘ —perhaps even yet you may fave our Geral-
‘ dine.’

‘ Let us ftudy moderation in every thing,’
replied Mr. Evans in his ufual dignified manner ; ‘ whether we grieve for the refpectable
‘ friend who feems leaving us for a happier
‘ world, or feek to affift the dear lady who ap-
‘ peared to be worthy of a better fate. Let us
‘ ever remember, that excefs offends. Do not
‘ you fee, my dear child, that Mr. Powerfcourt
‘ is exhaufted by diftrefs, and the fatigue of
‘ feven days’ inceffant travelling. We have no
‘ clue to direct us where to find the loft coun-
‘ tefs. Inftead, therefore, of wearing out his
‘ ftrength in impatient romantic wandering, let
‘ him referve it, till fome certain intelligence
‘ calls us forth to action ; and if *I* can ferve
‘ the

' the child of my benefactor, neither my age nor
' my function shall be pleaded in my excuse. In
' the mean time we will confole ourfelves with
' the conviction, that Fitzofborne cannot fecrete
' her from the fuperintendance of Omnipotence ;
' and we will confide her to the care of that Pro-
' vidence which never deferts thofe who, fenfible
' of their own weaknefs and the perils by which
' they are furrounded, fanctify the meafures
' which human prudence fuggefts by a depend-
' upon him who is able to fave.'' The weeping
Lucy acquiefced in the piety and the wifdom of
this reflection.'

Affairs continued in this ftate at Powerfcourt
till the following evening. Sir William grew
perceptibly weaker, and Henry in vain endeavoured to infpire Mifs Evans with the hopes
which he had himfelf abandoned. Every found
and every footftep feemed to her charged with tidings from her friend. About nine in the evening a note arrived, which I fhall tranfcribe.

To Miss Evans.

' Let not Mifs Evans ftart at the writing of
' her once–beloved Geraldine. The loft mifer-
' able wretch prefumes not to claim the friend-
' fhip which was the delight of her happier days.
' I only afk compaffion. Tell me, is my father
' yet alive ? If he is, exert that refiftlefs elo-
' quence which convinces every heart, and move
' him to beftow his parental blefling on his un-
' done child. And for this act of mercy, the laft
' I will ever folicit, my dying lips——but I dare
' not pray——I did not afk the protecting care
' of Heaven.—I did not liften to your counfels.
' —I was felf-willed, boaftful.—Ah ! what am I
' now ?

' now ?—I have no home, no name, no one to
" recognise or to protect me. Lord Monteith
'—but I deserve his accusations. Yet if I am
' the shameless being he calls me—I know not
' what I say.—O that eternal mercy would save
' me from the pangs of murdering my father!"

I spare all comment upon the feelings of Miss
Evans at receiving this incoherent epistle. Indeed it would be impossible to say, whether grief
or joy, rage or pity predominated. The messen-
ger stated, that the lady who sent him was at an
inn a few miles distant. The landlady told him
it was a great pity that none of her friends came
to her, for that she was quite alone, very ill,
and scarcely in her right mind.

Not an instant was lost in expediting the desired consolation. The carriage was prepared, and
the servants mounted, each contending, with all
their national impetuosity and humanity, who
should be the first to fetch back the respected
fugitive. Lucy had determined to go, but Henry persuaded her to change that resolution. ' Spend
' the time of my absence,' said he, ' with your
' your father, and consult his dispassionate judg-
' ment, whether it will be prudent to apprize fir
' William that we have heard of her. Try too,
' my love, to prepare your fortitude for the most
' excruciating trial it ever sustained. The dear
' unfortunate requires more than the tear of sym-
' pathizing sorow.'

' Restore her quickly to me,' cried Miss E-
vans. ' I will watch her night and day. She shall
' be all my employment, all my care.'

' The speed of my return will entirely depend
' upon her ability to bear the journey,' replied
Henry.

Let

Let the fufceptible reader, who has attended to the delineation of lady Monteith's character through the preceding pages, conceive the fituation of her mind at the time that her coufin joined her at the obfcure inn which afforded her a temporary afylum. Let them recollect her keen abhorrence of difgrace, her eager purfuit of fame, her acute fenfibility as a daughter, a wife, and a mother. Let them contraft the exquifite refinement of her ideas with her prefent calamities, and releafe me from the vain attempt of defcribing her mental fufferings.

She lay upon a couch; her eyes fixed and raylefs; her liftlefs arms hanging motionlefs; her face deadly pale, and half concealed by her redundant neglected hair. The attendant, who was fitting by her, announced a gentleman who wifhed to fpeak with her. Inftantly the ftupefaction in her countenance changed to extreme terror. She grafped the girl's hand, and entreated her to fave her, while her eyes rolled with frightful wildnefs. The terrified maid added, that his name was Powerfcourt; but that he fhould not come in unlefs fhe pleafed. The countefs relaxed her convulfive grafp, and funk fainting upon the couch.

Henry, who at that moment entered, contemplated, in mournful anguifh, the change fo fuddenly wrought in the lovelieft of female forms. While the remembrance of his youthful attachment gave a livelier impulfe to his fufceptibility, he rejoiced in the firm integrity which had preferved him from the infinuating enticements of an illicit paffion, and clafping his hands in an ecftafy of piety, gratitude, and regret, he exclaimed, ‘ Thank God! I have not this to anfwer.’

Geraldine

'Geraldine misinterpreted his emotion. ' I
' am a murderer then?—A parricide? He is
' dead.'

' No! he is still alive,' said Henry, in a faul-
tering tone.

' And has he,' exclaimed she with impassioned
frenzy, ' sent me any token of forgiveness?'

' I am come,' continued Henry, wetting with
his tears the feverish hand which she held towards him, ' to conduct you home.'

' Blessed, angelic, peaceful found!—My home!
' ——I never thought to have a home again.—O
' raise me up, let us go this instant.'

' Are you equal to the journey?'

' Yes. I can go home. O Heavenly found!
' —My father's house! And have I indeed yet a
' father?'

Unable to judge of her real strength during
this paroxysm of joy, Mr. Powerscourt proposed
waiting till the horses were refreshed. The uniform humanity of Geraldine shone through her
disorder. ' My heart is surely grown hard with
' my misfortunes. Are they my father's *old*
' horses that used to take me out when I was a
' girl? I talk foolishly, Henry. I did know it
' was you.—I thought you was lord Monteith
' come back again—or I thought you—I know
' not whom—I was so terrified.'

' Have you seen lord Monteith?'

' Yes. Don't blame me:—I hope for the last
' time. He used such horrid expressions. He
' would not allow me to speak to him. He will
' never let me see my children more.—Not once
' more, Henry.—I only asked for once, before I
' die. Is not this too hard even to such a wicked
' wretch as I am?'

Henry

Henry continued to bathe her hand with tears. They afforded fome relief to his full-fraught heart.

'Shall I ever,' refumed the plaintive mourner, 'fee your Lucy ?—You don't anfwer. Will 'fhe fpeak to me ? Don't let her fee me if fhe 'will not fpeak to me. Yet how fhould I re-'joice to hear her voice once more !'

'She waits your arrival at Powerfcourt, there 'to join with all your friends in the pious tafk of 'foothing your afflictions.'

I pafs over the remainder of this diftreffing con- verfation. No perfuafions could prevent lady Monteith from fetting off that night for what fhe termed her haven of reft. She bore her journey better than Mr. Powerfcourt expected; and he perceived with pleafure that the wanderings of her converfation were more the effect of weari- nefs, forrow, and indifpofition, than of deranged intellects. She feemed to ftruggle for fortitude, but her efforts failed her, when the carriage ftopped. 'The prodigal returns,' faid fhe, 'but 'where is the welcoming father ?''

Henry now inquired after fir William, and heard that he continued in the fame ftate. Mr. Powerfcourt fupported, or rather carried, Geral- dine into the breakfaft parlour; but no previous refolution could reftrain Mifs Evans's tranfport on feeing her. 'My more than fifter !—dearer 'than friend ! my love !—My Geraldine ! Open 'thofe fweet eyes—fpeak to thy faithful Lucy. '—Come, broken lily, reft upon my bofom.— 'Ever dear ! ever lovely !—Dearer than in thy 'hours of happinefs !—Give me but fign that 'thou doft hear me. Only prefs my hand if thou 'can'ft not fpeak.' The languid countefs feebly returned her friend's ardent preffure, and dropped

her

her liftlefs head on Lucy's throbbing bofom ;
while Henry, gazing on his deftined partner
with looks of affectionate admiration, gently
blamed the overflowing tendernefs which charmed
him to the foul.

Geraldine gradually revived. ' And this,'
faid fhe, ' is my father's houfe? And thou art
' Lucy?—And I hear no reproaches—no bit-
'' terly-remembered warnings.——O kind friends!
' —O ftill kinder Providence, thus to follow
' guilt with bleffings!—But when fhall I fee my
' father?'

It had been previoufly determined that this awful interview fhould be delayed till the next
morning; and Geraldine at laft reluctantly confented to try to obtain fome repofe. ' It has been,'
faid fhe, ' a ftranger to me——I know not how
' long.'

Her delirium feemed to return upon going into her apartment. ' Be fure,' faid fhe, ' you
' bar the doors and windows, and let fomebody
' fit up to guard me.'

Early the next morning, fir William altered fo
confiderably as to indicate immediate diffolution.
His daughter had juft dropped into a broken
flumber. Mr. Evans lamented the neceffity of
awakening her, but obferved, that as her father
was ftill fenfible, his forgivenefs would be a laft-
ing confolation. Prepared by the counfels of
this truly Chriftian paftor, Geraldine fupported
herfelf through the trying fcene with meeknefs,
piety and fortitude. Kneeling by his bed-fide,
fhe felt the preffure of his convulfed hand upon
her head, received from his quivering lips the
kifs of reconciliation and peace, and watched the
laft ftruggle of his parting foul, as it winged its
flight to join in Heaven thofe benevolent fpirits

VOL. II.   L   whom

whom it had imitated on earth. Univerfal dejection accompanied the news of his death, and
the tears of a grateful neighbourhood fpoke his
unequivocal eulogium.

CHAP. XV.

----One falfe ftep for ever damns her fame;
In vain with tears fhe may her lofs deplore;
In vain look back to what fhe was before;
She fets, like ftars that fall, to rife again no more.

ROWE.

THE obfervation of Solon, repeated by the
celebrated Crœfus at the moft interefting period
of his life, ' that we never fhould pronounce a
' man happy until we have feen his end,' was
ftrikingly verified in my heroine's hiftory. Her
morn of exiftence rofe with peculiar fplendour;
and even the contemplative philofopher, who is
accuftomed to look beyond the furface, and to ba-
lance hope with experience, when he confidered
the rare advantages of judicious education, amiable temper, difcreet habits, ample wealth, and
exemplary connections, united in the perfon of
the lovely Geraldine, muft have concluded that
no common viciffitude of fortune could demolifh
this goodly fabric.

The commencement of her married life was,
in the opinion of the generality of obfervers,
equally

equally aufpicious. United to the man of her heart, her fuperior in rank, and correfponding to herfelf in fortune, perfonal grace, and natural advantages, what 'a pity if aught'' had intervened to prevent the Hymeneal bond from infuring the happinefs of 'this matchlefs pair.' The latent fpark of vanity, lurking in her bofom, was undefcried; and no one could calculate how long it would be before the carelefs Monteith would drop the character of a lover. No one afked, where is the firm judgment, the manly tendernefs, which fhould guide and direct this attracting woman through the thorny maze of public life? Every admirer of equipage, vivacity, fplendour, and beauty, pronounced the perpetual happinefs of the earl and his bride.

Five years had elapfed fince Powerfcourt-houfe exhibited the fcene of feftivity with which I ufhered in this narrative; and the fun of Geraldine's peace is fet for ever. The fhadows lengthening, as the bright luminary defcends, point at laft to the tomb. The death of a revered father, full of age and honour, is not of itfelf an event to caft a fable hue over the fcarcely mature life of a dutiful affectionate daughter; but the circumftances attending fir William Powerfcourt's demife were fuch as lady Monteith could *never* overcome. She felt convinced that fhe had fhortened his exiftence; and though his parting fpirit, uniformly benignant, bleffed and forgave his involuntary murderer, a thoufand fatal indifcretions rofe to her remembrance, and, feen through the medium of their effects, they no longer appeared pardonable levities. She who had afpired to give delight and comfort to all around her, had brought difgrace on her hufband, infamy on her children, and death to her father. The pious confolations of of Mr. Evans alleviated the horrors of her firſt deſpair ; but mining grief confirmed the ravages which fatigue and terror had made in her delicate frame.   Each riſing morning ſeemed to announce ſome faded charm.   Uniform dejection uſurped the place of her faſcinating ſmile.   Feeblenefs and melancholy alike reſtrained her ſportively graceful movements ; and inſtead of the coruſcations of her ſprightly wit, ' ſorrow unfeigned and humiliation deep' ſpoke in all her accents.

Yet the heirefs of ſir William Powerſcourt's fortunes muſt ſtill poſlefs ſufficient charms to allure a mercenary heart; and Fitzoſborne (whom cowardice and chicane had preſerved from the vengeance which lord Monteith's pardonable fury firſt prompted him to require for his injured honour) encouraged the audacious hope, that the legal procefs which the frantic hufband immediately commenced to vindicate his wrongs would terminate in the accompliſhment of all his wiſhes, by putting him in poſſeſſion of a wealthy and admired wife.   Miſled by his own falſe maxims, which had taught him to believe that ' a woman ' pardons every inſult when ſhe loves the inſult-' er,' he ventured on the atrocious crimes which made him maſter of lady Monteith's perſon, while he knew her uncontaminated ſoul revolted at the idea of conjugal infidelity.   He was now perſuaded, that ſhe muſt feel anxious to repair her tarniſhed honour : and being convinced that grief and ſhame never proved fatal to youth and beauty, when its return to reputation and happinefs ſeemed not only poſſible, but certain, he determined to make my drooping Heroine, what he called, an *honourable* offer.   In the letter which he addreſſed to her upon this occaſion, he explained his ſentiments with more explicit freedom than

than he had dared to do while Geraldine, proud
in conscious innocence, felt no necessity of applying for consolation to the subterfuges of so-
phism. But he now thought her predominant
love of fame and horror of reproach would induce her to extricate herself from the disgrace in
which his infamous artifices and her own credulity had plunged her, by adopting those excuses
which were invented to enfeeble virtue, and to
sanctify vice. He knew indeed, that she had a
tale to tell, which would harrow up the hearer's
soul ; but he well understood the laws by which
public opinion is regulated, and the delicacy of
her sentiments. These reasons convinced him,
that she would never expose her defence to a
doubtful belief. I shall now subjoin his letter
written about two months after sir William's
death, with her reply.

     'To the COUNTESS of MONTEITH.

    ' Madam,

    ' When I reflect upon the melancholy event
' which has recently happened at Powerscourt, I
' feel that an additional odium devolves upon me,
' which reflection and candour must own I have
' not deserved. Could I possibly have foreseen,
' that when I felt the power of your irresistible
' charms, I was preparing the grave of your
' worthy father ! No, loveliest, and most-adored
' of women ! whatever of imperfection and frailty
' may be attached to my character, it is pure from
' the reproach of deliberate cruelty.
    ' I hear, with inexpressible concern, that your
' too susceptible mind sinks under the inconve-
' niences of your present situation. Suffer me,
        ' madam,

' madam, to remove the veil of forrow which now
' clouds your reafon, and permit me to direct
' your view to future profpects. Inconfideration
' like mine (for I, in juftice, claim that the
' blame fhould be folely confined to myfelf) is too
' frequent in this age to excite indignation ; and
' the known unworthinefs of lord Monteith forms
' an excufe which all ladies who have diffolved
' their firft marriage connection cannot plead.
' Some converfation will indeed be excited, while
' his lordfhip purfues the legal revenge which his
' vindictive temper will prompt him to adopt.
' But it will ceafe with the adventures of the
' day. Your prefent exemplary behaviour will
' reftore you to the efteem of the world; and
' permit me, Madam, to indulge a hope, (it is
' the only one which, fince I have heard of your
' extreme diftrefs, makes my exiftence fupporta-
' ble,) that you will deign to accept the repara-
' tion which it is in my power to make you, by
' allowing me to lead you to the altar the moment
' you are free from your prefent difaftrous tie.
' There, I truft with the moft aufpicious omens,
' will I dedicate to you a heart penetrated with
' your merits, and a mind capable of revering all
' the dazzling fuperiority of tafte, information,
' and difcernment, which you poffefs.

' I muft hope, that the happy moment will ar-
' rive, when we fhall look back upon our paft for-
' rows with complacency, and confider them as
' the progenitors of prefent blifs. But why
' fhould exceffive forrow *now* prey upon your
' heart ? It is but to fee you, adorned as you are
' with all that art and nature can beftow of lovely
' and excellent ; it is but to contraft your cha-
' racter with that of the imperious infenfible be-
' ing to whom a juvenile inclination unhappily
engaged

' engaged you ; and he muſt be loſt to the moſt
' amiable feelings of humanity who does not ex-
' cuſe and pity me.   The moſt enlightened lite-
' rati of the age have proved, that chaſtity con-
' ſiſts in the individuality of affection ; and when
' lord Monteith's conduct has forfeited your af-
' fection, the transfer of your perſon to another
' is equally delicate and juſt.   Marriage, being
' merely a civil engagement, cannot invalidate
' the great laws of Nature ; and the man muſt be
' a prey to the moſt narrow prejudices, who would
' deny a woman the right of flying to the protec-
' tion of a kindred mind, when her revolting
' ſoul ſpurns the tyrannical power of a huſband
' whom ſhe can neither reſpect nor love.

' O my beloved Geraldine ! ſuffer me to drop
' the hateful title of your former thraldom, and
' to call you mine.   I have been contented to
' ſuppreſs the keen indignation of wounded ho-
' nour, and have forborne to interrupt your filial
' ſorrows by an explanation of what muſt appear
' to you a baſe deſertion when I left you at the
' inn at ———.   Alas ! I only propoſed an ab-
' ſence of a few hours to procure you an honour-
' able aſylum in my ſiſter's family ; and during
' that interval Monteith, with the capricious cru-
' elty natural to his diſpoſition, bereft me of the
' treaſure I had riſked ſo much to obtain, and
' then abandoned it to an unfeeling world.   What
' anguiſh have I not ſuffered ſince that moment !
' Yet, ſtill more to convince you of the reſpectful
' delicacy of my unaltered love, I will not aſk per-
' miſſion to throw myſelf at your feet till the
' joyful moment of your emancipation.   Then
' will I lead you back to the world, nine-tenths
' of whom will not only juſtify but applaud your
' conduct.   That ſyſtem of univerſal benevo-
                                             lence,

' lence, which fuperfedes all written precept,
' gains ground. To that do we appeal, and
' not to the infane morality of fpecific injunc-
' tions, which foolifhly and even wickedly at-
' tempt to bring individual actions under the
' limitation of one general rule. Man in fo-
' ciety muft retain all his natural rights ; and
' the reftraints that circumfcribe thofe rights
' (if founded upon falfe principles) muft foon
' fubmit to the refiftlefs voice of public opinion.
' Nor does this fyftem tend to encourage gene-
' ral profligacy of manners. No ! it can only
' apply to thofe more intelligent characters,
' whofe refinement is a fecurity againft licen-
' tioufnefs.

' So acute is my own confcioufnefs of error,
' that my heart ftarts from the remorfeful re-
' collection of fome indirect means, not wholly
' confiftent with the lovely fincerity of truth,
' which my refiftlefs paffion for you urged me
' to adopt. For the deceptions which only love
' can excufe, I humbly entreat your pardon, and
' I faithfully promife you, that as they were the
' firft, fo they fhall be the laft inftances of mo-
' ral turpitude which you fhall ever difcover in
' the conduct of,

' Madam,

' Your entirely devoted

' EDWARD FITZOSBORNE.

' TO THE HONOURABLE EDWARD FITZOSBORNE.

' DOES Mr. Fitzofborne fuppofe the unhap-
' py victim of his treachery as meanly bafe as
' he has proved her to be weakly credulous,
' that

' that he affronts her with a a propofal, which
' atrocious guilt alone empowers him to make ;
' and from the indignity of which fhe was *once*
' happily fecured by infurmountable barriers,
' till he reduced her to the dire neceffity of fur-
' rendering the facred name of wife, and ming-
' ling her blufhes with her tears, when fhe hears
' the once-joyful honourable appellation of
' mother ?

' You feem, fir, to difown the charge of deli-
' berate cruelty. Account, if you can, for your
' conduct by any other motive. You know
' what I was when I had firft the misfortune of
' feeing you. You know how foon you formed
' a plan for my deftruction, and by what arts
' you have made me what I am. You know
' too, how your infidious friendfhip feduced
' lord Monteith, and made him unconfcioufly
' acceffary to my undoing. To you he owes
' the contamination of his once unfullied ho-
' nour. From you, my innocent, difgraced,
' deferted children, require their mother,
' their inftructor, the guardian of their in-
' fant years. From you I demand my ruined
' peace, my unfullied fame, my loft health, and
' ever blafted profpect, which, while they ren-
' dered life valuable, taught me to look on death
' with ferenity. I not only require of you the
' life of my dear venerable father, but I alfo
' charge you with having given inconceivable
' anguifh to the laft hours of one who lived but
' to make others happy ; whofe benevolence
' would not have hurt a worm !—He is at reft.—
' Would I were fo too '—O that I were now
' joined to his pure beatified fpirit !—But I muft
' firft pafs through many a purifying fea of for-
' row. How excruciatingly refined has your

I 3   cruelty

' cruelty been ! Life is infupportable, but I dare
' not afk to die.

   ' I fcorn to reply to the *arguments* urged in
' your infamous letter. Addrefs them, fir, to
' thofe who, while they lead a life of guilt, wifh
' *cheaply* to purchafe the reputation of virtue.
' Yet beware how you confide in them, when
' the awful fummons of death calls you to an
' invifible world. For me, all my temporal
' views have terminated. I feek no fubterfuges.
' I will endure the cenfures of the world ; they
' are my juft portion. Its vindications I would
' reject with difdain. I fubmit to whatever
' punifhment lord Monteith's lawful refentment
' inflicts. It does not belong to imprudence
' like mine either to juftify its actions, or to
' complain of fuffering. In repentance is all
' my hope.

   ' I will enumerate the offences which claim
' my conftant tears. You will then fee what
' portion of guilt falls to your fhare —Your
' artful adulation pleafed my vanity, and while
' I fuppofed myfelf merely amufed by your con-
' verfation, you excited a growing intereft in
' my regard. To you, by imperceptible degrees,
' I transferred the efteem of which I thought
' my lord undeferving ; and I foothed my re-
' proving confcience by fuppofing, that in ad-
' miring you, I honoured virtue. Blindly per-
' tinacious, I perfifted in rejecting the councils
' of my more difcerning friends, and purfued
' my own fallacious judgment, which taught
' me, that immoral actions were not the natu-
' ral confequence of relaxed principle. You
' know that you concealed the full tendency of
' thofe principles from me. You know that I
' always ftarted at what I thought feemed to
            ' militate

‘ militate againſt religion and virtue. You
‘ often aſſailed me, but I was your admirer and
‘ apologiſt, not your convert.

‘ Thus far have I contributed to my undoing ;
‘ and may my ſtory be an awful momento to all
‘ who, truſting in the ſuppoſed ſecurity of their
‘ own virtue, neglect the ſuggeſtions of pru-
‘ dence ; and, under the perverted name of
‘ friendſhip, admit a ſiniſter gueſt to diſpute the
‘ poſſeſſion of their affections with the lawful
‘ claims of connubial duty ! May it alſo warn
‘ thoſe wives, who, availing themſelves of the
‘ indulgence of faſhion, permit the marked at-
‘ tentions of an agreeable man of unknown or
‘ ſuſpicious character, however they may think
‘ themſelves ſanctioned by cuſtom, protected by
‘ the rules of decorum, or ſecured, as you taught
‘ me to think, by the bond of pre-attachment.
‘ I ſhall not then die in vain.

‘ Let me, though ſhame and horror alike
‘ agitate my trembling frame, this once allude
‘ to thoſe particulars of my misfortunes, which
‘ you alone can illuſtrate. You ſeem to allow,
‘ that it was to your artifices that I owed the
‘ fatal abſence of my friend and my huſband on
‘ the day I left Monteith. You know the ar-
‘ guments by which you influenced my elope-
‘ ment ; may your repentance enable you to
‘ eſcape the terrible malediction with which you
‘ cloſed them. You know how I hoped to over-
‘ take my lord at every ſtage ; but your heart,
‘ rendered callous by guilt, cannot conceive the
‘ agonies of mine when I firſt ſuſpected your
‘ nefarious purpoſe. My confuſed recollection
‘ can trace no more. I only know, that re-
‘ turning reaſon taught me, that I was a wretch
‘ for ever.

‘ And.

'And can you—who know that your life is
'in my hands, who are confcious that, by tell-
'ing my fad tale in a court of juftice, I could
'convict you of a crime more foul than mur-
'der—fuppofe me capable of plighting my faith
'to a monfter? - No! Fitzofborne; enjoy the
'fecurity which my own feelings, and not
'compaffion for you, allows you to poffefs;. but
'infult me no more. Know, that the moment
'which revealed your bafenefs tore from my
'heart every veftige of efteem, and taught me,
'by my deteftation of the offence, to hate and.
'to defpife the offender.

'From a wifh of roufing in your breaft the
'torpid feelings of compunction, I honour your
'letter with a copious reply. The compliments
'you pay to beauty are ill addreffed to the fad-
'ed form which pens this epiftle; and the
'praife of fuperior talents are equally inappli-
'cable to her whom you have proved guilty of
'the weakeft vanity, and the blindeft credu-
'lity.

'I have forfeited the name with which lord'
'Monteith once honoured me, and I will not
'difgrace the unfullied purity of my father's.

'GERALDINE.'

An interefting converfation took place between my heroine and her friend upon the fubject of thefe letters. The countefs had fhewn
them to Mifs Evans, and requefted her opinion
of the tendency of her reply. 'Worthy of
'yourfelf,' was the anfwer. 'But there is one
'part,' continued Lucy, 'which feems to afk
'for explanation: Some particulars of your
'ftory are unknown to me, nor do I wifh to
'hear

‘ hear what it will be agony for you to repeat.
‘ But why, my deareſt ! do you heſitate to do
‘ juſtice to your wounded fame, perhaps too to
‘ preſerve ſome other victim from meditated
‘ ruin, by giving up a villain to that puniſhment
‘ which the offended laws of his country would
‘ inflict upon his atrocious crimes ?’

‘ My reſolution,’ ſaid the counteſs, is fixed ;
‘ but you ſhall hear the reaſons on which it is
‘ founded. You know the fabricated tale
‘ which drew me from Monteith. My recol-
‘ lection, then not clear, ſoon grew more con-
‘ fuſed ; and it is only by comparing circum-
‘ ſtances that I can connect my narrative. I
‘ think I muſt have been firſt taken to an obſcure
‘ houſe in a lonely ſituation ; for I recollect on
‘ the horſes ſtopping I ſaw only trees and a
‘ mean building, and I thought how fooliſh it
‘ was to ſtop there, as my lord would never put
‘ up at ſuch a piace as that.—I ſuppoſe that I
‘ was detained there till my purſuers had paſſed
‘ upon the road. I remember travelling very
‘ faſt ; but my head was too bad for me to gueſs
‘ where. It was on a Thurſday that I left the
‘ caſtle. My lord found me in a ſmall inn in
‘ Lancaſhire on Tueſday. I was ſitting in a
‘ room by myſelf, and weeping bitterly, when
‘ he burſt in. He reviled me in the ſevereſt
‘ terms, and aſked me for Fitzoſborne. I told
‘ him that I did not know where he was, and
‘ wiſhed I never might ſee him more.—Indeed,
‘ Lucy, I ſpoke the truth ; but my lord redou-
‘ bled his ravings.—I know that I ſaid I was
‘ not ſo wicked as he ſuppoſed ; and I made an
‘ effort to kneel ; but whether he ſpurned me
‘ from him, or I fell through giddineſs, I can-
‘ not tell.—I hurt myſelf in my fall ; and, re-
‘ covering,

' covering, found myfelf covered with blood.
' But my head was relieved, and I was treated
' with compaffion. I kept afking for my lord.
' They told me, that he was gone after the
' gentleman who came with me. O what a
' found was that for me! The people at the inn
' were worthy characters. They believed me
' to be penitent, and affifted me to efcape from
' my feducer. I knew not where to go; but I
' thought you would advife me. I travelled
' rapidly towards Powerfcourt till I heard of my
' father's illnefs. You know the reft.'

The trembling Geraldine faltered as fhe repeated this melancholy tale, and then funk weeping on the bofom of her friend.

' Suppofe me now,' continued fhe, as foon as
fhe could recover compofure enough to proceed,
' repeating this narrative in a court of juftice;
' every eye fixed upon me with offenfive curi-
' ofity; infulted (at leaft in my own opinion)
' by that crofs-examination, which impartial
' juftice will require to difcover whether I was
' not the willing partner of the crime. The
' powers of eloquence will be exerted againft me.
' Confufion my make me prevaricate; and
' when life is at ftake, mercy pleads for the cri-
' minal whofe guilt appears doubtful. None
' of my own fervants were with me. I can
' bring no corroborating evidence. It will be
' proved, that I was feen with him on the road,
' and at feveral inns, and made no effort to ef-
' cape. My appearance may have caufed con-
' tradictory opinions; and art like his would
' certainly take care that the general impreffion
' fhould be unfavourable. To thofe who know
' not my ufual manner, I might feem paffive,
' or acquiefcent, as well as infenfible.

' But

' But fuppofe my character receives all the
' juftification it can by his condemnation, of
' what advantage will his death be to me, or to
' the world ? The vain beauty, who is not de-
' terred by my misfortunes from liftening to the
' adulations of a Fitzofborne, will not be dif-
' fuaded from encouraging the firen fong of
' flattery by hearing that a determined feducer
' can call in arts more unwarranted than illicit
' perfuafion. Lord Monteith can never be re-
' united to me. His honour and my delicacy
' demonftrate the impoffibility of oblivious for-
' givenefs. Wherever my children appeared,
' the fad tale of their mother would ftill be
' whifpered, and the blufh of fhame muft dye
' their cheeks.

' Nor,' continued fhe, wiping the tear which
maternal feelings called forth, ' can the mortal
' wound in my reputation ever be healed. I
' am confcious of a thoufand indifcretions, pro-
' ceeding indeed from the erroneous idea, that
' every virtue, as well as every accomplifhment,
' united in Fitzofborne's mind. Not an ac-
' quaintance have I in Scotland, or in London,
' who cannot relate thofe indifcretions, and tell
' with what marked preference I received his
' attentions; and when thefe corroborating tales
' are confidered, will candour fay, ' Perhaps
' the vain trifler ftopped at actual guilt ?' A
' thoufand incidental circumftances concur to
' overwhelm me. My mother's jewels are now
' in his poffeffion. They were not given with
' a culpable defign ; but who will acquit me ?
' who knows that lord Monteith's affairs were
' embarraffed ? Or fuppofe I ftate my motives :
' there again I am fole witnefs in my own
' caufe ; and fhe who beftowed on a ftranger the
' confidence

' confidence which she withheld from her hus-
' band, can scarcely expect belief. I gave him
' my picture too.—Good heaven, what blind
' delusion! No! Lucy; I must be silent. I
' have been too culpable to talk of innocence.
' The licentious would say, poor Fitzosborne
' was very hardly used at last by the woman who
' invited his attack; and the censorious would
' accuse me of taking a cruel method to redeem
' an irretrievable reputation.'

' Still,' said Miss Evans, ' there are advanta-
' ges which you have not considered. Your
' daughters would certainly be restored to your
' care.' A flood of tears burst from the eyes
of Geraldine, and she faintly uttered: ' Sweet,
' lovely, helpless girls!' Then, after a pause,
she added, ' Could I flatter myself with the ex-
' pectation that my protracted life would be
' advantageous to them, this suggestion would
' have weight; but a *transient* self-indulgence
' may be bought too dear.'

' At least,' urged Lucy, ' let Monteith know
' your story. Convinced of your comparative
' innocence, (you will not, I know, allow me
' to use a more favourable word,) Henry has
' been for some time employed in collecting
' the circumstances in your favour. The chief
' are the testimony and the confession of your
' servants at Monteith. Suffer him to add to it
' your narrative, before he transmits it to your
' lord.'

' By no means: use your influence with your
' generous Henry to abandon his proposed jus-
' tification. I know the disposition of him who
' *was* my husband. While he considers me as
' an adulteress, contempt preserves my gallant
' from

' from his vengeance ; and he can wait the flow
' proceedings of the law now his firft fury has
' fubfided. But if he knows the wrongs his
' once-beloved Geraldine has endured, not the
' united world could diffuade from taking a
' more fummary vengeance. He would pur-
' fue the ravifher of his wife to the remoteft
' corner of the globe, and only value his own
' life as it was the means of affailing his adver-
' fary. Chance, or fkill, my Lucy, and not juf-
' tice, determines thefe blind and audacious ap-
' peals to prefumptuous vengeance. And fhall
' my helplefs babes lofe their only parent ? No !
' let every document in my favour be fuppref-
' ed, at leaft till lord Monteith is fecure from
' the fword of my feducer.'

' Confider yet once more. Your lord has
' commenced proceedings in a court of juftice.'
—' I have deferved difgrace, and muft endure
' it.'

' The legitimacy of your little fon, I fear, is
' queftioned.'

Geraldine fhrank with horror. ' O wide ex-
' tended evil ! faid fhe. Three generations,
' blafted by me, may curfe the hour when I was
' born. Yet, my murdered father ! thy benig-
' nant fpirit, even in the pangs of death, for-
' gave me. Will my flandered babes be inexo-
' rable ? But I fhall not hear their reproaches.
' The time is not far diftant when I may fpeak
' with an expectation of being believed. I will
' juftify to lord Monteith the fufpected, becaufe
' premature, birth of his fon. O infupportable
' anguifh ? that fuch juftification fhould be re-
' quired of me.'

Mifs

Mifs Evans repeated this converfation to her
father and Henry. The latter praifed the great-
nefs of foul which dictated thefe fentiments.

 ' Your interefting friend, my dear child, does
' indeed repent,' faid Mr. Evans. ' No vindic-
' tive rage, no felf-acquitting accufations of
' others, mingles with her true remorfe. She
' properly appreciates the degree of her own
' culpability ; nor does any remaining affection
' for her feducer lurk in her paffionate reproach-
' es. She feems, like the penitent defcribed by
' our immortal bard,.

    ——' To repent her, as it is an evil,
 ' And takes the fhame with joy !'

 ' To fuch contrition we are warranted to hope.
 ' that the golden gates of mercy will be un-
 ' clofed.'

CHAP.

CHAP. XVI.

Hail wedded love !——by thee,
Founded in reafon, loyal, juft, and pure,
Relations dear, and all the charities
Of father, fon, and brother, firft were known.

MILTON.

GRIEF, the fwift anticipator of time, continued to prey on Geraldine's youthful cheek.
Her decay was vifible to every beholder. But
Lucy Evans, ftill liftening to the flattery of hope,
believed that another and another day would
bring the defired amendment. Paffionately admiring the beauties of nature, fhe wooed the
tardy fpring to approach, and continued to repeat the well-known defcription;

——Airs, vernal airs,
Able to cure all fadnefs but defpair.

Defpair was, however, the mortal difeafe, under
which her friend laboured. Like Shenftone's
interefting Jeffy, fhe faw in every object fome
reproach of her folly, or fome memento of her
former happinefs. ' What have I,' fhe would
fay to herfelf, ' to do with hope; and what
' without hope is life?'

Engroffed wholly by her friend's diftrefs,
Lucy dedicated all her time and thoughts to her
fervice and amufement. ' If I could fee that
' faded cheek blufh again!' fhe would fay.

' Surely

' Surely her appetite leaves her. I watch her
' fleeplefs couch till I fink with wearinefs. I
' wake, and the firft object which the lamp
' fhews me is her unclofed eyes. I offend my
' own feelings to affume cheerfulnefs. She
· fometimes fmiles, but it is fuch a fickly fmile,
' fo unlike its former exhilarating brilliancy,
' it fpeaks fo plainly, I will even feem diverted
' to footh my apprehenfive Lucy.'

Henry Powerfcourt often reproved this extreme folicitude; blamed her for being engroffed by one object; and pleaded his prior
right to her attention, and her promife of making him happy. ' O, talk not to me of feftal
' days and happy vows,' fhe would reply,
' when every hour prefents to me the affecting
' fpectacle of declining lovelinefs ! Surely,
' Henry, you never loved our Geraldine, if you
' can now think of any one but her.'

It was one lovely fpring-day, that Lucy prevailed upon her friend to accompany her into
the parfonage-garden, to look at the burfting
germs of the lilac, and the honey-fuckle's tender
green. They had proceeded to Nerina's bower
before the trembling knees of Geraldine required reft. When a little recovered, fhe read
with pleafure the infcription which Henry had
placed there, while Lucy energetically repeated
the laft lines ; and not infenfible to the charm
of praife, when offered by one fhe loved, fhe
exclaimed, ' There's a happy compliment for
' you. You ufed to fay, coufin Hal would
' never learn to make fine fpeeches.'

The fmile which Lucy's fprightly fally invited foon yielded to the bitter recollection of
former days. ' Happy blamelefs delight !' faid
the countefs gazing on her friend: ' long may
' it

' it be yours! May my sweet Lucy continue to
' receive the incense due to her worth, nor fear
' that a latent poison lurks in the grateful fra-
' grance! Ah, that I had never welcomed
' praise but from a husband's tongue!

' Let me,' continued she, ' here, in this
' your favoured retreat, disclose to you the his-
' tory of my errors. You need no warning;
' but the time will probably *soon* arrive, when
' the remembered confidence will still more
' endear this spot.

' I had not been long a wife before I disco-
' —vered that my eye had betrayed my judgment
' so far as to frustrate my expectation of ever
' finding in marriage that communion of well-
' paired minds, that feast of reason and that
' flow of soul which I had looked up to as the
' perfection of felicity. Every attempt to give
' lord Monteith a taste for intellectual pleasures
' was unsuccessful. But I was not unhappy.
' I remember your excellent mother's precepts,
' and reconciled myself to the limited enjoy-
' ments which this world affords. In every
' eccentricity I beheld myself the undisputed
' mistress of my husband's heart. In many
' instances I saw my power over his determina-
' tions; and often a genuine trait of native
' goodness appeared in something apparently
' inconsistent and irregular. I compared my
' situation with that of many married ladies
' whom I knew, and I found abundant reason
' to be contented with my lot.

' I then first saw Fitzosborne, and unhappily
' possessed sufficient consequence to attract his
' notice. He strove to please, and soon grew
' interesting. Yet, weak as I have proved
' myself to be, I think I should not have been
' the

‘ the victim of his arts, had not my lord's be-
‘ haviour to me been perceptibly changed.   He
‘ was no longer the man who engaged my
‘ youthful love, or the hufband who claimed
‘ my refpect and gratitude.   Then, and not
‘ till then, did I feel the power of contraft
‘ which I had hitherto indignantly avoided.
‘ The elegant commendations of Fitzofborne
‘ taught me, that I was not a being of a vulgar
‘ mould.   His graceful attentions indicated the
‘ homage which merit like mine ought to re-
‘ ceive.   His glowing defcriptions, though de-
‘ licate as the ear of purity itfelf could defire,
‘ pointed out a fairy region of felicity, the abode
‘ of congenial minds, where human foibles and
‘ human forrows never intrude.   Infatuated by
‘ this unreal vifion, the blamelefs occupations
‘ by which I had previoufly diverted painful
‘ reflections became infipid.   Wrongs were
‘ converted into unpardonable injuries, and in-
‘ attentions grew into wrongs.   I no longer re-
‘ collected thofe who were lefs happy than
‘ myfelf.   The pang of wounded love loft its
‘ tendernefs, while it affumed the indignant
‘ fpirit of offended pride ; and my rebel heart,
‘ imperceptibly alienated from its lawful pof-
‘ feffor, admitted an ufurped claim.

‘ O, Lucy ! if my tale were told, it would
‘ not only ferve as a warning to our weak fex,
‘ whom vanity or fufceptibility generally betrays,
‘ but alfo to thofe hufbands who are anxious
‘ to guard their honour from reproach.   I
‘ would bid them not entirely depend upon the
‘ ftability of our principles or the conftancy of
‘ our attachments, but to affift our virtue by
‘ that almoft invincible defence which their be-
‘ haviour to us would fupply.   Might they not,
                                                ‘ without

' without derogating from their own superi-
' ority, treat our foibles with generous lenity,
' and make even our faults conducive to our
' fecurity ? Praife is never fo grateful as from
' thofe we love. Attentions are never fo pleaf-
' ing as from our deareft friends. Let them
' not, when they neglect us, fuppofe, that the
' affiduity of an agreeable follower is only
' welcome to the *determined* wanton. The de-
' licate mind, that fhrinks abhorrent from the
' thought of guilt, may divert the pangs of
' unrequited affection by indulging the unfuf-
' pected feelings of efteem and gratitude for
' an amiable obfervant friend. Modern man-
' ners juftify thefe connections, and modern
' hiftory defcribes their refult. But let me not
' recriminate. My hopes of pardon are founded
' on my own penitence, not on the aggravation
' of my hufband's errors. The fuperior ad-
' vantages of my education, my habits of re-
' flection, my fenfe of fhame, the acutenefs of
' my fenfibility, were all entrufted talents ;
' and I recollect with terror the awful affur-
' ance, that where much is given much will be
' required.'

' Still, my Geraldine !' cried Lucy, ' ftill art
' thou the affociate of the pure in heart.'

' I might have been, had I liftened to your
' counfels. Have you forgiven me, Lucy ? I
' fear you have not.'

' Forgiven you ? O ! when did you offend ?'

' Then will you undertake to pay a debt
' which has long burdened my confcience ? I
' muft hope to live to fee it difcharged.'

Lucy's finances were not very abundant. She
could fcarcely underftand her friend's intention.

' Reward

‘ Reward Henry Powerfcourt,’ continued
the countefs ; ‘ for you alone can. And let
‘ my fetting fun contemplate the only objeĉt
‘ on which it can now look with pleafure. My
‘ contagious mifery has extended to all I love.
‘ Be you and your generous noble Henry ex-
‘ ceptions.’

Lucy could not refift this affeĉtionate appeal.
She only pleaded, that the death of their revered
benefaĉtor was too recent.

‘ His daughter,’ refumed the mourner,
‘ wifhes to perform the office which he would
‘ gladly have executed : I mean, beftowing
‘ you on a deferving partner. Look, Lucy, is
‘ there much time to lofe ? Will this hand be
‘ long equal to the pleafing tafk ?’

Geraldine, as fhe fpoke, held up her hand
againft the fun. Its fymmetry was formerly
one of her diftinguifhed charaĉts. It now exhibited a bare anatomy, loofely covered by a
fhrivelled fkin. Each meandering vein ánd ligature was vifible. It fcarcely obftruĉted the penetrating beam. Lucy flung herfelf into her
friend’s arms, and mingled compliance with
her tears.

On the day of celebration, lady Monteith,
in compliment to the bride, changed her fable
drefs for the tafteful elegance of her former
habit. She never looked more lovely. A hec-
tic bloom was fpread over her check, and the
accomplifhment of a favourite wifh gave to her
eyes the radiant emanation which they ufed to
poffefs. She was compofed, and almoft cheerful. She feemed to forbid the intrufive forrow
which preyed upon her own heart, and to drive
the remembrance of her woes from others. A
plain refpeĉtable neighbour of the Evans’s, and
his

his wife, were the only company. They were
ftruck with her appearance, and almoft feemed
to inquire, ' Was that Mifs Powerfcourt that
' was, or was it fome angel in her form ?' In
the overflowing of their hearts they talked of
the manor-houfe, the happy fcenes of feftivity
it exhibited when fhe lived there ; and then repeated their blunt wifhes, that it might *foon* be
as gay again. The countefs accepted the well-
intentioned compliment, and added, that fhe
hoped it would. Her eyes glanced upon the
bride's, who met them with an expreffion of
pleafure. ' She hopes to live,' whifpered fhe
to Henry. ' O furely that hope will be grati-
' fied !'

The morning after thefe aufpicious nuptials
was marked by a converfation peculiarly interefting. Lady Monteith had prepared the neceffary forms, and fhe took this opportunity of
delivering to Mr. Powerfcourt what fhe called a
pledge of her efteem. He faw with furprife
and regret, that it was a gift of that part of the
Powerfcourt eftate which was by her marriage
fettlement referved for her unlimited difpofal.
Henry exclaimed againft the profufe generofity
of her intentions ; affirmed, that her father's
bounty had gratified all his wifhes ; and pointed
out the propriety of prefenting it to lord Mon-
teih.

' What,' faid the countefs, ' to purchafe
' forgivenefs for me ? My lord would difdain
' to receive what I fhould blufh to offer."

' For your children then,' faid Powerfcourt.

' My daughter's fortunes are fufficiently am-
' ple, and lord Monteith's muft revert to his
' fon. Do not, Henry, reje.t this gift, if you
' would not add to my prefent forrows. I

' have been unjuft to your merits, even from
' my girlifh days. But though I may confefs
' my undifcerning caprice, I do not lament
' what has fecured your happinefs by uniting
' you to a mind fo much better adapted to the
' firm integrity of your own. Mine is not a
' difinterefted bequeft. How richly may you
' repay this fordid boon by the communication
' of unperifhing advantages! I have no right
' to the difpofal of my children. I gave them
' being, but I have forfeited all pretenfions to
' direct their education, or to difpofe of their
' perfons. Every requeft which I could make
' would but inflame lord Monteith's juft refent-
' ment. You have never wronged him: on
' the contrary, your difcrimination and inte-
' grity would have preferved me from the abyfs
' into which I have plunged. Perhaps a proper
' reprefentation might induce him to commit to
' your care thofe unhappy objects, whom
' wounded honour muft refufe to their wretched
' mother. They no longer can give him plea-
' fure, and he muft wifh to remove from him
' fuch lively mementos of former happinefs.'

Mr. Powerfcourt and his Lucy both promifed
to folicit the facred truft, and to difcharge it
with punctual fidelity.

' And you too will continue to refide with
us ?' inquired the bride.

The countefs fhook her head.

' Where do you mean to go ?' repeated Mrs.
Powerfcourt.

' There is but one afylum,' anfwered Geraldine. ' If I could but be received there."—
' Can we affift you in procuring it ?' refumed
her affectionate friend.

' I firmly

‘ I firmly believe, that you all have an in-
‘ tereſt there,’ continued the counteſs, looking
round her. ‘ Remember me in your prayers.’
Lucy, no longer able to miſtake her meaning,
burſt into tears ; while Powerſcourt, too much
agitated even to notice the diſtreſs of his beloved wife, attempted to relieve the gloom
which depreſſed lady Monteith’s proſpects. He
talked of the claims which ſociety had upon
her, and of the power of time in ſoftening
grief.

‘ What claims has ſociety,’ returned ſhe,
‘ upon a wretch whom every one that is tena-
‘ cious of reputation muſt abjure ? My huſ-
‘ band muſt caſt me off, or be degraded by the
‘ reproach of ſubmitting to wilful infamy. My
‘ children muſt be eſtranged from my ſight, or
‘ be ſuſpected of being infected by my conta-
‘ minating criminality. Time, Mr. Powerſ-
‘ court, will heal the wounds of common ſor-
‘ rows : it may redreſs the wrongs of inno-
‘ cence, or recruit the ſhattered fortunes of
‘ poverty. But what can time do for me ? Can
‘ it obviate the fatal effects of my errors ; recall
‘ my father from his grave ; give to my chil-
‘ dren that unſullied honour which my conduct
‘ has tarniſhed ; or reſtore to myſelf that peace
‘ of mind which I feel to be for ever forfeited ?
‘ If time can accompliſh theſe wonders, wel-
‘ come years of ſuffering ; welcome the ago-
‘ nies which lead to hopes ſo dear ; welcome
‘ the poignant regret which teaches the value
‘ of bleſſings that may be again enjoyed. But
‘ neither time nor ſorrow can reinſtate me in
‘ theſe loſt bleſſings, or reſtore to me the good
‘ opinion of the world. My ſecluded remorſe
‘ has no witneſſes ; and if it were oſtentatious,

K 2   ‘ it

'it would be fufpicious. Part of my ftory re-
'mains untold; but, judging of what is known,
'the world is right in its renunciation of me.
'No rules are prefcribed for my future con-
'duct, except feclufion, repentance, and
'death.'

Mr. Evans interrupted the pathetic paufe
which fucceeded the countefs's affecting conclufion with all the folemn earneftnefs which
fhould ever characterize the Chriftian prieft-
hood. 'One duty, lady Monteith, ftill remains,
'which you muft difcharge. Cheerfully fub-
'mit to your prefent calamities till Heaven fees
'fit to liberate you from them.'

'I do,' faid Geraldine, meekly bending her
head. 'I feel them to be the confequences of
'crimes. Betrayed by a vain confidence in my
'own ftrength, I fhut my eyes againft the
'cleareft difcoveries, and rejected the warning
'voice of Heaven, which fpake in the language
'of a faithful friend. I not only fubmit to live,
'I even cling to life, to that hopelefs life, which
'has no other aim but by recollection and pati-
'ence to atone for my youthful follies, and to
fmooth with meek refignation the painful
couch of death.'

'Remiffion of fins,' replied Mr. Evans,
wiping away a ftarting tear, 'is ever promifed
'to fincere contrition. Examine your heart,
'my dear lady! feparate the regret of paft plea-
'fures from the forrow for paft offences. Try,
'by a fevere fcrutiny, how far the lofs of fame
'may claim the tear which ftarts at the idea of
'remembered eminence; and, while the necef-
'fity fof forgivenefs finks deep into your foul,
compofe your anxieties by reflecting on the
mercy of your God.'

Mrs.

Mrs. Powerſcourt looked as if her father had
ſpoken with undue ſeverity ; but the counteſs,
after a mental ejaculation expreſſive of piety
and reſignation, proceeded : ‘ While I fre-
‘ quented the circles of faſhionable life, I par-
‘ took of their follies ; yet the glare of perpe-
‘ tual amuſement, and the hurry of conſtant
‘ engagement, did not ſo far vitiate my mind as
‘ to render me unfit for the duties of domeſtic
‘ life.   Reflection ever attended my pillow, and
‘ deſcribed, not the parties in which I was to
‘ appear, nor the adulation I ſhould receive, but
‘ the more grateful images of my children, my
‘ ſocial friends, my quiet occupations.   Theſe,
‘ therefore, were ever my deareſt delights ; and
‘ regret for theſe bleſſings will mingle with the
‘ tear that contrition claims.

‘ The love of fame was, I own, my predomi-
‘ nant error.   Impelled by this powerful paſ-
‘ ſion, I purſued diſtinction, and, though I only
‘ ſought it by praiſe-worthy means, I am now
‘ ſenſible, that this ‘ buſy paſſion’ mingled im-
‘ perfection with my ‘ faireſt aims,’ ‘ perplexed
‘ the genuine ſchemes of defective virtue,’ and
‘ ‘ ſlyly warped my unſuſpecting heart.’   Though
‘ in the ſight of man they may wear the ſame
‘ impoſing aſpect, the ſearcher of hidden things
‘ muſt diſcover an infinite difference between
‘ thoſe actions which originate from the dutiful
‘ deſire of pleaſing him, and thoſe the ultimate
‘ view of which was the applauſe of fellow-
‘ mortals.   Your firmer mind, my Lucy, early
‘ imbibed the noble ambition of gaining the ap-
‘ probation of the Supreme Good.   Your vir-
‘ tues ſhunned obſervation, and only courted
‘ the ſilent plaudit of conſcience.   For me,
‘ though not inſenſible to the innate lovelineſs

‘ of

' of virtue, nor callous to the feelings of com-
' paffion, I felt every faculty roufed to exertion
' by the idea of what the world would fay of
' me. Our hiftory is a comment upon the com-
' parative tendency of thefe governing principles.
' Happy Powerfcourt! how firm muft be your
' confidence in the integrity of a mind which
' always acts under the conviction that its moft
' fecret thoughts are noted by Omnipotence !'

' The merit was more in my fituation, than
' in myfelf,' returned the amiable bride. ' I
' was fecluded from temptation, and I had lei-
' fure to acquaint myfelf with my own frailties.
' Retirement, my Geraldine ! is the foil moft
' congenial to female virtue. How will yours,
' which even in the contaminating world ap-
' peared fo lovely, flourifh in thefe peaceful
' fhades ! What ample fupplies will your here-
' ditary poffeffions afford to your benevolence !
' Let not mortal forrow dry up the fource
' which would convey happinefs to all around
' you ; but enjoy the anticipated pleafure of
' widely-diffufed liberality.'

' You forget,' faid Geraldine, ' what I now
' am. The mercy of the law, or the bounty of
' lord Monteith, muft determine the means of
' my future fubfiftence. My marriage-articles
' made no provifion for contingent crimes. My
' dear father did not think his child could be
' guilty of any, and his conviction of my frailty
' was attended by death. The mortal forrow,
' my Lucy, which has to lament fo many de-
' privations, cannot ceafe, at leaft while me-
' mory holds her feat. Yet though Reafon
' fhrinks from the contemplation of my cala-
' mities, I muft continue to requeft, that her
' guiding ray may accompany me to the laft
                                          ' moment

'moment of my frail exiftence. My generous
'friends! I fadden you with my forrows. I
'feel your kind fympathy. Every day confirms
'the certain diminution of my ftrength and
'health; nor can I conceal from your difcern-
'ment my conviction that I have not long to
'live. Your pious offices, Mr. Evans, are
'doubly welcome. If any unwarrantable fen-
'timent efcape my lips, reprove me with the
'meek intrepidity of your function, and teach
'me yet further to explore the weaknefs of my
'own heart. Yet in one point let your can-
'dour credit my folemn affertion. It is not
'from any remaining infatuation, but from a
'deep fenfe of my feducer's atrocious crimes,
'that I not only, thus unfolicited, exprefs my
'forgivenefs of my deftroyer; but I alfo ear-
'neftly entreat, that Heaven would pardon his
'mifdeeds.'

'Let us leave him,' faid Mr. Evans, 'to the
'unknown mercies of his Maker. It is not for
'us finite mortals to decide; but as far as our
'views can extend, hope feems like prefump-
'tion. Dreadful, my dear lady, is the fituation
'of that finner who confides in the infidelity
'which deftroys his laft refuge; nor can your
'charitable prayers benefit him who difdains
'the mercy you implore.'

CHAP.

CHAP. XVII.

——What we have we prize not to the worth
Whilst we enjoy it ; but being lack'd and loft,
Why then we rack the value ; then we find
The virtue that poffeffion would not fhow us
Whilft it was ours.

SHAKESPEARE.

SOON after the foregoing converfation, lady Monteith received a letter from her lord's folicitor, informing her, that his lordfhip's meditated vengeance againft Mr. Fitzofborne having been difappointed, he had determined to purfue the legal means of redrefs which were in his power. He had, therefore, inftituted two fuits in the ecclefiaftical and civil courts, which he intended to follow up by an application to the Houfe of Peers for a divorce. The learned barrifter wifhed to know what fteps the countefs would take in her own defence, or if fhe fufpected that the evidence would affect the legitimacy of her fon.

Geraldine's anfwer was fubmiffive, yet not altogether departing from the dignity of her character. She had no defence to make. She acquiefced in the punifhment which the laws of her country would inflict. She only hoped, that her confeffion might prevent fome of the horrors of a public inveftigation. Her ladyfhip added, that fhe would addrefs the earl himfelf on the fubject of the birth of his fon.

Even

Even in the laft fcenes of her exiftence, the ruling paffion of my Heroine's mind predominated. Though perfuaded that her deep defpair could receive no addition ; though her imagination had long anticipated the courfe of law which her lord would purfue, yet the certainty of a legal procefs, and the apprehenfion of general infamy, antedated the crifis of her diforder ; and an excruciating pain in her fide announced the formation of an abfcefs, the rupture of which muft be mortal. Her fufferings were extreme, but the faint flumber which pain brought on was broken by more intolerable reflections. ‘ Not a corner in the kingdom,’ faid fhe, ‘ but ‘ muft now be acquainted with my fall. The ‘ village dame, who never heard of my cele- ‘ brity, will fhudder at my difgrace, and warn ‘ her daughters to avoid my crimes.’

She now pondered upon the only means of vindicating her character, and fhe queftioned the folidity of thofe arguments which had induced her to fupprefs the knowledge of every exculpatory circumftance. She had heard that Fitzofborne had fled from England ; a public difclofure would therefore have a fufpicious appearance. But that very flight, infuring in fome degree the earl's perfonal fafety, pointed out this to be the proper time for making an application to him in behalf of his fon, and endeavouring fomewhat to foften his refentment.— Impreffed with too deep a fenfe of her awful fituation, to deny the alienation of her affections previous to her flight ; fearful of exafperating him by faying any thing that might have an air of recrimination ; and deterred from entering at large upon her unhappy ftory, no lefs by her own weaknefs, than by a fear of urging him to

K 3 follow

follow Fitzosborne, she determined to confine herself to what related to her unfortunate child, and trust the partial vindication of her own conduct to the integrity and discretion of Mr. Powerscourt, who kindly undertook to be the bearer of the following letter.

' To the Earl of Monteith.

'IT is only in such circustances as those in
' which I write, that I could dare to intrude on
' lord Monteith. You will soon be released
' from your disgraced wife by an irreversible
' sentence; and I would entreat your mercy to
' stop your proceedings in the courts of law,
' and to spare my yet remaining sense of shame
' the horror of having my story bandied about
' in the public papers, exposed to indecent rail-
' lery and merciless reproach. I am in the last
' stage of a rapid decline, fully sensible of my
' offences, and fearing to add to their number.
' I declare upon the word of an accountable
' being, who knows she has not long to live, that
' lord Loch Lomond is your son, and entitled to
' be the heir of your honours. Compare the time
' of our fatal journey to London with the evi-
' dence which you may collect of his appearance
' at his birth, and your suspicions must be re-
' moved. And I beseech your justice, do not
' wrong an innocent babe from resentment to
' his mother.
' I entreat your forgiveness; at least do not
' follow me with your curses. Reconciliation
' I do not expect. I will, if you require me,
' for the little time I have to live, forbear the
' use of your name and arms. I restore your
' family jewels, which I had left at Powers-
' court.

' court. On my knees I beg your mercy with
' my dying lips. I shall commend you and my
' children to Heaven. Once more to see *them*
' would be the greatest comfort that I could
' enjoy. Perhaps, as I am past recovery, you
' will grant me that blessing.

' GERALDINE.'

Lord Monteith had been informed of the
countess's departure from his castle, without at
the same time hearing of those particulars which
would have allowed him to infer her innocence.
The rashness of his natural character precluded
reflection in circumstances less agitating than
those in which he was now placed. Nor can it
be wondered at, that, instead of going home to
receive more punctual intelligence, he immediately set off in pursuit of a faithless wife and a
treacherous friend. He took the direct road for
London, for the very reason which should have
decided him against it; namely, because Fitzofborne had stated that he should pursue that
route. Frantic with rage, and only meditating
how to compel his adversary to give him satisfaction for his wrongs, he had reached the con-
fines of Yorkshire, before repeated disappointments of hearing any tidings of the fugitives
taught him to reflect that they had certainly
taken another course. It now occurred to him,
that the family estate of the Fitzosbornes lay in
the northern extremity of Lancashire. It seemed probable that the neglected manorial house
might be the chosen residence of the guilty pair.
He travelled some miles westward with this persuasion, till an accident which disabled his carriage from proceeding compelled him to stop at
a small

a fmall inn fome miles diftant from the poft-
town. His impatience at hearing that the only
vehicle which this obfcure place afforded was
engaged, nearly affumed the form of frenzy;
and the landlord, whofe concern at the gentleman's being fo paffionate, was heightened by
his apprehenfions that he never might have an
earl call at his houfe again, determined to try
if his oratorical powers could allay the ftorm of
words; and, fince his honour could not proceed, perfuade him to remain contented. till his
own carriage could be repaired, or the poft-
chaife returned. With this view he endeavoured to engage his attention; and the Barber of
Bagdad was not a better ftory-teller in his own
opinion. He began by lamenting how unlucky
it was that the chaife fhould have juft drove
away, not ten minutes before his honor arrived,
with a gentleman, who came to his houfe with
his wife the night before. The poor lady was
one of the prettieft creatures he had ever feen;
but fhe feemed to be very ill, and was either always crying or fitting in a brown ftudy. The
footman who was left to take care of her whilft
his mafter went to make a vifit a little way off,
faid that fhe was off her head.——A fudden
thought fhot acrofs Monteith's mind. 'Where
'is fhe!'—'In that room.'—He would inftantly fee her. Words were vain; and the feeble
refiftance which the landlord made to prevent
him from rufhing into the apartment was foiled
by a force to which paffion gave Herculean
vigour. Monteith broke from his opponent,
and beheld his countefs.

The prefence of the wretched Geraldine
could no longer footh the ftormy paffions of her
lord. On the contrary, it now irritated him to
the

the moft ungoverned frenzy. He faw fhe was in diftrefs; but could the moft atrocious guilt affume compofure on fuch an occafion? She attempted fomething like a vindication of her conduct. But what extenuation could' her crimes admit? They were as apparent as his own difgrace. Did fhe not deny any knowledge of the adulterer, when fhe was recent from his arms? Why afk to fee the children fhe had deferted, wilfully deferted? Her feeming agony excited contempt, her entreaties infult; and as fhe flung herfelf at his feet, he fpurned her from him with abhorrence. Uttering a volley of imprecations againft her delufive beauty, he left her lifelefs upon the floor, and rufhed after Fitzofborne, whofe life appeared to be too poor a facrifice for his mighty revenge.

The effufion of blood which attended her fall fomewhat relieved lady Monteith's recollection from the effects of thofe infernal potions which her feducer had adminiftered; and her real ftory being now known, fhe was readily affifted in her earneft defire of proceeding to Caernarvonfhire. Pomade, who had been placed as a guard over her during his mafter's abfence, abandoned his charge, dreading to encounter the athletic arm whih had felled the landlord to the ground; and he flew after Fitzofborne to apprife him of lord Monteith's arrival. The abfence of the feducer proceeded from two motives: he fuppofed that he left his victim in perfect fecurity; and he was defirous of inducing his fifter, who refided in that neighbourhood, and was poffeffed of what the world calls a paffable character, to receive the unfortunate countefs, till, as he termed it, the affair was fettled. He was, befide, anxious to procure

fome

some medical aid; the effects of his nefarious arts were much to be dreaded, and returning reason was to him equally alarming. Pomade's intelligence transferred his solicitude to the care of his own life, which he determined to preserve by any means not *ostensibly* inconsistent with received opinions of intrepidity and honour. A chain of artifices preserved him from the meditated destruction; and after a vain pursuit, Monteith arrived in London.

Lady Arabella immediately hastened to him; but not with the pious design of soothing his anguish, nor of pleading in behalf of an unhappy woman. She was not of a temper to palliate a fault to which she herself had never been tempted; and Geraldine had too strongly awakened her jealousy and envy to allow her to suppose that her criminality admitted of any extenuation. By her malicious comments the account which his lordship had received from his servants in Scotland tended rather to exasperate than to ameliorate his rage; and because their letters did not criminate their mistress, he accused them of being participators in her crime.

Disappointed, by Fitzosborne's leaving the kingdom, in his intentions of either calling him out to combat, or of confining him in prison by the pressure of legal damages, the earl's fury pointed at the countess with an asperity which increased with every real or fancied insult to which her tarnished honour had exposed him; and he pursued the prescribed means of 'casting her off a prey to fortune,' with an avidity and acrimony proportioned to the violence with which he had once loved her and confided in her virtue. He had sent for his children to London, from the idea, that she might have the ef-

frontery

frontery to visit them at Monteith ; and his own
active suspicions, aided by Arabella's malignity,
soon taught him to believe, that his unfortunate
little son was the offspring of guilt. His memory continually tortured him with instances of
Fitzosborne's attention to the infant, whose ill
health, during its first month of existence, had
rendered it a yet more tender object of Geraldine's maternal care ; and the persuasion that a
spurious issue would inherit his lineal honours,
formed the climax of his misery. The dying
countess, worn by mental and corporal anguish,
was perhaps less an object of pity. Inebriety
was his wretched resource ; but even inebriety
was ineffectual. His burning passions kindled
with the feverish draught ; and his servants,
who once idolized their frank generous master,
now trembled for their own safety whenever
they approached him.

In this state of mind he was encountered by
Mr. Powerscourt, the benevolent advocate of
his unhappy wife. The proffered letter was rejected with disdain. The jewels were dashed
upon the floor. Every request was answered
by a sullen negative, and the representation of her
sufferings was treated as a false pretence, invented to excite compassion. The cruel Arabella,
who listened to the narrative of her present situation with more attention than her impassioned
brother could command, coldly observed, that
she really thought dying was the best thing
which the poor imprudent lady could now do.
Disappointed in his hopes, and even refused the
sight of the children, lest he should revive the
remembrance of a mother whom lady Arabella
said they must forget, Mr. Powerscourt took
leave with feelings of the deepest indignation
against

against the unjust, inhuman, self-approving cruelty, which denied forgiveness to one less criminal than themselves, and withheld from a dying penitent the only consolation which could relieve her mortal agonies.

On returning to his hotel, his attention was arrested by an accquaintance, who solicited him to contribute to the relief of a poor fellow who had known better days. He had formerly been his servant, but was now out of place; and the sudden departure of his last master from England had deprived him of a recommendatory character. Henry turned to look at the object of this exordium, and instantly recognized one of Fitzosborne's attendants. The confusion with which Pomade appeared to be overwhelmed was too extraordinary to escape his fixed observation. I shall not particularise what the reader's penetration will easily anticipate. The precipitation with which Fitzosborne had fled from England, joined to his natural ingratitude, and the embarrassment of his circumstances, had prevented him from rewarding the agent who had principally assisted his diabolical designs on lady Monteith. The pressure of poverty, and an accidental rencontre, induced the subaltern villain to discover what he knew of that iniquitous transaction, in hopes of obtaining temporary support. Lord Monteith was soon acquainted with every particular which specified the accumulated guilt of the perfidious wretch who, under the fair guise of friendship, had completed the destruction of a happy family.

The observations by which Mr. Powerscourt intended to have inforced this unequivocal testimony were now precluded by the vehemence of Lord Monteith's self-accusation. His once adored

adored wife was proved to be innocent in that
inftance which had appeared to fix upon her
the charge of deliberate perfidy. The final
views of Fitzofborne could only be obtained by
bafe falfehood and almoft murderous fraud.
Her delicate fenfe of honour, fhrinking with
horror from the imputation of crimes, of which
fhe had rather been the victim than the parti-
cipator, overpowered her feeble frame; and
the wronged innocent (for fo the quick tranfi-
tion of lord Monteith's paffions induced him
now to think her) muft with her life atone for
a hufband's credulous confidence and a traitor's
temerity. She was now dearer than ever to
his heart; and lady Arabella, convinced that
there was no refifting a torrent, endeavoured
to obliterate the remembrance of paft farcafms
by her lively commiferation for the fweet fufferer. Lord Monteith afked for the rejected
letter; bathed every fentence with tears; called
for the little outcaft, whom he had renounced
and banifhed from his fight; and recollected
with horror, that he had fent it to a diftant
county till the law fhould relieve him from the
fuppofititious incumbrance. His daughters were
now alternately folded in his arms. Their likenefs to their mother was recognifed with heart-
rending anguifh. In fine, the carriages were
immediately ordered for Caernarvonfhire; and
the tedious journey was fomewhat beguiled by
the hope, that a reconciliation to her lord, and
the prefence of her children, might ftop the
progrefs of decay. The filence of Henry was
intended to fupprefs that vain expectation, and
to prepare the unhappy hufband for the fcenes
which awaited him.

Compaffion

Compassion for the children, who suffered much from the fatigue of rapid travelling, induced Mr. Powerscourt to stop two stages short of their intended destination; and he was urging lord Monteith to try to obtain a few hours repose, when an express arrived from the manor-house to announce the increased danger of the countess, and to expedite his return. Fresh horses were immediately ordered, and the travellers set off with a rapidity which even the speed of the earl's former journey could not equal. His tortured memory continually recalled the occurrences of that journey, and his heart seemed somewhat eased of the pangs of self-reproach by the invectives with which he loaded the arch-hypocrite, who then acted the part of friendship, that he might be enabled with his scorpion fangs to transfix his breast with impunity. A ray of hope would sometimes break in. Geraldine had recovered from one dangerous attack; why not again? Henry had indeed affirmed, that the vital organs were irreparably injured; but it was presumptuous to affirm what human skill could not ascertain.—She might live, and they might yet be happy. Rash, misjudging Monteith! when happiness was not only in thy power, but absolutely in thy possession, the *common* blessing seemed unworthy preservation. All thy solicitude, all the anguish that corrodes thy soul, cannot now restore the slighted good. Could the healing art acquire miraculous energy sufficient to renew in the lamented sufferer the loveliness and the sprightly health which once captivated thy soul,

Not

' Not poppy, nor mandragora,
' Nor all the drowfy fyrups in the world,
' Can ever medicine to a mind difeafed. .
———' O now for ever .
' Farewell the tranquil mind ! farewell content.'

The path of reconciliation is impeded by infurmountable barriers ; and reflection would foon
convince even the uxorious hufband, that
wounded honour impofed the neceffity of feparation.

The morning broke before the travellers
entered the gate of Powerfcourt. The earl's
attention was arrefted by the atchievement fuf-
pended under the architrave, and a figh burft
from his heart, extorted by the remembrance
of the meek benevolence which it was defigned
to commemorate. Lights appeared at feveral
of the windows. He could difcern the fervants
gliding about when the carriage ftopped ; yet
all was filent, except the whifpering breeze.
The hofpitable doors, which ufed to fly open
at his approach, were now cautioufly unclofed. .
The attendants, whom the noife of the carriages had gathered in the hall, were dreffed in
the weeds of woe, and their countenances were
as mournful as their garb.

To the quick interrogatory of, ' Is fhe alive ?'
a faint affirmative was the only reply ; and
Monteith, gafping for breath, was rufhing forward, when the venerable figure of Mr.
Evans arrefted his fteps. ' I am fummoned,'
faid the good man, waving his hand. ' Let
' me perform my awful duty, and then you
' fhall be admitted. The countefs has fent to
' requeft my prayers. Join, fir, and recom-
' -mend .

' mend her parting fpirit to the Father of mer-
' cies.'

'' Pray for us both,' raved Monteith ; ' and
' if there be efficacy in prayer, entreat that
' my burning brain may be numbed by infen-
' fibility. If you have any mercy,' continued
he, raifing his voice after Mr. Evans, who had
made a fign to the fervants to detain him, ' let
' me fee my wedded love. Do not you know, that
' it is my feverity which has broken her heart,
' and my forgivenefs will yet reftore . her ?
' Think you that I can be patient when one
' loft moment may plunge me into perpetual
' anguifh ?' Mr. Evans promifed that he would
immediately announce his arrival ; and he
leaned againft one of the pillars, panting with
fufpence, expecting his fearful fummons.

It was to the death-bed of withering youth
and faded beauty, to the couch on which great-
nefs, difrobed of its diftinguifhing ornaments,
confeffed its defcent from the common ftock of
humanity, that Mr. Evans approached. '' Is
' it my extreme weaknefs, or fuperior intelli-
' gence,'' faid the countefs in a hollow voice,
' that makes me now attribute fuch powerful
' efficacy to a good man's prayers ?'

' A fellow finner,' replied Mr. Evans, ' re-
' commends you to Heaven.'

' Your hand, fir ! I fhall not long be able
' to thank you.—My fituation is very awful.—
' How my poor heart throbs with pain and
' terror !—Any news from lord Monteith ?'

' He forgives you.'

' And are my children well ?'

' They are waiting to be admitted.'

' I fear

' I fear my fight is now too dim to fee them.
' But I would blefs them, if I dare.—Would
' it be prefumptuous in me to blefs them ?'

A loud groan at this iftant iffued from the
door. It was Monteith's voice, and the dying
countefs caught the well-known found. The
bed fhook with her convulfive tremblings. ' I
' thought,' faid fhe, ' that nothing mortal
' would have affected me. But that voice—
' oh that I could proftrate myfelf before him.'

' My wife !' exclaimed the earl, who had
by this time broke from thofe who attempted
to reftrain him, and approached the bed ; when,
fhocked by the emaciated face where beauty
once refided, he fhuddering drew back his extended arms. ' Infernal villain, who hath
' brought thee to this ! Curfed traitor ! who
' firft feduced me from thee ;—plunged me in
' vice, then ftole my treafure ; and now laughs
' at my mifery !—may his guilty foul for
' ever writhe in tortures fuch as I now endure !
' Awake, awake, my love ! my Geraldine !'
' (for, over-powered by his appearance, fhe
' had fainted.)—' I forgive thee. Oh live,
' my love ! but I know all thy fad ftory. Do
' live, do but fmile upon me. Once more
' blefs me with thy tender fmile. Nothing,
' nothing then fhall part us.' The earl conti-
' nued raving till he was forced out of the
' apartment.'

The laft moments of lady Monteith's life
were marked by humble confidence and dignified compofure. She called for her daughters,
folded them in her arms, and then placed them
in her Lucy's. ' Be you,' faid fhe, ' their
' future mother, and transfer to them that
' love I once enjoyed. Wafte not your preci-
' ous

'ous tears upon my unconfcious corpfe. My
'exiftence is multiplied in thefe helplefs
'orphans; and they fhall flourifh under the
'care of the fifter of my foul. Infinite mercy
'may perhaps permit my feparated fpirit to
'witnefs your pious performance of this in-
'trufted charge.'

She again caught lady Arabella to her bofom.
'My eldeft darling,' faid fhe, 'you will not
'forget me. Give your aunt this ring, the
'pledge of reconciliation and peace. Keep
'this miniature till James can underftand that
'it is his mother's likenefs. Ye guardian
'angels, watch over thefe innocents!—All
'gracious Parent of the friendlefs, in mercy
'protect my babes from my faults and my
'forrows!'

'Watch,' faid fhe, addreffing Henry Powerfcourt, 'my unhappy lord. Do not abandon
'him to his firft forrows. Time will foften
'his defpair. Tell him that his repentant wife
'bleffes his goodnefs, and dies in hopes of
'meeting him in a better world. I would
'have told him fo; but the fight of him
'awakes infupportable anguifh. Urge him to
'comply with my laft requeft, and receive my
'children into your hofpitable dwelling. And
'you, my Chriftian monitor! (looking at Mr.
'Evans), early inftill into their minds thofe
'principles which repel temptation and fupport
'diftrefs. O that lord Monteith would feek
'confolation at the healing fountain of falva-
'tion!'

Her once-radiant eyes gradually affumed a
glaffy dimnefs, yet, though no longer able to
diftinguifh objects, they continued fixed on
that part of the room where her children ftood.
Her

Her clammy hands grafped Mr. Powerfcourt's with convulfive eagernefs, and the laft founds that quivered on her lips were fupplications for mercy.

So terminated the fhort exiftence of the lovely and amiable Geraldine, to whom nature, art, and fortune feemed prodigal of their favours; the faithful friend, the dutiful daughter, the obfervant wife, the tender mother. One fatal weaknefs, combining with the arts of a bafe feducer, annihilates all this excellence, blafts the fair promife of many happy years, and drives her to the refuge of a premature grave.

Does no folemn truth fpeak from her early bier? Does no warning voice repel the flutter of the heart which throbs for adulation, or arreft the career of thofe who, madly purfuing fame or pleafure, expofe domeftic happinefs, the only ' blifs of paradife which has furvived ' the fall,' to the cafual attacks of ignorance, the fubtle malignity of fyftematic depravity, and the certain ruin of indifference and neglect? In vain does perverfe human nature create fictitious bleffings, and wafte its reftlefs hours in the purfuit of vifionary delights, difdaining the pure and peaceful comforts which God and nature allow to all, a guiltlefs confcience, focial enjoyment, felf-poffeffion and content.

CHAP.

CHAP. XVIII.

Vain man ! 'tis Heaven's prerogative
To take, what firſt it deign'd to give,
   Thy tributary breath :
In awful expectation plac'd,
Await thy doom, nor impious haſte
To pluck from God's right hand his inſtruments of
   death.

                  WARTON.

MRS. POWERSCOURT, whoſe reſtrained
ſorrow had forborne to interrupt the parting
ſoul, ſunk upon the lifeleſs corpſe of her friend,
and preſſed the yet-warm lips with a fervid kiſs.
Then receiving the terrified children into her
arms, ' Ever dear and ſacred truſt,' ſhe exclaimed, ' living images of your angel mother :
' dear loſt companion ! pleaſing friend ! faith-
' ful partaker of all my youthful joys !—By all
' the anguiſh of this excruciating ſeparation,—
' by all the endearing remembrances which my
' impaſſioned memory ſhall ever preſerve,—by
' all my hopes of meeting thy approving ſpirit
' in a happier world, I will diſcharge my truſt
' to theſe ſweet innocents, and for their ſakes
' ſubdue the keen regret which would make life
' appear a barren deſert, bereft of thy endear-
' ing lovelineſs.'
   To the raving deſperation of lord Monteith
no pen can do juſtice. Unuſed to calamity, and
indignant of ſelf-reproach, his ſtubborn heart
                       refuſed

refused to submit to the righteous but severe
punishment; and his galled conscience started
from the terrifying accusation, that he, ' like
' the base Judean, had flung a pearl away richer
' than all his tribe.'

He sought to silence the horrors of remorse
by the most extravagant affection to his lady's
memory. Her funeral was conducted in the
highest style of pageant decoration; and he
wearied himself with examining designs for a
monument which he proposed to have executed in Parian marble, and that its magnificence
should rival the proudest structures which
sorrow, taste, or vanity have erected over ' fallen
' mortality.' He teazed his children with his
frantic caresses; vowed that he only existed for
their sakes; determined never to be separated
from them; and traced, with mingled ecstacy
and anguish, the various resemblances which
they bore to their mother.

' My little Geraldine,' he would say, ' is
' her perfect image. Just such a smile as that
' of my beloved, before I knew that accursed
' Fitzosborne. Lucy has her beautiful hair,
' and Arabella her melodious voice. Poor
' James too—but I have never seen him since
' he was three months old. They will all for-
' get her, except Arabella. Yet the murderer
' still lives.—But may I perish, Fitzosborne, if
' I do not pursue thee to the remotest corners
' of the globe.'

While the heart glows with sentiments of
just indignation, it is natural to inquire the
fate of the author of these calamitous scenes.
The last hours of Fitzosborne's life were not
sufficiently splendid to allure inexperience to
desert the plain path of rectitude, from the

hope of acquiring fame or fortune by indirect means. He had indeed plucked the forbidden fruit, but he had found it, like the bitter apples of Sodom, diftafteful and delufive, the origin of mifery and regret.

Difdainfully rejected by the victim of his artifices; compelled to fly his native country, or to languifh in hopelefs captivity; abandoned even by the licentious part of the world, who, though they enthufiaftically applaud triumphant vice, are ever firft to fhun indigent guilt; Fitzofborne was now left to meditate on the abufe of diftinguifhed talents, the wafte of perverted induftry, and the folly, as well as the wickednefs, of that knowledge which only afpires to organife depravity.

These infupportable reflections were, however, foon interrupted; and his miferable exiftence brought to a period by other means than the fword of an injured hufband and betrayed friend. Retributive juftice not only willed his fall in that country where he had imbibed his peftilent notions; it alfo decreed, that thofe very opinions fhould be the immediate occafion of his death. It is well known, that the mercilefs tyranny which Robefpierre erected on the tomb of the murdered Louis fpared neither friends nor enemies. Fitzofborne, as an Englifhman and a gentleman, became an object of fufpicion. In vain did he plead that he had difgraced his anceftors, and abjured his country; in vain boaft his contempt of fuperftition and abhorrence of prefcribed forms; in vain bend with mock adoration at the idol fhrine of liberty, or with fervile adulation load the new Romans with the falfified epithets of magnanimous and illuftrious: they,

who

who spared not a Roland or a Condorcet, could
not be expected to regard sanguinary *principles*,
unless attested by the repeated perpetration of
sanguinary *deeds*.

In the gloom of the Abbaye prison, exposed to
all the various wretchedness of want, disturbed by
the groans of fellow-sufferers, and surrounded by
the instruments of despotism, the wretched
Fitzosborne might have seen the refutation of that
false philosophy which, founded upon the vision-
ary perfectibility of the human species, rejects
the wise restrictions which Infinite Wisdom has
contrived as a barrier against the extreme atrocity
of a fallible creature. But Fitzosborne could neither commune with his own heart, nor seek forgiveness at that throne of mercy which he had
often presumptuously blasphemed. Amongst the
effects of these alarming doctrines, it is not the
least lamentable that they steel the heart against
contrition. The unhappy sinner, whom passion
betrays into guilt, trembles at the recollection of
those crimes which the systematic villain justifies.
But the sorrows of penitence lead to hope, while
the pangs of impiety end in despair.

Shrinking with horror from the disgrace of a
public execution, Fitzosborne applied to the un-
believer's last resource, and with his own hand
anticipated the stroke of the guillotine. He died
amongst men brutalized by guilt, or petrified by
suffering. He could not, therefore, expect the
poor consolation of pity ; but his last moments
were unexpectedly rendered more agonizing by
the intelligence (which the keeper of the prison
communicated with all the unfeeling cruelty of
his profession) that the Dictator, having received
a very favourable account of his talents, had not
only determined to liberate him from prison, but

L 2   also

also to advance him to some confidential employment. Shuddering at the idea of that eternal sleep, the reality of which he yet wished to believe; clinging to life with greater earnestness, in proportion as the possibility of living diminished; cursing his own impatience, which had irretrievably destroyed the fair prospects which he might have realized: stung by remorse and self-accusation, without one ray of hope; Fitzosborne's terrible unlamented exit appeared to anticipate the horrors of futurity. But here let me drop the awful veil; and while justice refuses the commiserating tear, let human nature, conscious of its own infirmities, humbly solicit the protection of Omnipotence against the magic of novelty, the delusions of sophistry, and the arrogance of human Reason, whenever, proud of her own supremacy, she presumes to pass the interdicted bounds prescribed to her finite powers.

The history of my remaining characters will be comprised in a few pages. Mr. Powerscourt prudently determined to let the first effervescence of lord Monteith's grief subside before he requested to be intrusted with the care of those children whose society the unhappy father fancied would alleviate his affliction. But the cheek of infancy is not always dimpled with smiles. Its little foibles require calm correction; and though it is delightful ' to teach the young idea how to ' shoot,' its wild luxuriance must be tenderly repressed. Calamity did not increase the number of the earl's virtues, and patience and application were never wanted in the list. He therefore soon found the prattle of childhood too mild an opiate to lull the tortures of corroding reflection. Lady Arabella too, who, on hearing that skill in education was the very highest ton, had determined

to

to be governefs to her fweet little nieces herfelf,
perceived that verbs and propofitions were very
dull reading, and that the engagements of the
fchool-room were abfolutely incompatible with
mixing in the world. In lefs than three months
after the death of their mother, the children were
fixed at Powerfcourt to the mutual fatisfaction of
all parties.

Love is faid to be the only paffion which can
conquer death. But friendfhip, as belonging to
the fame family, claims the like honour. Long
after the lamented death of Lady Monteith, the
following fonnet flowed from her Lucy's pen :

To FRIENDSHIP.

O Friendfhip ! folacer of grief ! whofe fmile
   Can calm the terrors of life's ruthlefs ftorms,
Come, with thy daughter's memory, and beguile
   My penfive hours. Recall the fairy forms
Of early pleafures. Bid them trip along
   Gay as the fanguine hope which youth infpires,
Renew my Geraldine's enchanting fong :
   That fong which warbles now 'mid angel
     choirs.

O be her peerlefs excellence difplay'd,
   True to the likenefs in my bofom worn !
O'er weeping error caft that lenient fhade,
   Which fcreens repentance from opprobrious
     fcorn.
Gild with thy lamp the cold fepulchral gloom,
And twine thy rofes round the mouldering tomb.

But it was not to the expreffions of vain regret
or elegant fufceptibility that this amiable woman
appealed for the atteftation of her inviolable affection. Her exemplary difcharge of the awful
L 3

truft which fhe had undertaken, unqueftionably
confirmed the fincerity of her regard. The
opening graces of the lovely children promife to
reward her pious care, but who that recollects
their mother's fate will dare to predict the event ?

Though the neighbourhood round Powerfcourt-houfe will long retain an affectionate veneration for the memory of their late benefactor, yet
they confefs with gratitude, that the prefent reprefentative of that illuftrious houfe is the true
heir of the good fir William's virtues. The
exertions of an intelligent cultivated mind fupply
the deficiencies of a lefs ample fortune ; and the
defires of Henry Powerfcourt to confer happinefs are only limited by his power of beftowing
it.

Though happy in his union with a woman,
whofe tafte and character is moft happily adapted
to his own, he has not entirely forgotten the attachment of his early years ; and he views the
adopted children of his once adored Geraldine
with all the fondnefs of paternal affection. He
traces with tender anxiety their refemblance to
their mother ; and he fympathifes with poignant
fenfibility in all his Lucy's regrets and cares.
Often as he wanders through the fhades which
derive a greater beauty from the interefting remembrance of youthful pleafures, he contemplates
the perplexed maze of paft events, and raifes his
eyes in grateful veneration of that Being who
kept him ftedfaft in the path of duty, and ultimately led him to tranquillity and content.

Mr. Evans continues to enjoy a ferene old age,
dignified by the exalted virtues which are com-
prized in the general term of chriftian philanthropy. He occafionally vifits at the manor-houfe,
and is gratified by the company of his children
and

and their young charge. But his time is generally spent at the rectory, meditating on the perplexities of the world he is about to leave, and the perpetuity of that to which he is journeying. His respectful gratitude to his late patron is exemplified by the care he takes to preserve among his parishioners the remembrance of those mild virtues conspicuous in sir William's character, which were ennobled by the song of angels, and are happily adapted to universal practice, ' Peace ' on earth and good-will toward men.'

Lord Monteith continues to drag a miserable existence. His intemperate habits have entirely obliterated all the graces of his person and the amiable qualities of his mind. He is now the associate of boon companions, and the dupe of sharpers; sought only by servile sycophants and usurers, and avoided by all who preserve any decent respect for character. His health rapidly declines. Prevented by legal restrictions from ultimately injuring his children's property, he has been driven by his thoughtless extravagance to the desperate resource of life annuities, which have been multiplied, till they so nearly reach the value of his rent-roll, that it is now become a favourite speculation whether his life or his fortune will hold out the longest.

Repeated matrimonial disappointments have given lady Arabella Macdonald something of a cynical cast of mind. Not that it appears in her conduct, for she still glitters in the first circles, and is always the best-dressed and noisiest woman of fashion in the room. But she has been heard to express several misanthropic sentiments; and her dislike to the male part of the species has arisen to such a degree of acrimony, that she affirms she will never part with her liberty, ' which ' is the zest of life,' to oblige any of those odious

mercenary

mercenary creatures. There are people who think that fhe will perfevere in her refolution, not on account of her having lately become a *belle efprit* of the firft clafs, but from the knowledge of fome *private* events which have lately happened at the pharo table kept by the right honourable lady vifcountefs Fitzofborne, wife of a Britifh *fenator*, and lady Arabella's moft *particular* friend.

The Author's intention of enforcing fome moral truths by an appropriate narrative is now complete. Whatever difregard of applaufe fhe may affect in her affumed character, or whatever indifference fhe may really feel for the fiat of the felf-conftituted guardians of literature, if they fhould pervert their important and highly refponfible office, by exerting the influence which learning and wit give them over the public tafte in recommending works injurious to public morals, fhe ftill recollects, that found fenfe, accurate difcrimination, and correct judgment, form a part of that public by which her merit muft be tried; and fhe cannot but feel anxious, that the rectitude of her *intention* fhould be admitted by fuch a tribunal.

If her apprehenfion of the dangerous tendency of fome popular productions fhould be deemed ill-founded, the *real* friends of morality and religion will ftill fay, "God fpeed!" to the enthufiaftic champion who fallies forth to refift even the delving mole that exerts its puny powers to undermine the facred edifice. Nor will her acrimonious cenfure of thofe falfe lights which lead the unwary aftray, induce the reflecting reader to fufpect that fhe is hoftile to the caufe of real candour, true philofophy, and judicious liberality. In common with every well-wifher to the happinefs and improvement of the world, fhe deeply

mourns

mourns the irreparable injuries which they have received from the blaſphemous pretenſions of thoſe hypocritical furies who have uſurped their hallowed characters.

She feels it neceſſary to add an apology to the lovers of propriety and decorum, for her frequent alluſions to religious ſubjects, and her intermixture of ſerious truths with fictitious events. It is not from any vain deſire of throwing her feeble gage in the crowded fields of controverſy, much leſs from a want of heart—felt reverence for ſacred themes, that ſhe adventured to make theſe digreſſions ; but as the moſt faſhionable, and perhaps moſt ſuccefsful, way of vending pernicious ſentiments has been through the medium of books of entertainment, ſhe conceives it not only allowable, but neceſſary, to repel the enemy's inſidious attacks with ſimilar weapons.

One, of the misfortunes under which literature now labours is, that the title of a work no longer announces its intention : books of travels are converted into vehicles of politics and ſyſtems of legiſlation. Female letter-writers teach us the arcana of government, and obliquely vindicate, or even recommend, manners and actions at which female delicacy ſhould bluſh, and female tenderneſs mourn. Traits on education ſubvert every principle of filial reverence : Writers on morality lay the axe to the root of domeſtic harmony : Compilers of natural hiſtory debaſe their pages with deſcriptions which modeſty cannot peruſe : Philologiſts diſpute the revealed will of God : Philoſophers and antiquarians deny its hiſtorical credibility : and Mathematicians define the non-entity of Him in whom we live, and move, and have our being. The muſe chaunts the yell of diſcord, and, under the pretence of univerſal ci-
tizenſhip

tizenfhip, founds the dirge of that *amor patriæ* which her claffic predeceffor fought to infpire. And laft, though not leaft in its effect, the novel, calculated, by its infinuating narrative and interefting defcription to fafcinate the imagination without roufing the ftronger energies of the mind, is converted into an offenfive weapon, directed againft our religion, our morals, or our government, as the humour of the writer may determine his particular warfare. The egotifm of infidelity, which guides the wandering pen, may be the undefigned caufe of fome of thefe effects ; but *repeated* deviations from an oftenfible fubject can only proceed from a fettled defign of *covertly* attacking whatever fcience once taught us to revere.

THE END.

BOOKS

PRINTED AND SOLD BY

WILLIAM PORTER,

69, GRAFTON-STREET, DUBLIN,

———————

A GOSSIP'S STORY, and a LEGENDARY TALE;
By the Author of the Advantages of Education.—
Price, bound, ...   3s. 9½d.

> " Nor Peace nor Eafe the Heart can know,
>   " Which, like the Needle true,
> " Turns at the touch of Joy and Woe,
>   " Yet; turning, trembles too."
>
> GREVILLE'S ODE TO INDIFFERENCE.

> " With calm feverity unpaffion'd age
>   " Detects the fpecious fallacies of youth,
> " Reviews the motives which no more engage,
>   " And weighs each action in the fcale of truth."
>
> MRS. CARTER'S POEMS.

EXTRACT FROM THE MONTHLY REVIEW.

> " *We recommend this ftory as uniting in a great degree
> of intereft the rarer qualities of good fenfe and an accu ate
> knowledge of mankind.   The grammatical errors and vul-
> garifms whi h difgrace many even of our moft celebrated
> novels; have here no place, and feveral of the fhorter poeti-
> cal pieces interfperfed through the work, have very confi-
> derable merit.   Amufement is com ined with utilit , and
> fiction is in ifted in the caufe of virtue and practical p hi-
> lofophy.*"

∽∾∽∾

ELEMENTS OF MORALITY, for the ufe of Children,
with an Introductory Addrefs to Parents.—*Recommended by the Committee of Education, belonging to the
Affociation for difcountenancing Vice, and promoting the
Practice of Religion and Vi tue.* Price, bound, . .
. . . . 3s. 9½d.

The PARENTAL MONITOR; By Mrs. BONHOTE.—
Price, bound, ...   3*s.*   3*d.*

> Virtue, for ever frail, as fair, below,
> Her tender nature suffers in the crowd,
> Nor touches on the world without a stain :
> The world's infectious : few bring back at eve,
> Immaculate, the manners of the morn.
>
>   *   *   *   *
>
> " Virtue alone out-builds the pyramids :
> " Her monuments shall last, when Egypt's fail.
>
>   YOUNG.

The LOOKING-GLASS FOR THE MIND, or INTELLEC-
TUAL MIRROR : being an elegant Collection of the
most delightful Stories and interesting Tales ; chiefly
translated from that much admired Work—the Children's Friend. Price, bound, ... 2*s.* 8*hd.*

FABULOUS HISTORIES, designed for the Instruction of
Children, respecting their Treatment of Animals ; by
Mrs. TRIMMER. Price, bound, . . . 2*s.* 8*hd.*

MORAL CONTRASTS, or the Power of Religion, exemplified under different Characters ; By WM. GILPIN,
Prebendary of Salisbury. Price, bound, . 2*s.* 8*hd.*

An easy INTRODUCTION TO THE KNOWLEDGE OF
NATURE, and reading the HOLY SCRIPTURES ;
adapted to the Capacities of Children ; By Mrs.
TRIMMER. Price, bound, ... 1*s.* 7*hd.*

ORIGINAL STORIES, from real Life ; with Conversati-
ons calculated to regulate the Affections, and form
the Mind to Truth and Goodness. Price, bound,
. . . . 1*s.* 7*hd.*

EVERY NEW PUBLICATION, AND A GREAT VARIETY
OF SCHOOL BOOKS, AND BOOKS FOR THE
USE OF CHILDREN, MAY BE HAD
AT PORTER's SHOP.